A Place Without Shadows

Book Two of the Deadlock Trilogy

By P.T. Hylton

ISBN-13: 978-1514352663
ISBN-10: 1514352664

WHAT WE KNOW

On March 27th, 2014, Rook Mountain, Tennessee, was attacked by bird-like creatures called the Unfeathered. The residents lived in fear for the next eight years, forced to abide by strict regulations as a price for protection from the creatures. Some citizens chose to embrace and even enforce the regulations, while others secretly fought against them. What most Rook Mountaineers didn't know was their town was locked outside of time. While they lived their eight-year nightmare, time stood still in the rest of the world.

Jake Hinkle fought against the regulations in secret. He and his friends (who referred to themselves as the Unregulated) were dedicated to finding the Tools, powerful objects disguised as everyday items, identifiable only by the broken clock symbol they bore. When Jake's cover was blown, he used one of the Tools, a mirror, to transport himself to an unknown land. He promised to find help for Rook Mountain.

Zed was a supposed drifter who gave quasi-spiritual talks to desperate losers in the town's parks. He always carried a pocket watch that bore the broken clock symbol. When the Unfeathered struck, he vowed to protect the town...if the residents would agree to a few regulations. Zed and his appointed **selectmen** ruled the town, making sure all regulation breakers were dealt with swiftly and harshly. During a battle on the roof of City Hall, Zed's pocket watch was destroyed, and he was banished through the same mirror Jake had passed through seven years earlier. His reasons for seeking the Tools and taking Rook Mountain out of time remain a mystery.

Sean Lee was a Rook Mountain police officer and a member of the Unregulated. He hid the coin, the most powerful of the Tools, in his home for years. After Zed was defeated, Sean and his friends destroyed all the Tools in their possession except for the knife, which remained safely in the hands of **Christine Osmond**.

Wendy Caulfield was a teacher at the Beyond Academy, a school for gifted students. While she spent her days teaching Zed's curriculum, she was secretly a member of the Unregulated.

Frank Hinkle spent eight years in prison for murder. When he was released, he reignited the fight against Zed. Frank learned he had the ability to make locks that could render objects invisible to unwanted eyes, a skill that allowed his friends to hide a number of Tools from Zed. After being captured, Frank was sent into a deep hole in time, a place Zed called the Away. He spent an unknown number of years in the Away, locked in daily battle with shadow creatures called **the Ones Who Sing**. He eventually escaped and led the charge to defeat Zed. He and his friends destroyed Zed's pocket watch, restarted time, and banished Zed. After the victory, Frank went into the mirror to find his brother, Jake.

PROLOGUE

Frank Hinkle drifted through the mirror.

Falling into the mirror had been a violent experience, like being pulled into a pool of cold water, but falling *out* of it was gentle. One moment, there was the strange coldness and the sensation of being suspended in liquid, his lungs burning and desperate for air, and the next, Frank was on a dirt path, dry and standing upright.

He stood in a forest of towering, twisted trees. It was eerily quiet; Frank felt the absence of all the expected forest sounds —no birds singing or insects buzzing. Even the wind was silent.

He leaned his head back and gazed up at the trees, trying to make out the tops of them, and a wave of dizziness washed over him. This place—wherever it was—it wasn't right. The silence felt like a sickness.

It'd been almost three months since he'd left prison—three months since he promised the Rook Mountain city manager he would find his brother Jake. Or had it? Time was tricky, especially for Frank. It had been three months of Rook Mountain time, but that didn't count the time—probably years—he'd spent in the Away, fighting for his life against the

3

Ones Who Sing.

However you figured it, it felt like he'd been searching for his brother for a long time. All of it had brought him here.

It had been seven years since Jake came through the mirror. Frank wondered how far his brother had wandered in that time. If Frank knew Jake, the man was doing everything he could to get back to his family, even if that meant walking halfway around the world.

Frank took in his surroundings. Ferns, bushes, and rhododendrons grew thick on the ground around him. He stood on a thin dirt trail on the side of a hill. Seemed odd, such behemoths of trees growing on such a steep slope.

As his ears began to adjust to the quiet of the woods, he heard something through the silence, and he licked his lips at the thought of it. A stream. He'd only been here a minute, but already he felt a powerful thirst. Something about the air here made him want to rinse out his mouth. He headed toward the sound, cutting his own path through the dense foliage. It wasn't long before he came upon a stream.

Growing up in the Appalachian Mountains, he had more than a passing familiarity with mountain streams. He'd drunk from them, fished them, and swam in them plenty of times. This one was a shallow little number, freckled with rocks.

He squatted at the bank and reached a cupped hand toward the water. A dark shape hovered near the bed of the stream. For a moment, he thought it was his own shadow. It was a black round thing no bigger than a basketball, and it seemed unmoved by the force of the water around it.

He craned his neck and looked up to see if something above him was casting this odd shadow. He saw nothing but trees. He passed his hand over the shape and didn't see the shadow on the back of his hand. That thing was under the water.

He held his breath, the pace of his heart suddenly quickening. He'd seen more than enough of shadow creatures in his time Away. But he didn't hear any singing now.

He cursed himself for coming here so unprepared. Why hadn't he brought a gun or a knife or, hell, a canteen?

Then he heard it. Not the buzzing, collective, mind-numbing song of the Ones Who Sing. This was something else. Something softer. It was like a light humming he could feel at the base of his skull. It was a disquieting but almost sweet sound.

He leaned back, away from the water. He'd have to move upstream and find somewhere else to drink. He started to rise, then felt a callused hand on his shoulder and heard a gruff voice say, "Don't move. It might look small, but that damn thing'll cut through you like a buzz saw."

Frank froze. He didn't dare turn around.

"Talking's alright though," the man continued. "They can't hear us, near as I've ever been able to tell. Or, if they can, they don't seem to care."

The man hunkered down on the river bank, and Frank got a good look at him. The guy had to be in his sixties. His skin was a leathery color that spoke of long hours outdoors. His jeans were baggy and tattered. He wore a faded blue Carolina Panthers baseball cap and a plain red tee-shirt, and he held a long pointed stick that had a knife lashed to the end of it.

"Okay, so what do we do?" Frank asked. "Wait for it to go away?"

The man's eyes were on the creature in the water. "Nah, I may not have that much time left to me. This thing has been sitting at the bottom of this stream for years, never hurting no one 'til you came by and caught its attention. You see the way it's quivering? It wants you dead like it's never wanted anything. You put all three of us in a bad situation."

Frank did see it quivering now. It seemed to have risen up off the bottom of the stream, though it was hard to tell for sure.

"Only thing to do now is to kill it." He grinned at Frank, revealing a smile speckled with holes where teeth had once been. "Might want to say a quick prayer. I miss and we're both dead."

Quicker than Frank could respond, the man pulled back the stick and stabbed it toward the shadow creature. He yelped and hopped to his feet, pulling the stick out of the water, and holding up the creature impaled on the knife. The thing looked like a huge black cotton ball. Thick strands of fur hung limply from its round body.

"You see that? Teach you to quiver at a man trying to enjoy a cool drink of water!" He held the spear high, and as Frank watched, the shadow creature melted, dissolving into a sludgy mess of ink-like ooze.

A thick glob fell onto the man's shoe, but he didn't seem bothered. He scraped it off with the heel of his other foot.

Frank put his hands on his knees and started to stand.

"Wait!" the man shouted. "You know how many of those things are in the water?"

Frank froze mid-crouch. His eyes darted back and forth along the stream.

The man bellowed out a laugh. "I'm just messing with you, man. Stand up."

Frank did so and looked the older man in the eye, not sure whether to punch him or hug him. He pointed at the sludge dripping from the spear. "Thanks. What the hell's that thing?"

The man shrugged. "I call them Larvae. Mostly I try to

leave them alone. They don't bother me much, unless I invade their space. They usually stick to quiet places like the bottom of that stream or up in the trees. It was different when I was young. Back then they were hungry. Now they keep quiet. Until someone or something like you comes along and gets them riled." He held out his hand. "I'm Mason."

Frank shook it. The hand was hard and rough with calluses. "Frank."

Mason leaned the spear over his shoulder, oblivious to the sludge running down onto his neck and shirt. "Frank." He said the name like he was skeptical of its authenticity. "I gotta ask you, what the hell are you doing here?"

Frank brushed his hands off on his pants and looked around. "I don't even know where *here* is."

Mason's smile suddenly looked a bit more artificial. "Oh, don't kid a kidder. No one gets here by accident. It's been a long, long time since anyone's gotten here at all. Who sent you?"

"No one sent me. I sent myself."

Mason squinted at him. "I've got bad news for you. Whatever your purpose, you've made a seriously bad decision. I need to know why you're here. If you don't come clean with me right now, I'm gonna let my spear here ask the next question."

Frank nodded. Makeshift spear or not, he was confident he could take down this weather-beaten man if it came to that. Still, the guy moved pretty fast. "Look, I'm not trying to be secretive. I'm happy to explain everything. I'm looking for a man. I'm not sure he's still in the area, but he definitely passed through here a while back. About seven years ago."

Mason shook his head. "Ain't no such thing as passing through here. No one came here seven years ago, I can promise you that."

Frank's heart sank. "You sure?"

Mason spat on the ground by way of an answer. "This man you're asking after. Tell me about him."

Frank ran a hand through his hair. This was getting him nowhere. "He's a little shorter than me. Blond hair. Wears it a bit shaggy, at least he did last time I saw him. Suffers from a distinct lack of a sense of humor."

The old man rubbed his chin and squinted at Frank. "Why, if I didn't know better, I'd say you were talking about Jake Hinkle."

Frank's pulse quickened. "Yes!"

Mason squinted at him. "You came here looking for Jake Hinkle?"

"Yes!"

"And what exactly do you want with him?"

Frank wondered if the man was messing with him. "I'm here to help him, if I can. He's my brother."

Mason grimaced. "That's what I figured, but I needed to hear you say it." He cleared his throat. "I'm sorry, but I've got some hard news. Jake Hinkle has been dead more than fifty years."

The air went out of Frank's lungs. No. It wasn't possible.

"Uncle Frank." Mason put a hand on his shoulder. "My dad never gave up on you. He told me you'd be coming."

CHAPTER ONE: THE CURBSIDE KILLER

1.

The man who killed Sophie's sister ran free for five years before they caught him. His victims were young and old, black and white, beautiful and ugly. He was an equal opportunity killer. His only criterion was convenience. He attacked pedestrians, a quick baseball bat to the head and he went on his way, leaving them lying in the gutter.

Still, even knowing that, Sophie Porter spent her high school years living in fear of him. Fear he'd come after her some day. Even though she never walked anywhere—her parents didn't let her and she wouldn't have wanted to anyway—it was always in her mind that he'd make an exception from his established pattern for her. Sophie never believed her sister's death had been random. She believed there was something special about Heather that had drawn him, and she believed maybe the same special quality was inside her, too.

The police caught Charles Dylan Taylor—the man the media had dubbed 'The Curbside Killer'—just outside Chattanooga in 2004. They pulled him over for an illegal U-turn, saw the bloody baseball bat, and took him into custody. His multi-state, half-decade-long voyage of terror was over.

No more names would be added to his already double-digit list of victims.

Sophie was nineteen years old when they caught him. She dropped out of Vanderbilt a month after the arrest. The combination of relief at the man's capture and dread over his upcoming trial left little room in her mind for coursework. She got a job at a jazz bar and stayed in Nashville rather than returning to her parents' home in Knoxville. She needed to be around people who were at least pretending to be happy.

Charles Dylan Taylor was sentenced to death by lethal injection four years later. Twenty-three year old Sophie Porter sat in the courtroom during the sentencing, promising herself this was the end of the story for her and Charles Taylor. He'd likely wait for years on Death Row, but she wouldn't let her mind and heart be held captive with him. She'd move on with her life. The Curbside Killer would wait for his final appointment with the needle at Northern Tennessee Correctional Complex in Rook Mountain.

On September 30, 2014, Taylor disappeared from his locked cell. The report showed he was in his bunk for the ten thirty bed check. When Officer Rodgers came around for the eleven fifteen bed check, he was gone.

The story made national headlines—'Death Row Inmate Escapes'—but most of the reports focused on how the disappearance had taken place in the weirdness capital of the nation. The other things that had happened there made a simple prison break, albeit a perplexing one, seem mundane by comparison. Most people chalked it up as another Rook Mountain mystery. Add it to the list, they said.

The families of the victims banded together and raised money to help bring attention to the manhunt. Sophie's parents reacted as they always did in a crisis: her mother leaping into action, organizing campaigns and committees, and her father withdrawing further into his own thoughts and distancing himself from the world.

Sophie had seen this all before. The victims' groups. The fund raising. The desperate pleas for a few moments of attention from the right media outlets. But Sophie wasn't a little girl this time, and she was no longer content to watch her parents try their broken-hearted best to cope with another chapter in an endless saga of tragedy. It all seemed so familiar and sad. That same old picture of Heather was being shown again and again.

Sophie knew their way didn't have to be her way. She needed to find her own method of survival.

On October 15, 2014, Sophie Porter drove to Rook Mountain.

2.

Sophie stomped on the clutch and downshifted into first, slowing to a roll as she approached the prison. The place was less menacing than she'd expected. Tall fences topped with coils of razor wire surrounded the complex, but what she could see inside the fence looked like the institutional version of quaint. The buildings were long and squat, gray and drab. They looked clean and freshly painted, not the grimy oppressiveness Sophie had seen in so many prison movies and television shows. It didn't look like the kind of place she'd want to spend the rest of her life, but the sight of it didn't cause her legs to go watery either.

There were seventy-six prisoners on death row at NTCC. Seventy-six people waiting around to die, some of them waiting decades. A few days before, there had been seventy-seven. Now Charles Dylan Taylor was walking free. Sophie didn't know exactly what she expected to do about that, but she had to try something. Someone had to be held accountable.

She'd never been to Rook Mountain before even though she had grown up two hours to the southwest in Knoxville. It hadn't been a hot tourist destination. Not until seven months ago, anyway.

It had been seven months since the weirdness. Seven months since everyone in this town had aged eight years in a single night. The residents of Rook Mountain had come back with wild and unbelievable stories, stories of giant birds and strange laws. They claimed they'd been led by a man named Zed. No last name. Zed had protected them, some claimed, from the things outside the town. Others claimed he'd been an oppressive dictator. Zed had apparently disappeared off the face of the earth around the time things went back to normal in Rook Mountain, and he hadn't been seen since.

Theories about what had really happened to Rook Mountain on the night of March 27 were as varied as you'd expect. Mass delusion with physical manifestation. Some sort of spiritual attack brought on to teach the town a lesson. And aliens. A lot of people theorized it was aliens.

Sophie thought of all the government employees and scientists still hanging around town, and she grimaced. Finding a place to stay would be a nightmare.

She took a deep breath and glanced at herself in the rear view mirror. Did she look professional? Like someone who might legitimately come calling on the warden? She thought so. She had done her best approximation of the pantsuit she imagined a government official might wear on a daily basis. And yet, she saw her own discomfort in the mirror. She wore the right clothes, but she didn't wear them with the casual grace of someone who was accustomed to business attire.

Nothing she could do about that now. She turned the wheel of her Civic and pulled up next to the guard station, stopping well behind the barrier arm blocking her path. She rolled down her window and waited for the guard to speak. He looked at her, his face blank.

When it became clear the guard wasn't going to initiate the conversation, she said, "I'm here to see Warden Cades."

For a moment, it seemed the guard still wasn't going to speak. Then he said, "You have an appointment?"

She waited a moment too long before answering. "Yes. He's expecting me."

The guard grunted, his expression unreadable. "ID please."

Sophie fumbled with the clasp on her purse. This wasn't going how she'd planned. She'd imagined she would be charming. That she'd win the guard over with her smile and friendly conversation. So naive. Charles Taylor could be anywhere by now, and here she was in the only place she knew he wasn't.

She handed the guard her driver's license. It still had the picture from when she was twenty-one years old. At the time she'd just bought a car and moved into a new apartment. It felt like a fresh start, a way to escape the past. No baseball bats would cave in the back of her head while she was driving her used Mitsubishi Expo, a vehicle that looked like a cross between Inspector Gadget's 'Gagetmobile' and a minivan. She'd quickly learned no simple vehicle or state-issued plastic card would be the answer to her problems. Nor would the various other solutions she tried over the years. Older men. Younger men. The Goth scene. The rave scene. Even the country music scene. Of course, none of it had made her forget the Curbside Killer. She didn't regret it, though. She had collected a wider array of memories than most people her age. Good as well as bad.

The guard looked at the ID for a full thirty seconds, squinting like it was written in Mandarin, and then he glared up at her.

"Hang on," he said.

He scooped up the phone and pressed a button, his eyes never leaving her. It was as if he was afraid she'd turn to smoke and disappear if he looked away. He muttered into the phone too quietly for Sophie to hear. Her stomach was doing flip-flops now. All the confidence she had felt minutes before had drifted away.

He handed the ID back to her. "Listen," he said. "I'm trying to get in touch with the warden. Visitor parking is over there. You can wait while I verify his schedule."

She hesitated, not sure where to take it from here, whether or not to push. She'd had a response ready for if he gave her a flat-out no, and she was ready to act unsurprised and confident if he lifted the one-armed barrier and waved her inside. She hadn't been ready for a maybe.

Sophie gave the guard a quick nod and shifted into reverse. She navigated the car backward fifty feet and then pulled into the visitor parking lot. She angled the car so she could see the guard's little hut of a station through her windshield.

She sat for five minutes, chewing her bottom lip and trying to make out the guard's movements through the tinted glass. She was staring so hard and gripping her steering wheel so tightly the vibration of her cell phone made her jump.

She fished the phone out of her pocket and saw a photo of a skinny, balding man on the screen. She groaned. Was this coincidence or catastrophe?

She took a deep breath and touched the green icon on the

screen.

"Hey, Dad! What's up?"

"Sophie, what are you doing?" His voice was matter-of-fact, but clipped. This was his get-down-to-business voice.

Sophie let out an exhausted breath. Catastrophe.

"You'd rather I was there with you and Mom manning the tip line?"

"Actually, I would."

It was always the same. It'd been this way when Taylor was on the run. Sophie got frustrated that Mom and Dad weren't doing enough, and Mom and Dad got frustrated that Sophie was distracting them from the work at hand. Fundamentally, her parents believed in the system. They thought Charles Taylor was a problem that could be solved through paperwork and phone calls. Sophie thought that was bullshit.

"You getting a lot of great tips on the hotline today?" she asked. "Did that guy who claims to have Heather's left foot in his basement call again?"

The number of crank calls to the hotline was overwhelming. Most of them barely even remembered the details of Heather's death. It was even worse this time. Not only did the crazy serial killer fans and wannabes call, now it was the Rook Mountain conspiracy nuts, too. Charles Taylor had been taken by aliens. Charles Taylor had been taken by giant birds. Charles Taylor had ascended into heaven to sit at the right hand of Jeffrey Dahmer. The crazy calls never stopped.

When her father didn't answer, Sophie said, "How'd you know I was here, Dad?"

"Somebody at the prison called Don Gurke. Don called me." Don Gurke was the family's attorney—a victim's rights advocate who had become a close friend of the family over the years. "Sophie, what exactly are you trying to accomplish? Did you really think anybody there would talk to you?"

She paused, trying to decide how to answer. What *was* she doing here? It had all seemed so clear fifteen minutes ago. "I had to try something different. Sometimes sitting and waiting for the phone to ring isn't the best approach."

"We've done a hell of a lot more than that. You know the money, the hours, the years we've put into capturing this madman?"

Sophie squeezed her eyes shut. She remembered. She remembered being shooed out of the room while her parents sat at the dining room table, a two-foot tall stack of files in front of them, when all she wanted was a hug. She remembered the painful, distracted looks in their eyes on every special occasion since Heather's death. Every milestone in Sophie's life was just another reminder of the daughter who wasn't there.

"We're trying our best here. Answering the phones might not sound like much. I know it's not flashy, like driving to a prison across the state, but this is how real cases get solved. Ask any detective, any criminal lawyer. Real investigations aren't sexy and they aren't exciting. They're long hours and paperwork. They're a grind."

"Yeah? How far has that grind gotten you this time?" She paused, the rest of her comment stuck in her throat. A tall man in a uniform was strutting toward the car, his arms swinging at his sides. His crooked smile revealed perfectly white, level-straight teeth.

"I gotta go," she told her father.

"Wait, we need to talk about this. Your mother and I—"

Sophie hit the END icon on her phone. Whatever authoritative, by-the-book resolution her father had been about to suggest would have to wait.

The closer the man got, the bigger he looked. Sophie gripped her phone tightly. Why hadn't she thought to bring a weapon? At least a can of mace or something.

The man reached the car, leaned over, and rapped on the driver's side window.

Sophie paused only a moment before she stabbed at the button to lower the window. As the glass descended, the man leaned forward, his smiling face getting uncomfortably close to hers.

"I'm hitting on you," the man said. He spoke in a low throaty voice. She smelled the freshly chewed wintergreen gum on his breath.

"Well, you're direct. I'll give you that."

His smile wavered. "No. I'm not really hitting on you. I mean, pretend I'm hitting on you. My friends are watching."

She struggled to keep her face even. Just what she needed. A horny guard. "Yeah? What did they want you to say?"

The man cleared his throat and looked away.

"It's okay," she said. "I worked in a bar in Nashville for five years. I've heard it all."

His eyes met hers, and she noticed his cheeks were red. "They, uh... they wanted me to tell you that if you really want to get into prison, you'll have to let me frisk you..."

"Go on."

"And you'll have to frisk me, too. Nice and slow."

"Lovely." She turned the key and started the engine.

"No. Wait. It's not like that."

She adjusted her rear view mirror and stepped on the clutch. "Oh yeah? What's it like?"

The man looked back and forth as if scanning to see if anyone was close by. He didn't look pervy to Sophie anymore;

17

he looked nervous. "It was an excuse to come talk to you. I know who you are. Who your sister was. I followed the case pretty closely back then."

She took her hand off the stick shift and set it on the wheel. "You and everyone else."

"Yeah, well, the difference is I remember. I remember what that monster did, and I never let him forget it while he was in here."

Sophie looked at him out of the corner of her eye. He wasn't bad looking. She glanced down at the ID badge hanging from his shirt pocket, and she saw the name Timothy Rodgers.

The man shook his head. "It's not right the way they're covering everything up. The way they pretend the last eight years don't matter. Taylor's proof they do. All the damn scientists and government types in town, looking in every old lady's cupboard for the secrets of the universe. And here a man, a killer, disappears and nobody sees the connection."

"Okay," she said, "what's the connection?"

He shook his head. "Not here. I'll talk to you, but if the guys find out I did, I'll wake up in a burlap sack being beaten with bars of soap, you know?"

"Not really. Listen, man, I want to hear what you have to say, but I'm not an idiot. Somewhere public, okay?"

He nodded. "There's a pizza place called Leon's downtown. We can grab a slice and I'll ruin your appetite with what I have to say. I'll be there at five thirty. Sound okay?"

It sounded like she'd struck gold and fallen into a trap all at the same time. "When you go back to your buddies, will you at least tell them I spit in your face?"

He grinned. "I don't like lying to my friends."

She spat in his face and threw the car into reverse.

* * *

3.

Sophie stopped at the first gas station she saw and grabbed two bottles of water, a bag of Doritos, and—after a moment's hesitation—a frozen burrito. No way was she showing up at this pizza place hungry. If she was hungry, she would order food, and then she'd be committed to sitting there eating it even if this Rodgers guy turned out to be a complete nut job.

She popped her burrito into the food-splattered microwave, hit the START button, and looked around while the microwave hummed. The gas station was oddly crowded for a Wednesday afternoon. The two cashiers were ringing up customers and handing out change and lottery tickets as fast as they could, but the line still snaked down the candy aisle and past the microwave station where she stood.

She eyed the kid in line standing closest to her. He looked like he was maybe fifteen years old. She glanced down and noticed a large tattoo on the back of his right hand. It featured the face of a clock with a jagged crack running down the center of it.

Sophie looked up and saw his eyes were on her. He'd caught her looking. Probably thought she was checking him out. With her slight build and her playfully-styled brunette hair, she was often mistaken for ten years younger than her age, and she constantly had to fend off guys far too young for her tastes.

She gave him a polite, thin-lipped smile. The kid grinned back at her.

He gestured to the long line in front of him. "This is crazy, right? It's always like this now."

Sophie gave him a disinterested look. She supposed it had

been hard for this kid, going from cut off from the world to being at the center of a media circus. "Yeah. Not like the good old days, I guess."

The look on his face changed at that. His smile narrowed, but something about it looked a little more genuine. The line in front of him moved forward. He gestured to the man behind him. "You can go ahead." He stepped out of line and held his hand out to Sophie. She gave it the briefest of shakes.

"I'm Grant. I'm pleased to meet you."

"I'm Sophie. I'm waiting for my burrito."

He pointed to the back of his right hand. "I saw you checking out my tattoo."

She shrugged. "Kinda jumped out at me, I guess."

Grant grinned. "I know, right? That's the whole point. To not live in the shadows anymore." He gave the tattoo a rub like it was a lucky rabbit's foot. "I like what you said before. About the good old days. I agree."

"Swell," she said. She stared hard at the timer on the microwave, willing it to move faster.

The kids nodded vigorously. Then he leaned closer and spoke a bit more quietly. "You know about the second coming, right?"

She raised one eyebrow. Maybe she had this kid's intentions wrong. Maybe he was about preaching rather than flirting.

"He's coming back. All these people want to pretend like he's not important, but they have a surprise coming. He'll be back, and there's nothing they can do about it."

"Yeah, man, that's cool. Jesus is coming back. I get it. I'm on board."

The kid looked confused. "What? No, not Jesus. I'm talking about the way things were, like you said. Zed's coming back to set things right. He's coming back, but there's work to do before he gets here. That's what my tattoo is about. We've done a lot already, but our work's just beginning and—"

"Grant!"

A bigger kid, probably a year or two older than Grant, marched toward them. He reached out and grabbed Sophie's right wrist. He pulled her hand in front of Grant's face. "You see a broken clock here?"

Sophie jerked her hand away, then pushed it against the kid's chest and shoved him backward. "What the hell, man?"

The guy regained his balance and shot Sophie a disgusted look. Then he stared back at his friend. "Well? Answer the question. You see a tat?"

Grant looked away. "No."

The bigger guy stood chin-to-chin with Grant and shoved him. "Then what the hell you running your mouth about?"

Grant rubbed his chest where the kid pushed him. "Look, Colt, I'm sorry. She was talking about the good old days. I got excited is all."

Colt leaned into the smaller guy's face. "You know who else talks about the good old days? My grandma. She lives in Fort Wayne, Indiana. Maybe you want to call her up, confide in her too?"

The microwave beeped. Sophie pulled out the hot burrito and ripped open the package. "Maybe lay off, Colt. Let's all pay for our burritos and—," she glanced down at the bottle in his hand, "—our Mountain Dews and call it a day. Cool?"

Colt looked her up and down as if she were something dead on the side of the road. He lifted his right hand, making sure Sophie could see the broken clock tattoo that matched Grant's. He held it there like Sophie was supposed to be impressed.

21

When Sophie didn't react, he said, "You're not even from Rook Mountain, are you?"

She shook her head. "Just here for the day."

Colt shot Grant a fiery look, and Grant's face reddened.

She moved to the back of the line, wanting to put as much distance as the gas station allowed between her and these weirdos.

Colt called back to her, "Get out of Rook Mountain soon. You won't like what's coming next."

4.

She slipped into the pizza place at five thirty-five and saw Rodgers sitting at a table in the corner, staring at a menu. He was wearing jeans and a tee-shirt, and his wet hair was slicked back, as if he'd either just stepped out of the shower or stuck his head under a faucet.

She marched to his table and slid into the seat across from him.

He nodded a greeting. "You want to order something? The calzones are great. They use fresh ricotta."

"I'm not eating. I just want to hear what you have to say about Taylor."

He shrugged. "Suit yourself. Me? I'm getting the calzone. With mushrooms and sausage." He set down the menu. "So, why'd you come here, anyway? Did you think you could bat your eyelashes at the warden and he'd hand over Taylor's files?"

"I wanted to get in the door. I thought maybe if I reminded him what my family's been through, he'd be willing to at least tell me what happened."

Rodgers chuckled. "Yeah, well, that isn't how Warden Cades works. He's a hard man. He had to be, the things that happened. You know how long I've worked at the prison?"

"Mr. Rodgers, you said you had information for me. Something about a cover up? Can we talk about that?"

Rodgers grimaced, and she saw the rough prison guard edge underneath his boyish good looks. "We are talking about it. I've worked at the prison thirteen years. Since 2011."

She started to correct him, and then stopped herself.

"Yeah, see what you did there?" he asked. "This town aged eight years while the rest of you experienced one second. Big deal, right? The news cycle moved on, and the only people still thinking about it are the scientists, the government, and the nut jobs. Nobody cares. Nobody from the outside, anyway."

She glanced around the crowded restaurant. "Looks to me like the town's still full of people from the outside who care."

He shook his head. "These are the bottom feeders. They're waiting for another fight to break out so they can write about how violence is on the rise in Rook Mountain." He shifted in his seat, and leaned toward her. He lowered his voice when he spoke again. "Let me ask you a question. You ever heard that urban legend about Sanctuary?"

She tilted her head, puzzled at the non sequitur. "Yeah, of course."

"When did you first hear it?"

Sophie thought about it for a moment, and then shrugged. "I'm not sure. It's one of those things I've known my whole life. Like saying Bloody Mary in the mirror. Kids talk about it to scare other kids. We'd dare each other to try it at slumber parties and stuff."

He leaned forward and looked into her eyes. She saw emptiness in those eyes, a hollow sadness.

"I'm gonna tell you something now," he said. "Something

23

you aren't going to believe. But I'd appreciate it if you'd hear me out anyway."

"Okay."

"That legend about the Sanctuary didn't exist before March twenty-seventh of this year."

She waited for some indication he was kidding, but none came. He sat there looking at her with those sad eyes. What he was saying wasn't true. There was no doubt about that. She had played Sanctuary with Heather when they were kids. They would stand on the balcony outside of their parents' bedroom and lean over as far as they dared. When they felt like they'd leaned a little too far, they would shout the word Sanctuary.

Of course, nothing ever happened. Just like Bloody Mary never came out of the mirror no matter how many times they said her name. Granted, the urban legend said your life had to be in danger. Leaning over the railing of a second story balcony wasn't exactly a death-defying situation, but still.

She took a sip of water before speaking. "Do you mean you hadn't heard about it before March twenty-seventh?" She asked the question even though she knew perfectly well that wasn't what he meant. "It's possible the story didn't make it out to these parts, I guess."

He shook his head. "I mean what I said. It didn't exist."

She smiled even as she wondered how to politely extract herself from this odd conversation. "Well, that's just not true. Like I said, I heard about it when I was a kid."

"When I was a teenager," Rodgers said, "I went through this phase where I was obsessed with urban legends. I had a shelf full of books on modern folklore. It was mostly garbage, people looking to make a quick buck by writing down stories everyone already knew. But I devoured those books. I knew it all. Candyman. The headless Lincoln. The song that steals your freewill. The standardized test that secretly checks you for psychic abilities."

Sophie had heard of the Candyman, but not any of the others. "You're telling me none of those books mentioned Sanctuary?"

He grinned his crooked boyish grin. "They didn't the first time I read them."

The waitress set a tall skinny beer glass in front of him. He thanked her and took a long sip before wiping the froth from his mouth with the back of his hand and continuing. "I heard somebody mention Sanctuary on TV back in April, so I looked it up online. There were a bunch of different versions, but they all had the same basic idea. If your life is ever in immediate danger, you can say the word 'Sanctuary' and you'll be saved. You'll be taken to some other place. No one knows where it is or what happens there, but you can never return. That sound like what you heard as a kid?"

Sophie nodded. This was all common knowledge, of course. There was even a saying people used when presented with a risk they couldn't help but take. *Close your eyes and ask for Sanctuary.*

Rodgers said, "You know that thing where you hear a word for the first time, and then you hear it a bunch of times over the next week or so? It was like that with Sanctuary. I started seeing references to it everywhere. In movies, online, in books. I felt like I was going crazy. So I brought it up to the guys at work. Most of them hadn't heard of it either. One guy knew of it, but he said he'd first seen it on TV a couple weeks back."

She grimaced. She wasn't here to learn about this prison guard's strange obsession with urban legends. "That's a weird story, but it happens. Sometimes stuff passes us by. We all have blind spots. They did an episode of *This American Life* about it. One lady didn't realize unicorns weren't real animals until she was thirty years old. Is it odd? Yes. But I need you to focus. Let's talk about Charles Taylor."

"We are talking about Taylor. This has everything to do with him. You don't see what the story of Sanctuary might have to do with a guy disappearing out of a locked prison?"

It was at that moment Sophie realized she was sitting with a crazy person. She put her hands on the table and pushed herself up to a standing position. "I appreciate you taking the time, but I better be going."

"No," he said. He grabbed her hand and pressed it tightly against the table. "Please. Listen for five more minutes. I can tell you what happened that night. It isn't what Warden Cades told the press."

She sank back into her seat and pulled her hand out from beneath his. "Talk fast."

"A few days before he disappeared, Taylor punched a guard, a buddy of mine named Brian Dayton. Taylor was on the wrong side of the prisoner/staff line, and Brian told him to step back. That was it, just told him to move. Taylor freaked out and punched him in the face."

"How has this not come out already?"

He looked away. "There are two ways we can deal with these types of situations. There's the official way, with the paperwork and the hand slapping and time in the SHU. But what the hell does a guy like Taylor care? It's not like we can extend his sentence for bad behavior. And he's pretty damn isolated on death row already."

"What's the unofficial way?"

He cleared his throat and leaned closer. "A few of us

decided to take our batons and pay Taylor a late-night visit. It's not something we do a lot, but guys like him have to occasionally be taught a lesson. It's hard to explain if you haven't worked in a prison, but it's really for the best."

"That asshole bashed my sister's head in while she was walking home from school. You think I'm gonna object to him getting a beat down?"

Rodgers scratched his chin and grinned. "Yeah, I guess maybe you wouldn't. When something like that happens, the smart prisoners curl up in the fetal position and take their beatings."

"I take it Taylor wasn't one of the smart ones?"

He shook his head. "Idiot fought back. After that, I'll admit, we got a little carried away. We whaled on him a bit too hard and a bit too long. The fight never went out of him, but he did eventually stop punching and kicking at us. When I thought he'd finally had enough, he looked up at us and grinned. It was creepy. We'd knocked a couple of his teeth out at that point. He looked like a jack-o'-lantern or something. And then he said it and disappeared."

"He said Sanctuary? And it worked?"

Rodgers spread his fingers out on the table like a magician showing there was nothing in his hands. "That was it. He was there one second and gone the next. He blinked out of existence."

She leaned back in her chair and pondered how far this man's madness went. Was there truth to his ramblings or was it all nonsense? "How much does the warden know?"

"He knows it all. We called him right after."

"Okay, say you're right. Despite the fact that who knows how many people have said Sanctuary in life and death situations and it's never worked before—"

"We don't know that. People disappear all the time."

She sighed. "Okay, fine. It happens all the time. Even if that's true, why would the warden cover it up?"

"Why wouldn't he? This is Rook Mountain. Secrets are what we do."

Sophie shook her head. "That's exactly why I don't buy it. This is the ideal place to claim something unexplainable happened. He had to know losing an inmate, a death row inmate, would make the whole prison staff look like idiots."

"You don't understand," he said. "You think this town wants more attention for being a hotspot for the unexplained? You think we want more weirdos coming here on sightseeing trips?"

"Seems like a 'Get Out of Jail Free' card to me. No pun intended."

He grimaced. "You're just like the rest. You know how many people died while you slept on March twenty-seventh?"

"But that's over now. It's time to find the man who killed my sister."

"That's where you're wrong," he said. "It isn't over. It's only getting started. You remember those urban legend books I collected as a teenager? I pulled one of them out a box in the basement a few weeks ago. Guess what story was featured on the cover?"

She pressed her lips into a thin line. "Sanctuary?"

He nodded. Beads of sweat stood on his forehead. He leaned closer. "We were gone for eight years, and we came back different. But you changed too while we were away. The world changed. That Sanctuary story's in every one of those books now. I can't prove it, but it wasn't there before. And that's only one example. This world we came back to is all wrong."

28

Sophie stood up, careful to keep her hands out of his reach.

"Wait," he said. "There's more."

"I've heard enough. Thanks for wasting my time."

He took a deep breath. "I'm asking you, Ms. Porter. Don't leave yet. Please."

"Sorry, man. Places to be." She turned and took long strides toward the door of the pizzeria, careful not to look back.

She'd almost made it to her car when she felt the gun against her back.

"Get in the car," Rodgers said. "We're going for a ride."

5.

They took her car, Sophie driving and Rodgers in the passenger seat, sticking the gun into her side harder than was necessary. She'd been sure he was taking her to his house so he could lock her up in his torture chamber or something, but instead he took her to the center of town. City Hall was closed for the evening, but Rodgers produced a key and walked them right through the front door. Why a prison guard had a key to City Hall, she did not know.

After directing her up three flights of stairs, he waved his gun toward a ladder. "You go first."

Sophie grimaced and pulled herself up. She counted ten rungs before she reached the trapdoor at the top. She twisted the handle and shoved it open, struggling against the heavy metal of the door. Sunlight poured into the dim hallway below. She squinted against the sun and climbed out onto the roof of Rook Mountain City Hall.

She looked around the rooftop, hoping to see another trapdoor she could escape through, but there was nothing.

Just a flat roof, some air conditioning units, and a long drop on four sides.

Rodgers pulled himself onto the roof, stood up, and brushed off his pants. He smiled at Sophie.

"Why are you doing this, Rodgers? What do you want from me?"

He pointed the gun at her. "That is an excellent question. And I'm not sure I know the answer. But I'm hoping to figure that out right quick." He reached into his pocket and pulled out a round object Sophie recognized as a compass.

"You see this?" he asked. He flipped it around so Sophie could see both sides of it. On the back was the symbol she'd seen tattooed on the two kids' hands. A broken clock.

He waved the compass in front of her as he spoke. "I found this compass in the prison yard about ten years back. Right after Zed came to town, actually. Back when we all thought he was a crazy drifter. No idea how it got in the prison yard. Shouldn't have been possible. But there it was. I thought it was beautiful, so I hung on to it rather than turning it into the warden."

Sophie backed away. Rodgers seemed to be losing control of the composure he had displayed earlier. He might freak out and shoot her at any moment. On the other hand, it also upped her odds of being able to take him out.

He continued, "Later, after the Unfeathered came, we had this rule that said we were supposed to turn over anything with the broken clock symbol to the selectmen. By then I thought of this thing as my good luck charm."

He looked at her, and she saw there were tears in his eyes. "That's my biggest regret. Not turning in this thing when I had the chance. Maybe if I had, maybe if Zed had this compass, things wouldn't have gone down like they did on this rooftop. That son of a bitch Hinkle and his freak show of a family somehow sent Zed away. I keep thinking maybe this compass could have helped."

Sophie spoke cautiously. "Maybe... maybe I can help. Charles Taylor and this Zed guy both disappeared, right? Maybe the disappearances are related. Maybe we can—"

"You don't understand!" he shouted. "You weren't here. To you, Zed's a name in a story on some news website. You never heard him speak or knew the way it felt when he smiled at you. He was a great man."

She held up her hands. "Okay. Great man. Got it."

He giggled, a surprisingly high-pitched sound coming from this big man. "You know the crazy part? This compass never even worked right. Instead of pointing north, you know where it pointed? At Charles Taylor."

She squinted at him. "What?"

"Until the day Zed disappeared and time started again. Then the compass started pointing here. Toward City Hall. The place where Zed disappeared."

"So that's why you brought me here?"

He shook his head. "No. The reason I brought you here—the reason I talked to you at all in that parking lot at the prison—is because the compass changed. The minute you showed up this morning, the needle stopped pointing at City Hall and started pointing at you."

She stepped back again. Her feet were close to the edge now, mere inches away. "Why the hell would it do that?"

"I don't know!" Rodgers screamed. "Look." He paced back and forth while staring at the compass. "Still pointing at you. Wherever I go, it's locked on you. I hoped if I brought you here, to the place the compass used to point, something would happen. But it's not working!"

He stomped toward her and pushed the barrel of the gun into the center of her chest. "Who are you really? What's so special about you? Why did you come to Rook Mountain?"

"You know." She struggled to keep the quiver out of her voice. "You know why I'm here."

He shook the compass wildly through the air. "Come on! I've done everything right, everything I possibly could do. Why aren't you working?"

Her eyes darted to the trap door. Rodgers stood between her and it, but there was a chance. If she took off running, darted around him, maybe—

He flashed a joyless grin. "He's coming back, you know."

"So I keep hearing," she muttered. "Some kids at the gas station were saying the same thing. They had these tattoos. Maybe you need to talk to them."

He groaned. "You think I haven't already? They've been loyal to Zed, I gotta give them that. But they're dangerous. People think they're nothing to worry about because they're kids, but the things they're planning are no joke, I promise you that."

"Okay. So let's go to them. Maybe they can help."

Rodgers gave his head a violent shake. She could feel the presence of the edge of the building. Her stomach clenched at the thought of the gun in front of her and the drop inches behind her.

"You don't understand," he said. "They still believe in the Regulations. Do you know what that means?" He pressed the gun barrel harder against her chest and vertigo washed over her. "It means they'd take my compass. It's one of the Tools. That's what they called them, Tools. And they'd kill me for hiding it all this time. No, we can't work with them."

She put her hand over his. "Rodgers... Tim... I can help

you. The compass is trying to tell you I can help."

He shook his head. "It's not like that. The compass has chosen you. I think it wants justice. What Regulations have you broken, Sophie Porter?"

At that moment, Sophie decided she'd had enough of being held at gunpoint by a crazy person. Heather had died when she was struck in the back of the head with an aluminum baseball bat. She probably never knew what hit her, and she never had the chance to react. Sophie did have the chance, and she was sure as hell going to take it. She sucked in a quick breath. The surge of adrenaline rushing through her gave the world an over-saturated quality.

She planted her foot behind her, hoping it would find solid ground rather than air. She pushed off that back foot and drove the heel of her hand upward into Rodgers' nose with all her strength.

He howled in pain and stumbled backwards.

She watched him stagger for only a moment before she took off toward the trapdoor. She pumped her arms and ran with all her might. When she was nearly there, she dove and slid as she'd been taught in softball so many years ago. But this wasn't dirt, and the rough concrete dug into her arms and hands as she slid. She felt her pants tear and the skin of her knees being stripped away.

It didn't matter. She was here. The handle of the trapdoor was in her hand. She pulled on it and found it was heavier than she'd expected. She wasn't about to let that stop her. She pulled harder and the door rose with a satisfying moan.

Something grabbed her around her waist. An arm was wrapped around her, flinging her backward, and suddenly she was on her ass six feet away from the trapdoor. She grunted in pain, surprise and frustration.

Rodgers glowered down at her, dark blood streaming from his nose into his mouth and down his neck. His face was streaked with wet lines of tears, but his teeth were gritted. He still clutched the compass in his right hand. The gun was jammed down the back of his pants.

"Leaving isn't an option. The compass wants you here."

She scooted backwards away from him as fast as she could, then stumbled to her feet. If she couldn't escape, she'd have to fight him. He took a step toward her, and she threw a punch. Her feet weren't set like last time, though, and her swing was wild and desperate. The blow ricocheted off his cheek, barely slowing him down.

He was almost to her now. She feigned another punch, and used the moment it bought her to set her back foot. She stomped, driving her front foot into his knee, putting all the adrenaline coursing through her into slamming her foot against him as hard as possible.

He yelped in pain and crouched down, grabbing for the injured knee.

She kicked again, this time aiming for his chin, but he ducked and she hit his shoulder. She staggered to keep her balance. Rodgers growled, and sprang up off the ground, crashing into her. She toppled backwards grabbing at him as she fell, hoping to bring him down with her. The expected impact with the ground never came, and she realized they'd gone over the edge a moment before she saw the side of the building rushing past her.

Her stomach somersaulted as the air rushed past her face. She clutched at Rodgers as they fell, groping for something, anything, to hold on to. Her hand closed around something hard and cold—the compass, she realized—and she gripped it hard, holding on as if the object could save her.

"Sanctuary!" he screamed.

Unbidden, Sophie's voice joined his. She whispered the word just as she had so many times with Heather on the balcony outside her parents' bedroom.

"Sanctuary."

And then it was nighttime, and she was lying in the mud in a strange and unfamiliar place as the rain fell around her.

IN THE WOODS (PART ONE)

Frank swallowed hard, pushing down the lump in his throat.

He looked at Mason. What did he really know about this man? He hadn't offered up any real information so far, other than claiming Jake was dead. He'd only used the term *uncle* after Frank revealed his own relationship to Jake. And saying Jake was dead? Seemed like a pretty good plan if you wanted someone to stop looking for him.

"You're lying." Frank was surprised at the choked, throaty quality of his own voice.

"I'm not," Mason replied softly.

"You say he's been dead more than fifty years."

Mason nodded.

"My brother's not even forty years old. You see how I might have some trouble believing he's been dead that long?"

Mason gave a weary laugh. "I've lived in these woods all my life. I've never set foot in Tennessee or any of the other places my dad and mom used to tell me about. But the way I understand it, time has its wires crossed between here and there."

"What the hell does that mean?"

"It means fifty years here doesn't exactly add up to fifty

years on the outside. The way my dad told it, you might have some experience with time getting weird."

Frank clenched his fists. The air felt thick in his lungs, hard to push in and out, and the sour taste in his mouth was only getting worse.

"You don't want to believe me, that's your affair," Mason said. "But I'm guessing you came through the mirror, same as my dad did. I'm guessing you were hoping to take him back to Rook Mountain. Back to his wife, Christine, and his son, Trevor."

Frank said nothing. He blinked back the tears pooling in his eyes.

"See?" Mason asked. "I do know a thing or two about a thing or two."

"H-How'd he die?" Frank asked. The words stuck in his throat like they didn't want to be said, like saying the thing might make it true.

"He died protecting his friends." Mason turned away from Frank and started down the trail. "Come on. Let's head to my place. I want to collect a few things. Then I can show you where it happened."

Frank nodded absently and followed the older man. His nephew. Frank heard his own feet thumping against the trail as he walked, but he didn't feel it. He felt numb. Hollow. If what this man said was true…No, he wouldn't allow himself to believe it. He'd come too far, endured too much, to be fifty years too late.

Something came back to him. While he was in the hell of the Away, the Ones Who Sing had revealed three truths to him, though they had seemed more like riddles than truths to Frank. The first was how to escape the Away. The second was how to defeat Zed. But to his third question, how to find

37

Jake Hinkle, they'd been unable to provide an answer.

"Ah, we know this name, too. We know it well. He is our—" Here the voices split once again and Frank heard multiple words at once.

"Friend."

"Enemy."

"Rival."

"Champion."

"Oppressor."

"Brother."

The voices joined back together. *"The one you speak of stands outside the river of time. He stands on its edge like a fisherman, pulling out those who swim by as it suits him...We do not know all, but we do know this: you will never see Jake Hinkle again."*

A chill ran through Frank.

Mason glanced over his shoulder and frowned when he saw Frank falling behind. He slowed his pace.

Frank had so many questions and this man with the weathered face had the answers. He decided to start with something generic. "Tell me what you remember about him."

Mason shrugged. "It wasn't easy. Growing up here, I mean. My dad tried, but spending time with me didn't exactly come natural to him."

"Jake could be distant at times...I'm sure he cared about you."

"There wasn't a lot for us to do together. Like I said, the woods were different in those days. Dangerous. So he couldn't exactly take me out for a hike. The one thing he did do was tell stories."

Frank tilted his head, trying to picture Jake sitting on the end of a kid's bed telling fairy tales. "What kind of stories?"

Mason chuckled. "Oh, King Arthur. Robin Hood. Luke Skywalker. Battlestar Galactica. Dune. All the classics."

Frank let out an unexpected laugh. Though few knew it, Jake was a hardcore sci-fi geek.

"But you know what my favorite stories were?" Mason asked. "The ones he told about growing up with you."

Frank stopped walking. "He talked about that?"

"Of course." He waved his hand as if batting away the ridiculous idea that it could have been otherwise. "How about the time you two snuck out of the house to go camping? Carried the tent and the sleeping bags on your bikes. How old were you when that happened?"

Frank hadn't thought about that in years. "I guess I was nine or so. Jake must have been eleven. We didn't take anything other than the tent and sleeping bags. No food. No matches for starting the fire. Not even a flashlight." They had left their bikes at the edge of the woods and hiked until they found a flat, half-way clear spot and set up camp. It wasn't until the sun went down and the temperature started to drop that they began to question the wisdom of their plan. They'd made it through the night, huddling together against the cold and the dark, and in the morning they'd broke camp and exited the woods to find their bikes gone and their parents beyond frantic at their unannounced night out.

"He talked about you a lot," Mason said. "I know he cared about me in his own way. I just wanted to make sure you knew he cared about you, too."

Before Frank could respond, something over Mason's shoulder caught his eye. It was so unexpected, so out of place, that he had to blink a few times before he was confident in what was right in front of him.

It was a man. His face was encircled in a wild nest of long hair, both on top of his head and growing out of his face. His eyes were a chalky gray, and there were deep lines around them. The rest of him was hidden in the foliage.

He looked at Frank with distant curiosity, seeming oblivious to the fact that Frank was looking back at him.

Mason squinted at Frank. His voice was quiet when he spoke. "Tell me what you see."

"A man," Frank said. "He has a beard and—"

As he was still speaking, the face disappeared into the foliage.

"He's gone!" Frank said. He stepped toward the place he had seen him.

Mason grabbed his arm. "We have to go. Now."

"You know him?" Frank asked.

Mason gritted his teeth. "I know *of* him. But he was banished back before my dad died. It seems to me you might have woken something up when you came through that mirror."

CHAPTER TWO: SANCTUARY

1. Rook Mountain

Officer Sean Lee was the first on the scene, which was saying something considering the police station was a block and a half away. For some odd reason, nobody was rushing to investigate the jumper whose broken body was now lying on the sidewalk outside city hall. The memories of what had happened on that roof last March were still too strong. Many of them had been in the street below when the Unfeathered attacked and Zed and Frank Hinkle faced off on the roof of city hall.

Many of them weren't sure how they felt about Rook Mountain rejoining the normal world.

Sean knew how he felt about it, though. He was damn glad Zed was gone. He hoped wherever the guy was now, giant bird creatures were pecking his eyes out. Even seven months later, you had to be careful saying things like that out loud. People didn't wear their colors on their sleeves. You had your Zed Lovers and your Zed Haters, not to mention the closet Zed Lovers and the closet Zed Haters. Everyone had been toeing the official Regulation line for so long most Rook Mountaineers didn't yet feel comfortable voicing their honest-to-God opinions.

That was fine with Sean. He'd never been one for over-sharing, even in the pre-Zed days.

The uncertainty of the situation made people uncomfortable. Most tended to shy away from anything the slightest bit controversial or any situation where they might be expected to voice an opinion. That was probably why the five cops on duty didn't exactly pour out of the station when word came in about the jumper.

Sean had been three blocks away, playing with his radar gun and trying to get up the gumption to drive out to the exit ramp off the highway, park under the sign, and ruin speeders' days.

The only thing he missed about the Regulations was the lack of speeding ticket quotas. Even thinking about radar gun duty made him glum. So, when the call came over the radio about the jumper, he answered double quick and hustled over to city hall.

There was a small crowd of five men and women standing around the body when Sean arrived. Of course, the dead guy was smack-dab in the middle of the concrete sidewalk. He couldn't have landed in one of the many grassy areas around the building. Someone had laid a coat over man's head and torso. Sean waved the spectators back, squatted down beside the body, and lifted the coat, using his body to block their view.

The man's head was lying on his shoulder at an unnatural angle. His skull was misshapen, like the shell of a hard-boiled egg dropped from a great height. His eyes were open, and blood seeped around the edges. The building was only four stories tall; he must have landed headfirst.

Even through the blood, Sean recognized the man: it was

Tim Rodgers. Tim worked over at the prison. The Rook Mountain police didn't have a ton of interaction with the Correctional Officers, but a little bit of path-crossing was inevitable. There was the occasional training session the two services did jointly in order to save money. And there were annual training exercises that let them practice how their teams would work together in the event of an escape or a riot at the prison.

Sean had never liked the man. The other CO's at NTCC looked at Rodgers like he was a big deal, and Rodgers looked at the Rook Mountain cops like they were all idiots. It had gotten a little better during the Zed years, when the police had been at least technically in charge of enforcing the Regulations, but it'd never gone away completely. The COs had a complicated relationship with police force. Many of them had aspirations of becoming cops. Some had even tried and been turned down. At the same time, the COs felt like they dealt with the worst of the worst everyday—which, in fairness, they did—while the police spent their time dealing with drunks and parking tickets. And Rodgers had been the worst of them.

Sean's stomach turned at the sight of the familiar face under the coat.

He rubbed his eyes, trying to remember the correct procedures for this type of situation. It was difficult after eight years living under the Regulations to re-adapt to the laws and guidelines of the great state of Tennessee. The State had brought in people to retrain them and even stationed a couple of advisors at the station to help, but old habits were tougher to break than COs' skulls. In the Zed years, Sean would have radioed for the hearse, had the body hauled to the clinic, and called Christine Osmond to give it a cursory inspection. Now there was probably some sort of investigation that should be done here at the scene.

He forced himself to take a hard look at the body. What he saw made him frown. By the time he covered it again, two other officers, Graves and Banks, were meandering up the steps of city hall. Sean felt his knees pop as he stood.

Graves and Banks nodded in greeting as they approached.

"Anybody we know?" Graves asked.

Sean gave the briefest of nods and leaned in close before he answered. "Tim Rodgers. The CO."

"Shit," Graves said.

"Listen," Sean said, his voice even quieter than before, "we need to close off the building. And question these looky-loos. And, hell, I don't know what else."

Banks raised an eyebrow. "This procedure or you got reason to believe Rodgers didn't jump?"

"He's got dried blood on his chin and his neck. On his shirt, too. Not splattered on there. More like it was running down his face. Thing is, he landed head first. He's on his side now. So unless blood runs sideways, we've got a problem."

Graves' eye drifted to behind Sean and suddenly grew wide. "Hey! Get away from there!"

Sean spun around and saw a teenage boy kneeling next to the body, his hand in Rodgers' pocket. The three cops sprinted toward him. The boy sprang to his feet and held up his hands, showing they were empty. Sean recognized the kid.

"Colt, what the hell are you doing?"

"Sorry!" he said, his hands still in the air. "I thought he was someone I knew and I panicked."

"So you went through his pockets?" Graves was in the kid's face, practically yelling.

He grinned sheepishly. "I was looking for his wallet. Trying to ID him."

"Christ, kid," Graves said. "Step back, will ya? We'll deal with you in a minute." Colt lowered his hands and Sean saw the broken clock tattoo.

Sean nodded toward the tat. "I didn't know you were one of those."

Colt smiled a little more widely, showing his orthodontically straightened teeth. Must have gotten those braces off recently. "I didn't know you weren't."

These young self-proclaimed Zed Heads were a new phenomenon in the past couple of months, and Sean wasn't sure what to think of them. His general philosophy was to let kids rebel a bit, let them have their music and their edgy hairstyles—whatever edgy happened to be at the particular point in time. Kids needed to blow off steam and, as long as they weren't breaking the law or hurting anyone, Sean was all for it, even if it did offend some of the more conservative sensibilities of the adult folks. Sean himself had dabbled in the rave scene in his younger days.

But this Zed Head thing seemed different. On the one hand, it was classic teen rebellion. Pick an icon that would freak out your parents and plaster him on your wall. On the other hand, Zed wasn't some ruler of the distant past to be used for shock value. These kids knew Zed. They'd seen the impacts of Zed's rule of law up close and personal.

And then there was the fact that most of these kids had been former students at the Beyond Academy. The government inquiry into Rook Mountain had taken special interest in the Academy, and terms like 'brain washing' and 'Hitler youth' were thrown around in the media. Sean didn't know everything that went on in that school, but he did know the curriculum went beyond the usual high school fare.

Graduates knew the Regulations like the backs of their previously un-tattooed hands, and they weren't slow to enforce them.

Sean had been spending a lot of time at the Osmonds' house over the past few months, and he tried to ask Trevor about his experiences at the school once. The kid hadn't wanted to talk about it. Like Sean could blame him. Everyone in this town was sick of answering questions by that point.

Whatever went on at that school, Sean did know two things to be true: Zed had spent almost as much time at the Beyond Academy as he did at city hall, and seven months ago the Beyond Academy kids had been fighting the Unfeathered while the majority of the town huddled inside waiting for it all to end. Now their guns had been taken away and they were supposed to go back to being normal kids. It was no wonder they were acting out.

Colt leaned forward and spoke softly. There was an odd light in his eyes that made Sean uncomfortable. "You find anything on that body?"

Sean squinted at him. "What? I don't think that's any of your business."

Colt grinned again, showing off his perfect teeth. "If you have anything to give me, or tell me, now's a great time. You're not a Regulation breaker, are you Officer?"

Sean stared into his eyes for a long moment, trying to figure out what the hell the kid was going on about. Colt met his gaze without blinking.

A squad car rolled to a stop at the bottom of the stairs and Chief Yates climbed out of the driver's seat. He left the lights flashing and trotted up the steps.

"Officer Lee, what did I miss?"

Sean nodded toward the building. "Our jumper might not

have jumped. We need to search city hall." By the time Sean looked back, Colt was gone.

2. Sanctuary

Sophie closed her eyes tight, whispered "Sanctuary," and waited for impact.

The material against her face suddenly felt different. A moment ago it had been the cotton of Rodgers' shirt. Now it was something else, something squishy. Rain pelted her back.

She opened her eyes, and what she saw caused her to experience the worst sense of disorientation she'd ever felt. She expected to see Rodgers in front of her and the bright sky behind him. Instead, she squinted into darkness. She was lying on her stomach, she realized. Her left hand still held the compass, but her right hand was resting on the muddy ground six inches in front of her face. Rain fell around her, splashing onto the wet ground with heavy plops.

She felt sick to her stomach, but she tried to rise. She quivered for a moment, trying to hold herself up through the shock, then gave in and collapsed in the mud below. She rolled onto her back and stared up in the sky. It was pure darkness. The smell of the rain was thick in her nose.

She breathed hard and let the raindrops splatter against her. Where was she? What was happening to her? She held the compass in front of her face. Did this have something to do with what had happened?

But she was alive. A smile crept onto her face.

A light fell across her, and a voice said, "What the hell?" Then, louder, "Baldwin, get over here!"

The man crouched down next to her. He was tall and thin, and he wore a headlamp strapped to his head, the kind Sophie used when she went camping. The light coming from

47

his forehead made it difficult to look at him. "You okay?" His voice had a soft breathless quality that barely reached her over the sound of the rain.

Sophie groaned, then struggled to her hands and knees. It wasn't easy with nothing but slippery mud to cling to and her mind still spinning.

"Where are we?" she asked.

The man scratched his head. "Lady, I wouldn't even know where to start."

Another voice came from the darkness. "Leonard?"

"Over here!" the man crouching next to her yelled. Then to Sophie, "You got a name?"

She nodded and started to answer, but then another beam of light fell on her.

The man next to her shifted the beam of his headlamp toward this new arrival. He was short and stocky, and he had an umbrella. He too wore a headlamp. He froze when he saw Sophie.

In the glow of the headlamps, Sophie was able to make out a bit about her surroundings. A tree stood next to her, a thick tangle of roots at its base.

"What the hell's this?" the new arrival asked.

"That's what I'm wondering," said the other man. "She was lying here in the mud."

The short man scratched at his nose. "We weren't expecting anyone, right?"

The crouching man snorted. "You really think they wouldn't let us know?"

He reached down and held out a hand to Sophie. "I'm Leonard. This here's Baldwin."

She squinted at the hand for a long moment before taking it. She gripped it hard, her hand slippery with mud. "Sophie

Porter."

Baldwin gave a little nod, and then looked at Leonard. "Can we do this, please? You know how I feel about this part."

Leonard patted Sophie's shoulder. "Stay strong for a bit. Things'll be better tomorrow." He looked back at Baldwin. "You want me to do it?"

Baldwin nodded.

Leonard rose to his feet. "Alrighty." He cleared his throat. and when he continued it was as if he were speaking for an audience of a hundred people rather than a single woman less than five feet away. "Do you seek sanctuary and protection?"

She raised herself up on her elbows. "Are you telling me this is the actual real Sanctuary? Like in the urban legend?"

"He's not telling you anything," Baldwin said. "He's asking you a question. Did you come here for sanctuary?"

Sophie thought for a moment. She'd said the word. In the stories, once you'd said the word, you could never go back. But it sounded like they were giving her a chance. "What happens if I say no?"

Leonard said, "We leave. You're free to get up and go... wherever. I wouldn't recommend it though. These woods aren't the safest place. Especially after sun up."

She gazed out into the darkness. If this was really happening, if it wasn't some weird afterlife or hallucination, that meant Sanctuary was real. And if it was real, maybe Rodgers wasn't as crazy as she had assumed. If Sanctuary was real, Taylor could be here. He might be in these woods at this very moment. And she had the compass. If it pointed to Taylor as Rodgers had said, she could find him.

"Yes. I want Sanctuary."

Leonard cleared his throat loudly. "Your request is denied."

The men stepped toward her.

Leonard said, "Until you're accepted into Sanctuary, your belongings will be confiscated and you'll be held for questioning."

Baldwin bent down and grabbed her legs. She twisted, trying to squirm out of his grasp. At the same moment she felt another arm, it had to be Leonard's, wrap around her waist.

Her arms flailed as she desperately felt in the darkness for something to hold on to. Her fingers laced around a tangle of roots at the base of the tree next to her. She knew she wouldn't be able fight them much longer. Wherever they were taking here, they wouldn't get the compass. That was her key to finding Taylor, and they wouldn't take it from her. She shoved the compass under the roots just before Leonard grabbed her arms and wrapped them up under his own, pinning them to her side.

She kicked and thrashed wildly, but their hold on her was too strong. She felt weak; the fight with Rodgers on the rooftop seemed like it had happened both moments before and a lifetime ago. She wasn't going to be able to squirm out of their grasp, even as wet and slippery as she was.

They carried her through the darkness in near silence, only the dim beam of men's headlamps illuminating the trail ahead; the only sound was her own groaning and cursing and the labored breathing of the men. They moved slowly, Baldwin going first, one of her legs held on either side of him like he was pulling a wheel barrow. They stopped a few times, and she could have sworn they doubled back more than once.

After what seemed like ten minutes of trudging through the rain, the men stumbled to a halt, and she heard a sound like knuckles rapping on wood.

"Yeah?" The voice was muffled and distant.

"It's Baldwin and Leonard. We've got a new arrival."

There was a long pause. Then, "There's not one tonight."

"Open the door, Frasier," Leonard yelled. "We found her in the woods."

Another long pause, then the squeal of metal on metal as the hinges reluctantly opened and a slowly widening rectangle of light appeared. The door was only a quarter open when Baldwin pushed into the room, shouldering it open the rest of the way.

They brought her into a sparsely furnished room. Leonard shut the door behind him.

Sophie squinted against the light, not wanting to wait until her eyes adjusted before taking in her new surroundings. There was a card table in the center of the room. A checkers game that appeared to be in progress was set up on the table. There were four wooden chairs, a half-empty bottle of Jack Daniels, and an open paperback on the floor. The room had the look of an old log cabin.

The man standing next to the card table was rail thin and looked older than Baldwin and Leonard put together.

Leonard said, "Get the door. Then get Logan."

The old man nodded and rushed to a door on the other side of the room. Baldwin and Leonard carried her into a new room, which was empty but for a garden hose on the ground and three work lamps clamped to the exposed overhead beams. And a chair with four sets of handcuffs attached to it, one on each leg.

The fear that had been racing through Sophie's veins since Rodgers pulled the gun outside the pizza place suddenly reached a new pitch. The men dropped her into the chair.

Leonard held her down while Baldwin snapped the handcuffs into place, one on each wrist and one on each ankle.

Leonard smiled. "Look…," he paused and scratched his head. If Sophie didn't know better, she'd have guessed he was embarrassed. "We'll talk soon, okay?"

She hurled a few of her more creative strings of curses at him by way of response. Baldwin shook his head and chuckled. "Logan will be along."

The two men marched out of the room without another word. The door shut, she heard a click, and the lights went out. She was once again in darkness.

She took a deep breath and tried to stop the panic racing through her brain. She had to think clearly now. No telling when this Logan person would arrive. She tested her wrists against the handcuffs and choked back her desperation. She couldn't so much as twist her arm in the cuff, let alone slip out of it. She took a deep breath and pulled as hard as she could with both hands, then cried out in pain as the cuffs cut into her wrists. She tried the same thing with her feet and achieved the same painful result.

Sophie squirmed and felt her rain-soaked pantsuit squish wetly on the seat. She'd been so proud of the outfit only a few hours ago. Picked out special to impress the warden, a man she would never even meet.

The chair was bolted to the floor. The cuffs were too strong to escape. She'd have to talk her way out of it when Logan arrived. Appeal to his sense of humanity. Or something.

The years spent under her mother's optimistic tutelage— even in the hard times—suddenly came back to her. She tried to think of something positive. "A happy mind is a clear mind," her mother had always said, and, God help her,

Sophie believed it.

So, happy thoughts.

For one thing, she wasn't splattered on the pavement outside city hall. That was something. She wasn't dead or even hurt much. Best of all, there was a chance Charles Taylor, the Curbside Killer himself, was here in these very woods. Or, at least he'd been very recently.

The work lights clamped to the ceiling suddenly turned on, flooding the room with hot white light and shooting daggers of pain into her skull. She snapped her eyes shut and then opened them a little, squinting to see what was happening.

She heard the creak of the door opening, and the click-click of footsteps. She saw the silhouette of the new arrival, but couldn't make out any of the features.

A woman's voice said, "Do you seek sanctuary and protection?"

Sophie relaxed a little at the female voice. But only a little. "Yeah."

"Request denied." The woman's voice was cold and hard. "What's your name?"

"Sophie Porter."

A spray of ice-cold water hit her in the chest and she yelled in surprise.

"No!" the woman shouted. "That's not your name. We don't use full names here. How'd you get here? What were you doing when you said the word?"

Sophie spat the cold water out of her mouth. "I take it you're Logan?"

Another stream of water blasted her.

"Answer the question! What were you doing?"

The water was still slamming against her and she shouted to be heard over it. "I was falling! I fell off a building."

The water shut off, leaving her shivering. The woman said, "Sophie Porter's as good as dead. She might as well have hit the ground and died on impact. All that's left is you, a new person. You have the chance to start fresh here. You can be Sophie or Porter. Take your pick."

Sophie shook her head hard to clear the water out of her face. "Listen, I'm happy to answer any questions you have, but can we behave like civilized human beings and stop spraying me with water?"

A blast of water to the face was her only answer.

"Okay! Okay! Sophie! I'll go by Sophie." The spray stopped, and she spit out another mouthful of water. "Listen, there's something you need to know. There's a guy named Charles Taylor around here. He was on death row, and—"

Water hit her in her open mouth, causing her to cough and choke.

"There's not any Charles Taylor here. Charles Taylor's dead, just like Sophie Porter. No one here has a past."

"Are you kidding me?" Sophie screamed through the water. "He was the Curbside Killer! He smashed strangers' heads in with baseball bats!"

"You're not listening! We don't care if you were the pope or Satan himself in your past life. All that matters is whether you can follow the rules."

"Some comfort that'll be when he kills you in your bed."

The angle of the water changed and it shot up her nose. She twisted her head, but the water followed.

"Do yourself a favor, and shut up," the woman said.

The door creaked open and another silhouette darkened the doorway.

"Really, Logan?" a male voice said. "Is this necessary?"

"She's lippy. Talking about people's pasts. I'm telling her

the rules."

"That's not your job."

"You weren't here."

"True enough. What's she go by?"

"She goes by Sophie," Sophie muttered through the water.

"Will you turn off the water, please?" the man asked. "And get the lights?"

The water stopped, and Sophie gasped for air. A moment later the work lights turned off, and the softer light of an overhead bulb replaced them.

The man walked over, his feet squeaking as he came. Sophie squeezed her eyes shut tight to blink away the water, and then opened them. He looked to be in his late-thirties. Most of his hair was gone and an expansive belly hung over the front of his pants. His smile shone bright as he leaned down toward her.

"I'm sorry about all that. Logan gets a bit carried away with the whole hazing thing."

Sophie was shivering hard now. "Apology accepted. You gonna unlock me now so I can kick her ass?"

He shook his head. "Not yet. There's one more thing."

She gritted her teeth and waited.

"Sophie, do you come here seeking sanctuary and protection?"

She glanced over the man's shoulder and got her first good look at Logan. The woman was tall with fiery red hair, and she wore a tank top that showed off her well-muscled arms.

Sophie looked back at the man. She'd asked this question before, but she had a feeling she might get a straight-forward answer this time. "What happens if I say no?"

He waved toward the door. "You walk out of here and go on your merry way. Though, I must say, I seriously doubt you'd survive long in those woods. And you'd never be welcomed back into our fold. This is a one-time offer."

Sophie looked at the pool of water around her feet. "Your fold, huh? That's what you call it?"

"Answer the question, Sophie," Logan said.

Sophie bit back a snide retort. "I'm looking for a man named Charles Taylor. Is he here?"

"I won't answer that question," the man said. "Not until you answer mine."

Sophie took a deep breath. "Yes. I want sanctuary."

The man broke out in a wide grin. He bent down and unlocked the cuffs around her ankles, and then the ones around her wrists. He held out his hand to her. "Sophie, my name's Nate. Welcome to Sanctuary."

3. Rook Mountain

The doorbell woke Sean. He looked around the room frantically, filled suddenly with a mix of adrenaline and confusion. He glanced at the clock. 3:12 AM. He sat up, swung his feet out of bed, and rubbed his eyes.

Had that really been the doorbell? Or had it been the tail end of a dream that spun so neatly into reality he thought he'd heard something?

He stood up and stretched. Only one way to find out.

The doorbell rang again, a series of three chimes that each felt like ice picks driving panic into his chest. There were few things scarier than an unexpected caller at three twelve in the morning.

He hurried to his dresser and grabbed his service revolver from the top drawer. Maybe not the best idea considering the adrenaline rushing through his veins and the sleep still clouding his mind. This was the exact type of situation where the wrong person could get shot. Still, he'd feel mighty dumb if he interrupted a home invasion and left a perfectly good gun in a drawer in the bedroom.

But, really, how many home invaders rang the doorbell?

Sean crept out of the bedroom, down the stairs, and toward the front door. He kept the lights off, not wanting to ruin his night vision. He slid his feet along the ground, moving swiftly and carefully to avoid anything he might have left on the floor.

As he moved through the house, he thought about the last time he'd woken in the middle of the night to find an unexpected visitor at the door. It had been his old friend Frank Hinkle. Frank had a crazy look in his eyes that night, and he'd been blabbering about the items with the broken clock symbol. At least this couldn't be any worse than that. An hour after that visit the Unfeathered had made their return to Rook Mountain.

He took a deep breath and flipped on the porch light. Pushing aside the curtain, he looked out. A single, thin figure stood on the porch. Colt Bryant. The kid from the crime scene earlier that day.

He pulled the door open. The chain was still latched, and he opened it wide enough to look out at the kid.

"Colt, what is it?" Sean asked. He tried hard to mask the irritation in his voice, but he wasn't sure if he succeeded.

Colt wore only a tee-shirt and jeans. His arms were wrapped around his chest, and he looked much younger than he had this morning. "Hi. I'm really sorry to wake you up."

Sean shook his head. "It's okay. What's going on?"

The kid stared up into Sean's eyes, a pathetic look of despair on his face. "Remember when you told me I could come talk to you if I was ever in trouble?"

Sean searched his memory for when he might have said that to this kid, but he came up empty. To the best of his knowledge, he'd never even spoken with Colt Bryant before today. Maybe he'd said it when talking at Colt's school or something. Of course, if that was the case, he would have been talking to the class about the Regulations, telling them to turn in any Regulation Breakers to the first police officer they could find.

"Yeah, I remember. Are you in trouble?"

Colt shook his head. "No. Well, maybe. I'm not sure yet."

"Okay. Tell me what you need."

Colt squinted into the black space between the door and the door frame. "Can I come in and talk?"

Sean paused, suddenly aware that all he was wearing was his boxers. "How about I come out there?"

"Okay."

"You want me to bring you a jacket?"

The kid shook his head. Sean shut the door and unhooked the chain. He grabbed his blue hoodie off the back of the recliner where he'd thrown it last night and slipped it on. He hesitated, and then shoved the gun into the pocket of the hoodie, keeping his right hand in there with it. Just in case. Something about Colt Bryant creeped him out a little, even when it wasn't 3:12 AM.

He stepped outside and gestured to the two rocking chairs on the porch. "Have a seat."

Colt shook his head. "This won't take long. I wanted to talk about the crime scene today. I have some information that might help you. With the case."

They needed all the help they could get on this one. The blood and the injuries made it clear Rodgers had taken a beaten before plunging off that roof, but their search of the building and interviews with bystanders had turned up nothing. A little help could go a long way. He'd prefer to not have evidence handed over on his porch in the middle of the night, though.

"That would be great," he said. "Why don't I get dressed and we can head down to the station?"

"No, I want to talk here. I don't think the station would be the safest place for me. Like I said, I might be in some trouble."

Sean nodded. "Okay. Let's talk here."

Colt paused, looking out into the night. "First, I have to ask you a question. Did you find anything on the body?"

Sean gripped his gun a bit harder. Was this why Colt had gotten him out of bed in the middle of the night? "We already talked about this at the scene. I can't give out that information."

Colt lowered his head, and his voice came out choked when he spoke. "I know he had something. Please. I need it."

"Tell me what kind of trouble you're in, son."

"Everyone's gonna think he killed himself because that death row inmate escaped while he was on duty. But that's not what happened."

Sean raised an eyebrow. "And you know what did happen?"

Colt's body shook for a moment as if he was crying. He cleared his throat. "You...you remember Regulation 2? The items with the broken clock symbol?"

Even hearing mention of that Regulation sent a jolt through Sean. That was the last thing he had expected to hear. "Yeah. Of course."

"Rodgers had one of the objects. A compass."

"How do you know that?"

Colt shrugged. "He wasn't exactly subtle about it. Ever

since so-called Deregulation Day, he's been drinking in bars, running his mouth. The wrong person overheard him."

"And how exactly did you get involved?" Sean asked.

"I've been running with Zed Heads lately."

"Yeah, I saw the tat."

"The Zed Heads want that object. Day before yesterday, they sent me and a couple of the younger guys to take it from him. Thing is, we didn't expect him to be armed."

"What happened?"

"We asked for the item. He admitted he had it. Even told us it was a compass. He pulled out a gun and I chickened out and left. He must have realized the Zed Heads would never let it go and offed himself."

Maybe this kid didn't know as much as he thought he did about what had happened. "Thank you, Colt," Sean said. "That's valuable information."

Colt nodded, and then he smiled a crooked smile, and a sudden light danced in his eyes. "The thing is, Officer Lee, Rodgers wasn't dumb. I respect him for that. He understood his situation and he acted on it. See, the Zed Heads aren't the kind of people to let something like this go. This joke of a government, these arbitrary laws we follow now, they're meaningless. The Regulations are the true law. They must be upheld. Regulation 2 is no exception."

Sean felt a chill in the air.

Colt continued. "Take you, for example. You were the first one at the scene today. Everyone there saw you bending down, pawing at the body. I happen to know the Zed Heads have friends in the police department, friends who are still loyal to Zed and what he stands for. Those friends tell us the compass wasn't on the body. I also happen to know the Zed Heads searched Rodgers' house. And his car. And a Zed-loyal guard searched his locker at the prison. The compass wasn't in any of those places. Some people might think you decided to keep the compass for yourself."

Sean leaned in close. "Is that why you came here? Are you trying to threaten me?"

"Officer Lee, it would help me out, and you too really, if you would hand over the compass. We would highly appreciate it."

"I don't have the compass. I think it's time for you to leave."

Colt's smile widened a little. "Okay. I'll go. I can't speak for my friends, though." He gestured toward the road.

Sean squinted out into the night. It took a moment, and then he saw them. There must have been two dozen dark shapes standing on the sidewalk facing the house. The Zed Heads. How long had they been there, silently watching, listening to the conversation? Sean's heart raced. He pulled the gun out of his pocket and held it down at his side, making sure Colt could see it.

He spoke loudly so they all could hear him. "Everyone needs to move along now. I don't have what you're looking for."

Colt nodded toward Sean's gun. "You gonna shoot us, Officer? Kids standing on the sidewalk at night? For what? Being out past curfew? Pulling a gun on kids breaking curfew sounds a little Regulationy to me."

The words were sharpened like a dagger. The department had zero-tolerance for officers enforcing Regulations. Two cops had been fired in the last few months for minor Regulation enforcement, and one had been fired for publicly stating that some of the Regulations might have been a good idea. The department was doing everything it could to distance itself from the perceived police state that existed under Zed's rule.

"Of course I'm not going to shoot anyone. But I will write citations for each and every person who isn't gone in the next thirty seconds."

"Citations?" Colt spat the word back in Sean's face. "The rules used to mean something. This town used to mean something. You think we care about your citations? Your pieces of paper are meaningless against what's coming. And I'll tell you something else: your gun isn't gonna be so helpful either. When the second coming happens it ain't gonna be like last time. There's gonna be a clear dividing line between those who upheld Zed's message and those who stood against it. You want to be on the right side of that line."

"It's time to go," Sean growled. "I'm not asking again."

Colt nodded. "You'll be seeing a lot more of us. Real soon. I gave you the chance to hand over the compass." With that, he turned and walked away. The rest of the Zed Heads followed, seeming to melt into the darkness.

Sean stood on the porch, his heart racing. He gazed out into the street, watching for any shapes that remained on the sidewalk. He saw none.

He was about to go back into the house when he heard a crash, quickly followed by the blaring of a car alarm. He leapt off the porch, skipping over the three steps and landing on the sidewalk mid-stride. He sprinted toward the driveway and then froze. The window of his police cruiser was shattered and a brick lay on the driver's seat.

He spun on his heels, searching, listening for some sign of which way the perpetrators ran. There was none. He was alone.

* * *

4. Sanctuary

Nate led Sophie along a broad path through the woods. His flashlight was small and he walked in front, so the beam of light was too far ahead of her to be of much help. She concentrated on his back, trying to follow him as he zigged and zagged toward wherever he was leading her.

At least she was dry. The rain had stopped, and the only reminder of it was the way her feet squished into the mud with each step. Nate had given her dry clothes: underwear, a tee-shirt, jeans, sneakers, and a light jacket, all the right size. They'd been waiting for her in another room in the cabin along with a towel, a hairbrush, and even a ponytail holder. Nate had shown her to the room and told her to take her time, to come out whenever she was ready. He'd waited outside while she dressed.

And now he was taking her somewhere. Nate had been quiet since they left the little cabin, simply plodding along the path, not even looking back to make sure she was still with him.

They rounded a sharp corner, and Nate paused. "This is it," he said. He turned and looked at her, as if watching for her reaction.

The building in front of them was a large, Victorian-style home. The lights inside illuminated the many windows, and she saw movement upstairs. The wrap-around porch was dotted with at least ten rocking chairs. Large white columns stood along the front of the house.

"Is this where you live?" she asked.

"Nah, not me. This is the boss's place. He lives upstairs, and most of the business that needs doing gets done downstairs. I have a much smaller, less obnoxious house down the path a ways. You'll get your own too, in time." With that, he turned and strode toward the house. Sophie looked at it for another moment and then followed.

The trail led straight to the front of the house. As far as she could see, there was no driveway, sidewalk, or garage, unless it was behind the house. She ran her hand along the banister as they ascended the stairs to the porch. This place was in perfect condition. The white paint was clean and unchipped. The bushes in front of the house were carefully manicured. The rocking chairs on the porch looked like they'd been hand built, considering the intricate details in the woodwork. The house seemed out of place in the dense forest. It was like finding a teacup in a tree branch; she knew there had to be a crazy story behind how and why the house had been built here.

Nate gestured toward one of the rocking chairs. "Nice night. You mind sitting out here and talking for a couple minutes before we head inside?"

She shook her head and eased herself into the rocking chair closest to her. It had been a long day/night, and her body was beginning to complain from the beating it had taken. In the last few hours, she had experienced the fight with Rodgers, been carried through the woods by Leonard and Baldwin, and gotten cuffed to the chair and hosed down by Logan. She hurt all over. And Nate was right; it was a nice night. A cool breeze cut through the trees. There wasn't the usual humid muggy haze that hung in the air after it rained. She hadn't been bitten by a single mosquito on the walk through the woods, and mosquitoes were generally drawn to Sophie.

"You doing okay?" Nate asked. "It must have been quite a shock. I know it was for me. First almost dying, then showing up here, then Logan with the hose."

Sophie nodded. "I'm doing okay." And she realized it was true. She was doing okay. She'd set out this morning to find Charles Taylor, and, whatever other craziness had happened, she could honestly say she was much closer to finding him than she'd thought she'd be at this point. For all she knew, he could be in that house right now. "You know, it's funny. I don't even know why I said the word. I didn't believe Sanctuary was real. Not even a little. But the word still came out of my mouth."

"It was the same for me," Nate said.

Sophie suddenly remembered something. "The man I was with. His name was Rodgers. He said the word, too. Is he here?"

Nate shook his head. "You think everyone who shouts 'Sanctuary' in their hour of need shows up here? This place would be overrun. We're the lucky ones."

"How's that work? Why us?"

He smiled. "The boss picked us. The way I understand it, he hears the cries of 'Sanctuary'. Every one of them. He can't save them all. We don't have the room. But every once in a while he plucks someone out of wherever they are and brings them here, gives them a new life." He reached forward and patted Sophie's knee. "We're truly a chosen people."

She gritted her teeth. How many good, decent folk had called for Sanctuary and had their call go unanswered? And the Curbside Killer gets chosen instead. "It certainly doesn't seem to be based on merit."

A shadow fell across Nate's face. "No. It isn't."

"How'd it happen for you? The almost dying thing."

"Well, Sophie, that's not something we talk about."

"Why not? I'll bet you're missing out on some hilarious stories. Who wouldn't want to talk about their near death experience?"

"It's not like it's against the rules. You can talk about yours if you want. It's sorta considered rude to ask. That's the way it is here. I don't know anyone's past but my own, but I'd guess most of the folks here didn't have it easy. You can see it in their eyes. They've seen things. Done things, some of them. But that's the beauty of this place. It doesn't matter. Everyone gets a fresh start."

She felt her face grow hot at the thought of Charles Taylor getting a clean slate. He might have his own little house in these woods. Probably laughed himself to sleep every night. "Maybe some people don't deserve a fresh start."

"I won't say I disagree with you. But the boss does. Everyone here starts with the same blank slate. He makes sure of it."

"Is that why you brought me up here? To meet the boss?"

"Yeah. Just a quick hello for now. We'll do that in a few minutes, but there are some things we need to discuss first. I need to prepare you."

She paused. "That sounds ominous."

"Nah. Quite the opposite, actually. Some people find him to be a little... let's say, intimidating. He takes his work here very seriously, and he gets a little intense about it. But underneath it all, he's a sweetheart. Really. And it's important work, so maybe he has reason to be intense about it."

"What work is that?" She suddenly envisioned herself hauling stones over a mountain to build a statue to the great and mysterious boss.

He nodded toward the woods. "We tend to the forest. We maintain the trails."

"What if I don't see myself as the park ranger type?"

"What do you see yourself as?"

She thought for a moment. That was a tough question. She was twenty-seven years old, and she couldn't say she had much of an identity. For years, she'd concentrated on not thinking about what happened to Heather. But she'd thrown that away when she drove to Rook Mountain.

Rules weren't her thing. She'd walked away from jobs when she'd butted heads with her bosses. There were always other jobs, and no paycheck was worth her freedom.

"I guess I see myself more as the type who steals picnic baskets," she said.

He chuckled. "There's room for all kinds here, bear and park ranger alike. We'll help you find your place, and in time I think you'll find it's far more rewarding than anything you did in the outside world. The boss believes in hard work, but he also believes in letting people figure out what type of work they should be doing. What type of work fulfills them."

"Where are we? I mean, like, where in the world? These trees are huge. Are they redwoods?"

He paused for a moment before answering. "Sorry, I've been here so long I forgot the crazy things that go through your head when you're new."

"Let me guess," she said. "I'm not supposed to ask that question."

He held up his hands. "No, no. You can ask. It's not something I spend a lot of time thinking about these days. Fact is, I have no idea where in the world we are. And I don't care. We're never leaving. Most of us wouldn't want to. So why's it matter?" He nodded toward the house. "Listen, he's probably waiting for us, so let me tell you about the rules."

Sophie smirked. "Rules, huh? I was waiting for that part ever since you mentioned a boss."

"Chill, Yogi. It's not a big deal. The boss isn't a fan of rules and regulations. For the most part, it's live and let live around here. I guarantee you've never had as much freedom in your life. But there are two rules you cannot violate. We take them very seriously." He nodded toward the house again. "*He* takes them very seriously."

Sophie leaned forward in her rocking chair. What kind of a place was this?

"Rule one. Don't hurt anyone. Simple as that. Fist fights, unprovoked attacks, murder. We treat them all the same."

"Except hosing down new recruits. You let that slide."

"That was different. You were an outsider. You've been accepted into Sanctuary now. But don't even think about getting back at Logan or Leonard or Baldwin. When we say don't hurt anyone, we mean it. It's a hard line rule, but it works. We don't have any fights, because everyone understands the consequences."

"And the consequences are?"

"Banishment. Understand the rule?"

She nodded.

"And you'll follow it?"

She pictured herself driving a knife into Charles Taylor's chest all the way to the hilt. "Yeah. I'll follow it."

She gazed at the window and wondered if this mysterious boss was looking out at her through one of those curtains. Did he know? Did he know what Taylor had done to her? Was he watching her, waiting to see how she'd react?

"What's the second rule?"

Nate smiled. "Never go into the boss's office. Except now." He stood up. "Come on. He's waiting to meet you."

She clenched her fists. She felt the anger welling up inside of her, the familiar rage she'd felt so many times over the years. But she had become an expert at suppressing it, at smiling through the pain and going to class or going to work and no one being the wiser. She'd do it again now. She'd follow their rules and be the perfect citizen of this creepy little commune until she saw her way out. It didn't seem likely she'd be able to haul Taylor through the woods and back to civilization. If she could, she'd leave this place and bring the authorities back with her. But if she had to, she'd carry out Taylor's sentence herself. It made her a little sick thinking about it, but she would do it if it came to that.

She followed Nate through the double doors on the front of the house and into a large living area. The room was decorated in a simple and rugged style that didn't exactly fit the old southern charm of the exterior, but she had to admit the furniture looked top quality.

She glanced at the chandelier overhead with its many glowing light bulbs. Was this house running off a generator or was it on the grid? Even if it was a generator, they had to be getting the fuel somewhere. Maybe this place wasn't as cut off from the outside world as Nate implied. And where there was contact with the outside world, there was a chance at escape.

"This way," Nate said. He led her to a door on the far side of the room. He rapped on the door three times.

"Come," a voice from within said.

Nate winked at Sophie. "Don't worry. He'll love you." He opened the door and went into the room. Sophie took a deep breath and followed.

The office was dominated by a large oak desk. The man behind the desk stood as they entered. He was a tall, solid looking man with shaggy blond hair streaked with gray. He was handsome in an unkempt kind of way, and his wide smile added to his boyish charm. He wore a simple plain black tee-shirt and jeans.

He held out his hand to her.

"Sophie, welcome to Sanctuary. My name's Jake."

IN THE WOODS (PART TWO)

They waited in Mason's cabin until nightfall.

The exterior was rough, with trees growing uncomfortably close and boards covering most of the windows. But the inside was nice, if not exactly spacious. The large main room was decorated with a couch and an easy chair. There was a king size bed in the corner, and one of the walls was lined with boxes sporting the logos of everything from Hormel to Ramen to Nike.

When Frank asked him where he got all this stuff, Mason shrugged and told him they'd been here his whole life. Whatever that meant. Frank didn't press the matter. Not now. He was still reeling from the news that his brother was dead.

According to what Mason said, Frank had arrived at least sixty-five years after Jake. It seemed crazy, but it did make a certain amount of sense. The mirror had the broken clock symbol on it, just like the pocket watch. Frank and his friends hadn't discovered any time-altering properties of the mirror —or any of the other Tools—but Zed told them they had only scratched the surface of what the Tools could do.

Then there was always the possibility time passed differently here, wherever here was. Frank thought back to

The Chronicles of Narnia books he'd read as a kid. Peter, Susan, Edmond, and Lucy spent years in Narnia while only a few hours passed back on Earth. He supposed fictional wonderlands probably weren't the best way to find the truth, but maybe they could help him find new ways to look at it.

Mason stood near the one window that had glass covering it instead of boards.

"Who was that man with the beard?" Frank asked. He'd kept quiet about it on the walk here since Mason clearly seemed disturbed by the sighting, but Frank needed to know.

Mason shook his head. "Not yet. It's hard to explain unless you understand what happened to my parents. And *that's* hard to explain without showing you."

He looked out the window, then waved Frank over.

Frank shuffled to the window and looked out, following Mason's gaze. They had a view of the nearest mountain top through a thin gap in the trees. The sun was slipping behind the peak.

"We should be good to go now," Mason said. "The Larvae aren't the bravest of creatures. They don't come out of their hidey holes once it gets dark."

From the almost defensive way he said it, Frank could tell Mason had affection for the creatures. And why not? He'd spent his whole life around them.

"If they're larvae, does that mean they're babies?" Frank asked. "What do they grow up to become?"

Mason shook his head. The way his shaggy hair brushed the tops of his eyebrows reminded Frank of Jake. "They grow to a certain point, and then they leave. I don't know where they go or how they do it. Hell, if I knew I would have followed them years ago."

Mason picked up two flashlights and handed one to Frank.

They left the cabin and headed down a trail that had been worn down, Frank guessed, by Mason's feet alone. It was wide enough that they could walk side-by-side with room to spare.

"How far is it?" Frank asked.

"Not far. Probably."

Frank decided to let that odd statement go for now.

After five minutes of walking, Mason said, "It's right ahead." They rounded a bend and Frank saw it, a hulking shape in the dark. He pointed his flashlight at it to reveal more.

From the bits that weren't covered in vines and ivy, Frank could see it had once been a beautiful home. Old dilapidated columns supported the sagging roof over the wrap-around porch, and long blades of grass grew through the slats.

"This is it," Mason said. "My dad's house."

Frank's eyes scanned the area. "Tell me what happened."

Mason took a long moment before speaking. "You gotta understand, he could be a difficult man at times."

Frank grinned. "You don't have to tell me. I used to share a bunk bed with him."

Mason chuckled. "He never told me that. At least not that I remember. I was so young. Sometimes the memories get fuzzy." He stared into the ruins of the house.

"You were saying he was difficult?" Frank prompted.

"Yeah. Sometimes he was. But he was also dedicated. If he believed in something, he'd fight for it."

"What did he believe in?"

Mason smiled. "That much I remember. He believed in his friends."

Frank cocked his head at that. Obviously, for Mason to exist there had to have been a woman here at some point. But friends? How many people had lived in these woods?

"My dad led a little community here. They called it Sanctuary. They worked together to keep the forest safe. They kept everything in place, if that makes sense. It wasn't always perfect, but it was always peaceful. Until I was eight."

"So what happened?"

Mason sighed. "New people would show up here occasionally. My dad always took them in and put them to work. He was kind like that. But one day a woman showed up, and everything changed."

"Changed how?"

"Dad kept me sheltered from most of it, but even I saw what was happening. She had new ideas, a new way of dealing with things. There were a couple fights, and I know my father had to punish some people. And there was a tension in the air. Like something bad was coming."

Frank looked out over the rubble and tried to imagine it as it was then, groups of people fighting and squabbling and living their lives right here in these woods. And Jake leading them.

"One night," Mason continued, "there was a battle. Mom told me to go lock myself in the bathroom and not to come out until she came to get me. I waited what felt like hours. When I finally came out, there were bodies everywhere. Including mom's."

Mason pointed his flashlight toward a stand of trees twenty yards away. "I ran and hid in the woods and waited, praying for it all to end. I heard yelling, so much yelling."

He waved his hand towards the woods to the right of the house. "There used to be cabins all along here, a couple dozen of them. The woman and her friends burned most of them. The fires burned for hours. I could feel the heat of it from where I sat. I hid in the woods and watched the flames. I kept waiting for my dad to come find me. It wasn't until later that I found his body in the woods."

"I'm sorry that happened to you, Mason," Frank said. "I'm sure Jake did everything he could to protect you."

"I know he did," Mason said. "He was a good father. The best I've known, anyway. Besides, it wasn't all bad luck. They left a few cabins standing, including the storage cabin. So I had shelter and supplies. Supplement that with plants and berries and I've managed to get by. As I grew a little older, I hunted when I had the opportunity. Sometimes deer wandered into these woods. Or squirrel. We had a bear once. I just had to kill the animals before the Larvae got at them. Like I said, the forest was more lively back then."

Frank was still trying to decide what to think of his nephew.

"Let me ask you something," Frank said. "Have you been alone all this time? Because you don't talk like someone who hasn't had human contact since he was eight."

Mason grinned, showing yellowed teeth with plenty of gaps between them. "Oh I never said I was alone. There's a man who comes sometimes. I might have sat in the woods looking at those fires forever if not for him. He taught me how to live out here. Which plants to eat. How to hunt on the odd occasion an animal showed up. I spent a lot of time with him when I was growing up."

Frank felt a cold chill. "Who was it? What's his name?"

Mason's grin widened. "The way he tells it, you know him already. His name's Zed."

CHAPTER THREE: ARTIFACTS

1. Sanctuary

It was two days later the first time Sophie saw him.

They kept her isolated. Jake told her she needed time to adjust before meeting the others. She lived in the cabin where she had been hazed by Logan. The handcuff-enhanced chair and the hose had been replaced with a nice queen-size bed, a dresser stocked with simple and practical clothes, and a small bookshelf stocked with popular fiction from a variety of eras.

She spent the first day mostly unsupervised. She could hang out in the house. She could work in the vegetable garden out back. As long as she didn't step outside the tall wooden fence that caged off the backyard. She occasionally heard people walking past the fence, usually alone and quiet, only the sounds of their feet shuffling on the hard dirt giving them away. But sometimes there were groups, and she heard talking and laughing. She was forbidden from calling out to them. It was against the rules to talk to anyone outside this cabin. She got the feeling climbing the fence and peaking over it at them wouldn't be appreciated either.

Just for now, Jake told her.

So much for there only being two rules.

Jake had been much like Nate had described. Friendly and pleasant, but in a surface way. There was something distant about the man, like he was only partially there in the room with her. But it wasn't like his mind was wandering. She never got the sense he wasn't paying attention. It was more like a vital part of him, of his personality, his soul maybe, was missing.

Her only companion in isolation was Frasier, the man who had been in the cabin when Leonard and Baldwin brought her in. He was always around, not following her, but not avoiding her either. He was a quiet man, and she was dying for some conversation.

"Was Frasier your first name or your last name?" she asked him. They were in the garden. She had already pulled all the weeds she could find, and not having a lot of gardening experience, she didn't know what else to do. She wanted to talk to Frasier, and she hadn't been able to think of a good question despite wracking her brain for the past twenty minutes.

He grinned a toothy grin. "See, this is exactly why you need time to adjust before joining up with the rest of the crew. It's not polite to ask that kind of thing."

"I didn't ask about your past. I asked about your name. Your name is who you are. Always."

Frasier shook his head. "Not anymore. Now it's just the one name. Get it through your skull. The old life's gone."

Sophie grunted. "Man! You're a stone wall." Her eyes combed the garden for the twentieth time, hoping to find a weed to pick.

"It's kind of freeing though, isn't it?" he asked. "Not having the weight of the past on you. You can be anything you want here. Look at it as an opportunity to reinvent yourself."

Sophie looked at him. "Am I allowed to ask about Jake?"

The old man stretched, cracking his back loudly. "Sure. No rule against that."

"Does he bring us here? This is gonna sound stupid, but does he have some kind of machine or something? Or, I don't know, some power?"

Frasier chuckled. "You figure that one out, you tell me. He's pretty tight lipped. All I know is he has this book. I think it lets him know when a new person is coming. He tells us a couple of days in advance. Usually anyway."

"I remember Leonard saying they weren't expecting anyone the other night."

Frasier nodded. "Either Jake didn't know, or he had some reason for not telling us."

"If people get here by asking for Sanctuary in unexpected, life-threatening situations, how does Jake know it's gonna happen ahead of time?" Sophie asked. Frasier started to speak, and she held up a hand to stop him. "I know. He's tight lipped. I'm making conversation. Asking you to speculate."

Frasier shook his head. "Like I said, if you figure it out, you let me know." With that, he turned and went into the cabin.

Sophie groaned. Of all the people to be stuck with for an indeterminate amount of time, she got Stonewall Frasier.

If the purpose of this time in isolation was to make her more comfortable in Sanctuary, it was having the opposite effect. She had far too much time to think. She thought about her parents, the way they'd already lost one child, and how they must be frantic at the disappearance of their remaining daughter. It made her sick to her stomach. She had to find a way to get back, and not just to bring Taylor to justice. Her parents deserved better than to be left wondering for the rest of their lives.

The next day, Frasier let her sit on the front porch with him. It wasn't much, but it beat the hell out of being stuck in the backyard, fenced in like an animal. Here she had a view.

The trees in front of her were unlike any she'd ever seen. They were unbelievably tall, and the trunks were as thick around as her Honda Civic. They first reminded her of redwoods, but they were different. Part of it was the color. The bark reminded her of butterscotch. And they were twisted. The trunks bent and spun and angled out in odd directions in their journey skyward. The shadows of the massive trees fell over everything.

The trail, she assumed the same trail she had been carried up three days ago, snaked out of the woods, past the porch where they sat, then wrapped around the back of the cabin, off to who knew where. The people she'd heard the day before must have been walking on that trail.

It was dusk, and people occasionally passed the cabin. Either they knew not to talk to newcomers or this was an especially introverted community. Most of them didn't even acknowledge her. A few gave a curt nod. One, a boy who couldn't have been more than eight, waved at her shyly.

Frasier introduced her by proxy after the walkers disappeared around the corner. "That woman in the red tee-shirt's Abby. She's a hard worker. Had a baby about six months ago. Cute little girl. Named her Gavin. The man with her is Vance. They're together. Though he's not Gavin's daddy. Baldwin's the father."

Sophie reached over and playfully slapped his knee. "Guess there's no rule against gossiping."

His face turned beet red. "Just giving you the lay of the land," he muttered. "Thought you might want to know."

Sophie smiled. "No, no, please continue. Who was the kid who waved?"

He cleared his throat, making a show of his reluctance to gossip further. "Him you're gonna want to know. That's Jake's boy. Mason."

"Huh," Sophie said. "Who's the mother?"

Now Frasier grinned. "You met her." He leaned forward, clearly enjoying this. "Logan."

Sophie groaned. "Doesn't surprise me. She gave off a queen bee kind of vibe."

Frasier shrugged. "She comes on strong at times, that's for sure. Officially, she and Jake are broken up, but unofficially not much has changed." He gave her a wink. "She's good people. You should cut her some slack. She's been through a lot."

"Considering how people get to Sanctuary, I'd say *been through a lot* applies to every person here."

Frasier chuckled. "Yeah, I guess it does."

That was the moment it happened. He rounded the corner, and there he was, right in front of her. Charles Taylor.

He looked older than Sophie remembered. His scraggly beard was as much salt as pepper now. But that made sense. It had been nearly a decade since she last saw him. The picture they'd been flashing on the news the past few days was the old one, the famous one from his trial, where he was sitting behind the defendant's table, smirking as if the proceedings were a joke. But his most defining characteristic, his thick arms and his huge, catcher's mitt hands, remained the same. Sophie could never look at those hands without picturing a baseball bat in them, couldn't look at those arms without imagining them swinging a bat into the back of Heather's head so hard her skull broke into a hundred tiny shards of bone.

He froze when he saw her. The sun was behind Sophie, and Taylor's squinted into it, as if not sure of what he was seeing. He took a few steps forward and fell under the shadow of the cabin. He stared at Sophie for a long while, his head tilted slightly, as if trying to place her.

Sophie felt the old familiar anger flow through her. She wanted to leap out of the rocking chair and dig her fingernails into his throat, to squeeze the breath out of him, to stand on his face as he died. But she felt something else too. Something stronger. Something unexpected. Fear.

She wanted to move, but she couldn't. She was frozen under his terrifying gaze. All the old fears came rushing back. The Curbside Killer had finally come for her.

Charles Taylor slowly smiled. He tipped his baseball cap at her. Then he moseyed down the path. Sophie's eyes followed him. She didn't breathe until he rounded the corner and disappeared from sight.

Frasier gently cleared his throat. "That was Taylor. But I'm guessing you already knew that."

Sophie kept her eyes on the path, as if Taylor might come charging back around at any moment. "We don't talk about the past," she said.

"Fair point," Frasier said. "And I wasn't going to ask."

She felt the life come back into her limbs, and with it something else: shame. It was a moment she'd been waiting for the last seven years. She'd planned a thousand things she'd say if she ever got the chance. A thousand things she'd do. But, instead, she'd acted like a scared child who saw the boogeyman. Worse still, Taylor had seen her fear.

She'd lost the element of surprise. She'd lost her edge. Taylor knew she was here, and he knew she was afraid.

"Piece of advice." Frasier spoke slowly and softly, his fatherly side coming out for the first time. "Taylor? The man's not right. I don't know what's between you, and I don't want to know. Whatever it is, let it stay in wherever the hell you came from. Steer clear of him as much as possible. When you do see him again, pretend like you're meeting him for the first time. If he has any smarts, he'll do the same."

"Easier said than done."

"Maybe, but it's what you need to do. I can help."

Sophie looked at him, finally pulling her eyes away from the spot where Taylor had disappeared. "Help how?"

"I can keep you busy. It's time we start talking about the work we do here. But first, an important question. You any good with a knife?"

Sophie raised an eyebrow. "Are you asking me to cook?"

Frasier stood up, a noisy process involving groans, cracks, and pops. "No, I'm not. We use our knives for more than cooking here. I think it's about time I showed you."

2. Sanctuary

Jake stood, as he often did these days, staring out his office window toward the trees at the edge of the woods.

The one benefit of living in a clearing in the middle of a constantly shifting forest was that your view was new every day. But over time, he had learned to identify some of the trees. The way a low branch crooked out a certain angle, the way the trunk took an unnatural twenty degree turn about fifteen feet off the ground. These were the things that distinguished one tree from another. It always made him a bit queasy looking at those trees. Each one of them represented another memory he couldn't forget.

There was one that was worse than the others. He paused at the window each morning before he looked out, hoping he wouldn't see that particular tree. When it was at the edge of woods, it cast the shadow of a foul mood over him for the rest of the day. Something about that one tree, a tree a bit taller and a bit gnarlier than the rest, disquieted Jake at a deep level.

Thankfully today that tree was not at the edge. It was buried somewhere deeper in the forest, which was fine with Jake. It could stay buried in there forever for all he cared. He glanced over at the small book shelf in the corner. How long had it been since he'd gotten himself a new book? In the old days, he had torn through novels like it was a mission from God to get to the last page as quickly as possible. But in the last few years he'd had a hard time concentrating while reading. The top shelf currently contained two John Scalzi books, one Scott Lynch, and one Patrick Rothfuss, all unread.

Sometimes Jake wondered if maybe the book with the broken world symbol had somehow sapped his love of reading anything else.

There was a knock at the door, three quick taps. Jake never locked the office door unless he was leaving the house, and everyone respected his privacy. People rarely disturbed him, and, when they did, they always knocked. Everyone but Mason. Mason burst into his father's office like it was his own bedroom. Which was as it should be, as far as Jake was concerned.

Sanctuary. Had any father every given his son a more awful birthright? A childhood of isolation in a place he would never be able to leave.

From the sound at the door, Jake knew it wasn't Nate, who

83

always used a distinct knocking pattern to identify himself.

"Come in," Jake said.

The door opened and Yang walked in, a sheet of yellow legal paper in his hand. Yang was a thin man who was quick with a smile but generally kept to himself. He seemed happiest when he was in the kitchen preparing the communal meals.

He handed Jake the legal paper. "Just dropping off the shopping list, boss."

Jake grimaced. It seems Nate's nickname for Jake was catching on with some of the others. "Thanks. You need it today?"

Yang shrugged, a wicked smile playing on his lips. "If possible. If not, I can always make meatloaf tonight."

Jake couldn't help but smile himself. Yang knew Jake loathed meatloaf. "Message received. I'll get to work."

Yang winked and ambled out of the office, swinging the door shut behind him.

Jake pulled the curtains shut, returned to his desk and took the book out of the faded red lockbox. He ran his hand across the symbol on the front of the book, a globe with a jagged crack running through it. The image was slightly raised and running his hand over it somehow calmed him.

He'd found the book only moments after arriving in these woods, and for a long time—close to two years by his calculation—it had been his only companion. The first time he'd looked through it, it had been nonsense, a series of strange, seemingly unrelated drawings surrounded by text composed of letters unlike anything Jake had ever seen. But, slowly, the book revealed itself to him. Line by line, page by page, the nonsense words became English. It was as if the book were learning to trust him.

The book showed him how to survive here. It instructed him in uncannily specific terms on how to find water and food. And it was the book that finally convinced him that he would never leave this place. That his mission in coming here would fail. Instead of saving his family back in Rook Mountain, he had abandoned them.

And, years later, it was the book that had helped him realize there may be a way home after all, but that it would be a very long road indeed.

Eventually, the book had taught him how to bring objects from elsewhere into Sanctuary. Pages of the book could transform into windows to the world. When he saw something he wanted, he could grab it and bring it through, like a kid pulling a toy out of a toy box. At first, it had been only small things. A little food here. An item of clothing there. But as more of the book was revealed to him, he found the size of the object didn't matter. He felt like Luke Skywalker struggling to raise his X-Wing ship out of the bog in *Empire Strikes Back* the first time he brought something large through, but he slowly got the hang of it. He found he could bring through anything from a can of soup to the house he was sitting in right now. And eventually, he'd learned he could bring people.

In his weakest moments, he'd considered trying to bring Trevor and Christine to Sanctuary, but he knew subjecting his family to that wasn't love; it was sickness.

And then the book began to reveal people asking for help in their moment of most extreme need. Asking for sanctuary. So he had started helping them.

Every person here represented a life Jake had saved. He'd pulled each of them through the book and granted new life. Every person but one, the most recent addition. Sophie.

Jake couldn't think about that now. He had spent most of the last few days worrying over that. Worrying came natural to him and he had to consciously fight it lest it overtake him.

He picked up the piece of legal paper off his desk, opened the book, and began tracing a window on the page with his index finger.

3. Sanctuary

A week later, Frasier said Sophie was ready. He handed her a knife and told her to hook it on her belt. It was the knife she'd been practicing with all week, a week where she'd learned more about knives than she had ever wanted to.

It was a six-inch fixed blade knife made of tempered steel with a coating of hard chrome.

"It's the same model the Navy Seals use," Frasier had proudly told her.

Sophie took the knife and looked at it sadly. "Not sure why I'm taking this. I'm just as likely to stab one of my team as I am anything else."

"Well, if you do have to stab someone, make sure it's not Logan. She's irritable enough already."

She'd grown fond of Frasier and his dry sense of humor, and she thought he enjoyed her company too, though he'd never say it. He had been a hard nut to crack, but she felt like she'd finally managed it.

Frasier put a hand on her shoulder. "Relax. You won't see anything. It's the middle of the night. The Larvae are in their deepest sleep now."

Sophie nodded. The way she understood it, their mission was simple: walk the trail. There were dozens of trails through the woods that Sanctuary crews maintained, but tonight Sophie and her team would be walking the biggest and most highly traveled of them. It seemed stupid to her, but Frasier claimed it was the most important job in Sanctuary.

"These woods are hungry," he told her. "If we don't walk the trails for a few days, they disappear."

"You mean they get grown over?"

He shook his head. "They disappear. They're not there anymore. It's like they never were. Like I said, these woods are hungry."

He'd explained it to Sophie a dozen times over the last week. According to Frasier, the purpose of the Sanctuary was to keep the woods at bay. The reason it existed was so it could keep existing. It seemed like circular logic to Sophie. Frasier insisted it was important. If they weren't vigilant, the forest would envelop them. It would swallow them whole.

"The forest's always shifting, always moving. It's changing every moment. The trees you see tonight through your window won't be there tomorrow when you look out. The forest changes its strategy and shifts its angle of attack. The only constant is the trails. And they only remain if we force them to. We keep them nailed down by walking them each and every day."

When he saw the skeptical look on her face, he said, "Well, maybe it'll be easier to understand once you've walked a few trails yourself."

Now she was preparing to do just that. A group of three was gathered in front of The Welcome Wagon. All of them wore headlamps like she'd seen Baldwin and Leonard wear that first night. She strapped on her own headlamp and walked over to them.

She recognized two of the group: Baldwin and Logan.

She was happy to see a couple of familiar faces, and at the

same time angry she had to work with two of the people who'd hazed her. Baldwin gave her a sheepish nod, perhaps feeling her out to see if she'd punch him on sight. She returned the nod, squinting in a manner she hoped looked cold and angry. In truth, she was mostly glad she would soon be talking to someone other than Frasier. As much as he'd grown on her, it would be great to meet other folks.

But she had to be careful not to form any attachments. She didn't intend to stay at the Sanctuary long. Once she got the lay of the land and figured out how to escape, she'd grab Taylor and bring him to justice. One way or another.

Logan had yet to acknowledge her existence, and that was fine with Sophie. She had nothing to say to the woman.

The group stood in the light of The Welcome Wagon's porch, and Sophie introduced herself to the other member of the group, a man named Carver. He couldn't have been more than twenty. He had a buzz cut and wore a tank top that displayed his well-defined arms. He gave Sophie a look that was a bit more than friendly. There it was again, the way she attracted younger men. Not that Carver was too young, necessarily. She had to admit he was pretty cute.

She cast a wary eye toward Logan. The woman was probably in her early forties. She, too, wore a tank top and, while her arms didn't quite compare with Carver's, they were certainly impressive. Sophie made a mental note to ask about the workout regime here. The 30 Day Sanctuary Shred?

After the introductions were over, Logan cleared her throat. When she spoke, it was all business. "Listen up, Sophie. I'm lead on this walk, so that means once we cross the tree line, my word's law. Understood?"

Sophie nodded.

"Good. You have one job and one job only tonight. Watch

and listen. That's it. This is the safest walk we have. This is the most populated trail and the Larvae are deep in their sleep cycle now. However, that doesn't mean we're gonna screw around. Things have gone south on this walk before. Not often, but the forest occasionally throws us curve balls. Any questions?"

Sophie shook her head. The Larvae. Frasier had told her about them, too.

"Good. Keep your headlamp pointed at the trail. Keep your knife in its sheath unless I say to draw it. Most of all, watch and listen." She looked around at the others. "Okay, let's go. Fall in behind me."

She turned and headed down the trail at a brisk pace. Baldwin went next. Sophie came behind him, and Carver went last.

"You excited?" Carver asked.

Sophie shrugged. "I don't know. I'm excited to be getting out of that cabin. But I've been on hikes in the woods before."

"Not like this."

Baldwin and Logan were pulling ahead. Sophie couldn't help but notice the way Carver was hanging back with her, sticking a bit closer than he probably needed to. "Geez," she said. "They go fast, don't they?"

Carver said, "It's a ten mile walk, sometimes more. Got to move fast if we want to get done while the Larvae are still in their deepest sleep."

Sometimes more? Sophie thought.

A few minutes later, Baldwin dropped back and pointed his headlamp at a tree past the edge of the trail. "Hey Sophie. You see that tree over there? That's the one we found you next to."

She shined her own light on the tree. "No. We were much deeper in the woods. That's not it."

"Oh, it's the one alright. Didn't Frasier tell you? The trees move here. After a while, you'll be able to identify some of them. This one you can recognize by the tangled roots."

Sophie stared at the roots. If this was the tree, then Rodgers' compass was under there. The compass that pointed to her and, according to Rodgers, pointed to Taylor. She'd always be able locate Taylor with that compass.

"One sec." She stepped off the trail and bent down next to the tree.

"Whoa!" Carver yelled. "Sophie, get back here!"

She ignored him. With her light, she searched for an opening in the tangle of roots. She saw the spot and thrust her hand into it. She felt around, and her hand passed over dry pine needles and sticky clay earth, but not the compass.

"Sophie, what the hell?" Baldwin shouted.

She ignored him too. She leaned forward, sticking more of her arm into the gap until her shoulder touched the base of the roots. She felt cold metal, and closed her hand around it.

Suddenly, she was yanked backwards. Her first insane thought was, *Rodgers!* She landed on her back on the trail, and she saw Logan standing over her. Logan lifted her foot and set it on Sophie's throat.

"What in the name of holy God was that?"

Sophie struggled to speak with the boot on her throat. "I...Sorry...That's the tree where..."

"Didn't Frasier do his job? Didn't he warn you to stay on the trail?"

"Yes! I'm sorry! I forgot!"

"Forgot?" Logan asked through clenched teeth. "There's no forgetting. Forgetting is how people die. No one dies. Not on my team."

"Logan," Baldwin said, his voice almost a whisper. "Eyes on the tree."

Logan spun, turning her light toward the tree. Sophie's eyes followed the beam of light, and her breath caught in her throat when she saw it. A black round creature the size of a basketball was sluggishly squeezing out of the hole where her arm had been only moments ago.

Logan whirled toward Sophie. "On your feet. We're all gonna back away slowly and head down the trail. It should go back in its burrow."

Sophie eased herself to her feet, her eyes never leaving the creature at the end of Logan's headlamp beam. She shuffled her feet with the others, heading down the trail as quickly as they dared.

She almost allowed herself to believe they were safe. Then, with no provocation that Sophie could see, the creature gave itself a violent shake.

"Shit!" Logan yelled. "Let's move!"

The creature contracted to half its original size and launched into the air. It spun with a freakish speed. As it flew, the soft-looking fur on its body stood up into clumps that resembled spikes. It was heading toward Logan, but then it slowed in the air, made an impossible turn, and shot toward Carver.

Carver screamed as the Larva hit him in the upper arm. It struck him with a sickening thud. The creature gave another violent shake, burrowing deeper into Carver's arm, and he screamed again.

Sophie was frozen with fear. She glanced around and saw the others had their knives out. Sophie clumsily pulled her own from its sheath.

She took a deep breath and reminded herself what Frasier had said. He'd told her exactly what to do in this scenario. The Larvae were, for all practical purposes, indestructible. They were bulletproof, which was why the teams of walkers didn't carry guns. The only thing that could be damaged was their thick spike-like fur. Hence the knives.

"One of your buddies gets stuck by one of those bastards, you gotta cut through the spikes one by one. There will be dozens of them, and it's not the easiest stuff to cut through. It'll take ten, fifteen minutes of cutting, all while your buddy's screaming and bleeding all over you. Your best bet's to work as fast as you can and pray he doesn't bleed out before you get the creature off him."

Logan ran to Carver and went to work on the spikes. The Larva gave another shiver and pressed itself tighter against Carvers arm.

Carver grabbed at the thing, trying to pull it off his arm, but he only succeeded in impaling his hands on the spikes.

Logan grunted in frustration and kept cutting. "A little help?"

Blood seeped around the edges of where the Larva was attached to his arm.

Sophie realized she still had the compass in her left hand. All this because she'd wanted the stupid thing. If only she'd listened to the rules, Carver wouldn't have a monster burrowing into him. She squeezed the compass as hard as she could, and she felt something click like a button had been pressed.

She opened her hand and saw the needle of the compass was pointing at Carver and the Larva. But somehow Sophie knew more specifically where it was pointing. It was like a needle in her mind was pointing too. Pointing at the spot she was supposed to...

She gripped her knife and took three quick steps forward.

"Start at the top, Sophie," Logan said. "Cut as fast as you can."

Sophie ignored her. The needle in her mind pointed to a specific spot on the Larva. It a small bulge on the bottom of the creature, almost invisible to her eye. Somehow she knew it was the closest thing the creature had to a head.

She pulled her knife back, and then drove it upward with all her strength. She felt her blade sink into the creature and stick there. Then she felt her blade wiggle a little, and the Larva began to melt. Its black flesh ran down her blade. She pulled the blade away and took a step back.

The black sludge ran down Carver's arm and chest. He stared at the disappearing creature, his mouth agape as the ooze ran down his legs and onto the ground. He grabbed his arm and fell to his knees.

"Carver," Baldwin said. He sank to the ground next to his friend.

But Sophie barely noticed. The needle in her head was pointing somewhere else now. She spun and pointed her headlamp toward the tree. Another creature was squeezing out of the hole in the root structure. Sophie sprinted for it.

Now that she knew what to look for, she saw the head immediately. It was like an exposed wound.

The Larva was wiggling free of the last root when Sophie reached it. She drove the knife into it like a hammer, and the creature melted even faster than its brother had.

"My God," Logan said. "You killed it. You killed two of them."

But Sophie wasn't listening. Her internal needle was pointing elsewhere now. It was pointing at the tree itself.

She circled around the back of the tree. She looked up and saw something carved there. Four little words.

Don't trust them Sophie.

She froze, staring at the message that had been carved into the face of this tree for all time. A message apparently meant for her.

The bark around the words was bent outward, almost as if the words had been carved from the inside.

The words wouldn't be visible from the trail. They were hers and hers alone.

Logan and Baldwin stared at her. They both wore troubled looks on their faces. But something else danced behind Logan's eyes, something gleeful.

"How'd you do that?" Logan asked. "How'd you kill them?"

Sophie shook her head. "I don't know. I just...saw where to stab them."

Baldwin gritted his teeth. "You asshole. Carver's hurt bad thanks to you. We need to get him back to the house now."

4. Rook Mountain

Sean parked his squad car, complete with shiny new windshield, in the empty lot next to an old gnarly tree. He sat for a long moment looking at the building. It was a little sad. This place had been state-of-the-art a few years ago. Still was, really. But the new powers-that-be weren't keen on using facilities that had so recently served as the headquarters, armory, and military hospital for an army of students fighting a war against bird monsters.

Understandable, Sean supposed. It seemed like a waste the way the facilities stood unused.

He reached into his pocket, pulled out the key, and

unlocked the door. Technically, he was supposed to fill out a request form before checking out a key, but over the last eight years he'd learned sometimes it was easier to lie than to ask permission you knew would be denied.

The chief had been less than pleased after the incident at Sean's home. Colt and his parents had been called in, and Colt had been questioned. The boy admitted to showing up at Sean's house that night, but he denied having anything to do with the brick through the windshield. And, of course, he had a half-dozen friends who claimed they had been with him the whole time and not one of them had seen a brick in his hands.

In the pre-Zed days, Colt would have been looking at some time in juvenile lockup. In the Zed era, he'd probably have lost an ear. Now? The chief gave him a two-hundred dollar fine for breaking curfew and sent him on his way. Maybe the Zed Heads weren't so wrong about the good old days after all.

"You have any idea how many eyes are on us?" the chief had asked Sean after Colt and his parents left. "You know how many people read each and every incident report I file? The State and the Feds are both looking for an excuse to come in and take over Rook Mountain law enforcement. Kids running around smashing cruiser windshields isn't something they need to see. We'll get it fixed off the books. And, please, let's not go starting a war with these junior Zed Heads, okay?"

The chief wasn't completely wrong. There was so much going on in town. Maybe vandalism, even against a police vehicle, shouldn't be the priority right now. Sean knew the police should be concentrating on the string of disappearances.

There had been five since Deregulation Day. The first had

been a former selectman. Then it had been a teenage boy and a teenage girl, both Zed Heads. Then the death row inmate. And now Sophie Porter, who had been visiting town to investigate the disappearance of her sister's killer. Her parents were raising all sorts of hell and appearing on cable news eight times a day asking for help finding their missing daughter.

Some of the things Colt said on his porch last week stuck with Sean, nagging at him like a bit of popcorn in his teeth. The Zed Heads were planning something, and it was going to be a lot bigger than a brick through a windshield. The chief might be content to look the other way, but Sean knew that was the wrong move. If they didn't stay on top of this thing, filling out incident reports would be the least of the chief's worries.

Sean clicked on his Maglite and entered the Beyond Academy. Most of the Zed Heads had gone to school here, and it had popped into Sean's mind this morning that they could be using this place as a sort of club house.

The hallways were long, dark things that seemed to stretch for miles. No one had bothered to clean out this building, and remnants of the Zed era that had been scrubbed from the rest of the town remained in place here. Sean passed under a banner hanging from the ceiling that read, *Trust is a Must.*

He took his time, searching each classroom for signs it had been recently used. They all wore coats of dust, like blankets. Most of them looked like they had been abandoned mid-session. Words like *RESPY* and *Regulation* were still written on dry erase boards.

Sean paused at the door to the auditorium. Somehow he knew this was it. If the Zed Heads were congregating at the school, this is where it would be. He opened one of the double doors and stepped inside.

He almost fell down the steps leading toward the center of the room. He'd only been here once before, and he'd forgotten about the stadium seating. He shined his flashlight toward the front of the room and saw a white board had been rolled to the center of the stage. It stood next to a podium. He saw a something written on the board in crooked handwriting.

He squinted at the board as he approached. What he saw sent a chill up his spine.

It was a list of names.

Trevor Hinkle. Will Osmond. Ty Hansen. Christine Osmond. Gus Hansen. Frank Hinkle.

The last name on the list was crossed out: Timothy Rodgers.

What was this? Some kind of hit list? A tally of those who hadn't been faithful to Zed? A list of those who had helped bring him down? If that last theory was true, why was Rodgers' name there?

Sean climbed the steps to the podium, willing the dry erase board to tell him something more. Would the chief even care when Sean showed him this? Would he take any action at all? Sean wasn't sure. The man was in full-on job retention mode these days.

He saw a notebook on the podium. He picked it up and flipped through it. The handwriting was tiny and slanted. Probably written by the same hand that scrawled the list on the board. He'd need to get in some better lighting to read this mess.

He took one last look around, confirming there was nothing else of interest here. He snapped a quick picture of the whiteboard with his cell phone, though he wasn't confident it would turn out in the dark auditorium. He scooped up the notebook and headed for the door.

He made his way to his car, and he had his hand on the door handle when something caught his eye. The old, gnarly tree next to the car. Something was carved into the bark of the tree, staring him right in the face.

He reached for his radio. This would definitely get the chief's attention.

The words carved into the tree could be a joke, a clue, or a strange coincidence. He read the four simple words one more time.

Don't trust them Sophie.

IN THE WOODS (PART THREE)

"Zed?" Frank asked. "He's here in these woods?"

Mason nodded. "It's hard to tell exactly where. He wanders. But he's around here somewhere."

Frank stared at Mason in the dim light of his flashlight. If this man had really been raised by Zed, who knew what had been done to his mind? For all Frank knew, it could be twisted beyond repair.

Frank thought back to his last meeting with Zed on the roof of city hall. If Zed knew, or even suspected, that Frank would come after him, what would his move be? Would he try to kill Frank? Try to use Frank to find a way back to Rook Mountain? As usual with Zed, Frank had no idea.

"Mason, does Zed ever talk about me?"

Mason chuckled. "Of course. He talks about how bravely you fought against the Unfeathered. And how you protected the town when he had to go away that time. And how you even found your way back from the Away. Which, according to him, had never been done."

Frank grunted. "Did he say anything else?"

Mason shrugged. "He said you two didn't always see eye to eye. He told me about how you stood up to him on the roof of city hall and helped send him here. But, from what I can tell, he has nothing but respect for you."

"Huh. Well, just so you know, the feeling isn't mutual."

Mason chuckled again. "He said you weren't friends. Not like he was with my father."

Frank let that one slide. He didn't want to push things too far. Mason was practically raised by Zed, from the sound of it, and he'd only just met Frank.

Frank had come here to find Jake, but Jake was long dead. He'd come to make sure Zed couldn't return to Rook Mountain, but now it seemed he was the one who wouldn't be able to return.

He surveyed Jake's dilapidated old house. "Did your dad build this? Or did he find it here?"

"He found it."

"Jake never was much of a builder."

"He was a finder though." Mason's eyes lit up as he spoke. "He used to do this thing where he'd choose someone in Sanctuary, a different person each week, and he'd let them pick an object. Anything at all. As long as it wasn't large enough to cause a spacing problem here. They could pick anything they wanted, and he'd bring it here."

"What do you mean he'd bring it here? How'd he get it?"

"He had this book he used." Mason trotted through the open door and into the house. Frank followed. "He'd go in his office. It was right over here. He'd shut the door. A few minutes later he'd come out of the office with whatever the person had requested. Sometimes it was a nice bottle of wine or a nice article of clothing. Sometimes it was something more exotic. We had a painting by Da Vinci once. I guess that was a big deal."

Frank felt a dull ache in his chest. Not only had Jake not

needed to be saved, he'd spent his time playing some mystical version of 'pull the rabbit out of the hat'. Why hadn't Frank stayed in Rook Mountain? He could have built a life for himself. He had friends there. He had family.

Instead, he was standing in the ruins of an old house in the middle of the night with a crazy person.

Frank shuffled over to where Mason stood and looked into the room that had once been Jake's office. An old desk stood in the middle of the room. He shined his flashlight on a box sitting on the desk. "What's that?"

Mason paused. "Sorry, what's what?"

"That box."

The older man paused longer this time. He shined his flashlight beam around the entire area. "I'm not sure what you mean."

Maybe Mason's eyes were getting old. Frank guessed the woods didn't come equipped with a vision plan. From the look of Mason's teeth, he certainly didn't have dental.

He brushed the dirt off the old lockbox. Most of the paint was gone, but there were still flecks of rusty red clinging to the metal. The box looked like the one Jake had as a boy. He'd eventually upgraded and handed the older one down to his kid brother. Frank had spent many hours with that box. It had served as baseball card storage, piggy bank, Matchbox car garage, and tackle box. Seeing this one sent the memories flooding back into Frank's mind. Racing toy cars down the sloped driveway with Jake. Fishing with their father. Fighting with Jake over their favorite lures. He felt the beginnings of a lump in his throat.

He saw something dangling from the front of the box, and he understood why Mason hadn't been able to see it. It was one of Frank's original designs. The Cassandra lock. In fact, it looked exactly like the one in Frank's pocket. He paused, wondering how Jake had gotten the Cassandra lock in wherever-the-hell they were.

There was something else. Frank's locks could be used to hide things from people, at least that's how it worked back in Rook Mountain. Why would Jake want to hide the box from his own son?

Frank turned back to Mason, holding the box in the air. "You really can't see this?"

Mason shook his head, his faced scrunched in confusion.

Frank rapped on the box with his knuckles, and the box gave out a ringing clang. Mason jumped back a little.

Frank performed a quick twist on the Cassandra lock, squeezed it, pulled at just the right angle, and it popped open. Mason gasped.

"You see it now, I take it?"

Mason reached a shaky hand forward and brushed his fingertips against the box. "I've been out here hundreds of times. Thousands, probably. How have I never seen this?"

"It didn't want to be seen." Frank unhooked the latches and lifted the lid. It opened with a high-pitched squeak. Frank shined the flashlight inside. The first thing he saw was a picture of Jake, Christine and Trevor. Trevor was a baby in the picture. Frank had the same one hanging on the wall of his cabin back home. He had before he went to prison, anyway.

Frank moved the picture aside and saw another photo, this one of the previous generation of Hinkles: Jake, Frank, and their mom and dad.

There were other items in the box. An old pocket knife. Some guitar picks from a band Jake played in during college. Under all of that, there was a book. The symbol on the cover was partially obscured, and Frank almost gasped when he saw it. He moved the pictures aside. It wasn't a broken clock symbol as he had first thought. The crack was exactly the same, but the image under the crack was different. It was a circle with roughly shaped continents sketched inside it. Instead of a broken clock this was a broken world.

Mason craned his neck to see what Frank was looking it. Frank quickly shuffled the pictures to cover the book.

"What's in it?" Mason asked.

"Old pictures," Frank said. "It's Jake's old family. From Rook Mountain."

Mason was quiet for a long moment. Then he said, "I think I'd like to see those."

Frank nodded. "Look, he probably didn't want to make you feel bad. I'm sure that's why he hid them."

"Yeah, no big deal. You can show me at the cabin. We better start heading back if we're gonna make it before sunrise."

Frank blinked in confusion. The walk here had only taken fifteen minutes, and they'd left at sundown. "What do you mean?"

"My parents told me about your world," Mason said. "The way things are always in the same place. It's not like that here. Things change. They move. I know my cabin was close by when we left, but it might be all the way across the woods by now. Could be a five or six hour walk. We wouldn't be able to find it at all if it weren't for this thing."

He reached into his pocket and pulled out a round object. He held it up for Frank to see. Frank pointed his flashlight at it and saw it was a compass. Then Mason flipped it, showing Frank the backside of the thing.

It was the broken clock symbol.

Mason smiled. "It's more than what it looks like, I'll tell you that. All I have to do is think about where I want to go. The cabin. The stream. Whatever. I click the little drawing of the cracked clock on the back, and the needle on the compass points me in the right direction."

Frank stared at the object. Though it seemed hard to believe, just earlier today in Will and Christine's house he had destroyed those objects with the broken clock symbol. Now, here was another one, and he didn't exactly have access to Christine's knife.

"Does Zed know you have this?"

Mason chuckled. "Of course. He's the one who showed me how to use it when I was a kid. I wouldn't have survived out here more than a few days otherwise."

Frank tried to wrap his mind around the idea of Zed as a kindly mentor figure, showing the boy how to use this Tool like other men might teach a kid to fish. Why hadn't Zed taken the compass for himself?

"Where'd you get it?"

"You remember the woman I told you about? The one who came to Sanctuary and ruined everything? I pried this compass from her dead hand."

CHAPTER FOUR: THE PULSE

1. Sanctuary

Jake walked through the forest, a cold beer in his hand. He wouldn't open it until he got to the tree.

It was the dead of night, the time when he was least likely to be disturbed by Larvae. He'd made sure no patrols would be walking this path tonight. He needed to be alone. Alone with the tree.

A few minutes later he reached the tall tree with the trunk so twisted it looked like it was spinning toward the sky, and he leaned his back against it, cracked open his beer, and saluted the upper branches with the can, same as he did every week. "Here's to ya, you gnarly old bastard." He took a long drink and remembered better times.

He closed his eyes for a long moment and enjoyed the sounds of the forest. The buzz of the crickets. The rustle of a light wind through the trees. In the distance, the chatter of a fast-moving stream.

He needed this. Leading the Sanctuary, being the boss, took its toll on him. He'd only wanted to save people's lives. He hadn't realized at the time that he was also signing up to take care of them forever. To give structure to their lives. To help settle their petty squabbles. And, worst of all, to provide for them. He had the endless job of bringing over food, clothing, furniture, and all sorts of other necessities for every resident of Sanctuary. And it was getting more difficult. At first, the book had been fun to use—each new page it revealed to him was a new toy to play with—but it was growing more difficult over time. First, the book had revealed its secrets to him, and now it seemed to be using him up. Bringing over the weekly food supply tired him and the bigger jobs drained him completely. Sometimes he felt like Frodo carrying the ring to Mordor.

At the same time, he was grateful to the book, and not just for the food and clothes and supplies it allowed him to bring here. He was grateful to it for giving him the tree he was leaning against.

He knew he would eventually have to teach someone else to use the book. He should have done so already. If he suddenly dropped dead of a heart attack, they would all be in trouble. He'd considered teaching Logan. Or Nate. Or Mason, now that he was old enough to read but still young enough to be teachable. But each of those candidates had their drawbacks.

As much as he had come to dread using the book, he knew it had a hold on him. Deep down, he liked the power it gave him. He was the sole provider for this place. They needed him and he provided for them.

Jake turned and stepped back so he was facing the tree. "So…how was your week? Another seven days buried in the dirt. Hope you're enjoying it as much as I am."

He sighed. Having your worst enemy be a tree was great from a practical perspective, but it did make the banter less fun.

"I know I always say it, but I hope you're comfortable. You're going to be here a long, long time. See, I'm getting out of here. We all are. I can't tell them that, not yet. But I'm getting closer to finding the answer every day."

Jake could read almost ninety percent of the book now. Every little bit revealed was another step in the right direction. Currently he could pull objects through the book, but not send anything back in the other direction. Which meant there was no way home. But he was confident that if he stuck to his plan this would not always be the case. And these trees were the answer.

"I'll be back in Rook Mountain and you'll still be cooling your heels here in the dirt," he continued. "Until one day hundreds of years from now when a tree disease, or a lighting strike, or the weight of your own branches brings you down. And then you'll decay into nothing but a home for insects and small animals. How you feel about that?"

The tree didn't respond, and every time that happened, every time he asked the tree a question he knew it couldn't answer, it made him smile. Childish maybe, but there it was.

Jake finished the beer. It would be morning soon. He needed to go back.

He gave the tree trunk a pat. "Good talk. I'll see you next week. In the meantime, don't go anywhere."

2. Rook Mountain

Sean sat in his car with Wendy Caulfield, parked a block away from the Post Office.

"This place is special to Zed," Wendy said. "This is where you first saw him, right? Weren't you there when he was arrested?"

Sean nodded. "Yeah. He was naked and confused. And he

had that pocket watch of his clutched in his hand."

"Do you think he brought the pocket watch with him or found it here?"

Sean shook his head. "I don't know. But he was holding it in a death grip. He wouldn't let it go for anything."

Wendy shook her head. "Remember what he said when you first approached him? You told me years ago at that party at Jake and Christine's."

"Yeah. He said, 'this will do nicely'. I thought it was weird even then. He was looking around like he was surprised by his surroundings."

"Exactly. And remember the stilted way he talked at first? It was so formal. He was even like that when I first started to hear him speak in the parks."

"He really reinvented himself," Sean said.

"He got better every time I heard him speak. It was like...he was learning. Like he didn't know how a person was supposed to act or something. Like he was adapting to his environment."

Sean and Wendy had been dating for over a month now. After the Tools were destroyed and they had no reason to keep their distance from each other, Sean noticed the feelings creeping up. It was like a wall between them suddenly came down. As far as Sean was concerned, Wendy was the hottest girl in town. When he got up the courage to ask her out, he quickly found out she thought he was pretty hot, too.

And, today, having a kinda/sorta girlfriend with insider knowledge of the Beyond Academy didn't hurt.

Chief Yates had his best men investigating the carving on the tree outside the Beyond Academy. Sean wasn't one of them, so here he sat. At least he still had the book. It was the book that had brought them here. There was a rough map of

Rook Mountain drawn on one of the pages, with an 'X' near the Post Office.

Wendy was paging through the book now.

The first half was filled with Regulation violations. Each Regulation had four pages dedicated to it, front and back, and the pages were filled with lists of names and descriptions of their violations.

The first page, devoted to Regulation 1, said simply: "Only the Zed Heads remain faithful."

"They still consider the Regulations to be law," Sean said. "And, from the looks of this, they won't even leave town."

"Hardliners," Wendy said. "Nice to know Zed's legacy isn't dead. He succeeded in creating a weird new political party, if nothing else."

She looked up from the book. "So what do we do? Should we tell Christine and Will they're in danger?"

"No." The word came to Sean's lips quickly. "They've been through enough with Jake and now Frank. They need to concentrate on building a normal life together. They don't need to get pulled into..." he gestured toward the book, "whatever this is."

"I agree. But if they're in danger—if Trevor's in danger..."

"We'll tell them if we have to. But not before."

Wendy nodded. She leaned in close to him. "You're cute when you're protecting people." She gave him a long, slow kiss.

He pulled away and grinned. "Serve and protect."

She elbowed him in the ribs playfully and went back to paging through the book.

"You know, I've been thinking," Wendy said. "There was a group at the Academy. Kind of a like an Honor Society, but less..."

"Honorable?" Sean asked.

"Yeah," Wendy said. "Zed used to come talk to them every couple of weeks. He'd pull them out of class and take them into the auditorium for a private pow wow. The teachers were always welcome if it was during their free period. I went once."

"What did they talk about?"

"It was about what you'd expect. Zed told them they were the next generation of leaders. That the future depended on them. That they'd be tested."

"You're right," Sean said. "That's what I expected."

"Thing is, I've been noticing that a lot of the kids with the broken clock tattoos used to be in that group. Colt. Sam. Megan—all the leaders of the Zed Heads now."

"What do you remember about Colt from the Academy?"

"He was always popular. I remember him being a leader even before he was in the Academy. Other kids looked up to him and followed him. He was a bit of a goody two-shoes though."

"How do you mean?"

Wendy thought about that for a moment. "He was a stickler for the rules. He was always quick to turn in his friends for the smallest infractions."

"I don't hardly see how that would make him popular. Snitches wind up in ditches, and all that."

"Rats get hit with bats."

"Exactly. People who talk get outlined in chalk."

"Tattlers get bit by rattlers." Wendy smiled. "You're thinking about it wrong. That's how it worked when we were kids. But things were different for kids who went to school under the Regulations. Not turning someone in was seen as a truly shameful act."

"Nobody likes a tattletale. That's just human nature, right?"

"Maybe so," Wendy said. "I'm sure some kids would have taken shit for doing the things Colt did. But everyone liked him. He was charismatic. I remember thinking he'd be able to run through as many girls as he wanted in high school."

"Guess he's decided to use his charisma for other things. Anyway, whatever he was like back then, he certainly has no problem breaking the rules now."

"That's not how he sees it," Wendy said. "For us adults, the Regulations were a sudden seismic shift in our lives. Every man and woman in Rook Mountain knew the laws we were following were wrong, even if we didn't want to admit it. But it was different for the kids."

"They grew up with the Regulations."

"Exactly. Colt would have been, what, eight years old on Regulation Day? His brain was still developing. The Regulations are buried in there, rooted deep. And now the world's telling him the Regulations are wrong. It's like if tomorrow morning someone suddenly told us it was okay to kill anyone we wanted, and our friends and neighbors started murdering random people in the streets. We'd probably push back too."

"I would hope so," Sean said. "So Colt's a true believer. I saw that in his eyes when he came to my door the other night." He thought for a moment. "You know, in a way, I kind of admire Colt and his friends."

"Because they can throw a brick through a police car windshield with no consequences?"

He smiled. "Not exactly. It's their resolve. They're standing up for their beliefs."

"That isn't always a good thing. Look at terrorism. It's generally motivated by strong beliefs."

111

"Yeah. But if we would have had a little more resolve when Zed came to power, if we would have stood up to him like those kids are standing up to us, maybe none of this would have happened." He rubbed his eyes. "Makes my head hurt just thinking about it. I guess everything has its possible positive and negative outcomes. And its gray areas."

Wendy nodded. "That's exactly what these kids are missing. An understanding of gray areas. Do you remember how black and white morality seemed when you were young?"

A chill went through him at the thought.

"Yeah. I do."

She shifted in her seat to look at him. "Have you ever stopped to wonder what Zed really is? How he was able to do the things he could do?"

"Yeah. Of course." He paused, trying to think of how to continue. "Whatever he was...is...I think we can agree he's not human."

"Exactly. So why should we assume he walked into town or drove into town like a human would? I think maybe this spot is more than just the place you ran into him. I think maybe he somehow entered the town here."

He nodded slowly. "That would make sense. That could be why the Zed Heads have this place marked in their little book. Maybe they think if he entered the town here once—"

"This is where he'll return," she finished.

He suddenly sat up straighter in his seat. "Wait. That's not right. When we first got the call about the naked man downtown, he was two blocks east of here. Over near the pawn shop. He had wandered over here by the time we arrived."

She arched her eyebrows. "So, you gonna take me there or what?"

He shifted the car into drive and pulled onto the street. When they reached the pawn shop, he jumped out of the car. He stood and looked around. It seemed like any other street corner in this small downtown. A boy of no more than ten stood leaning against the brick wall outside the pawn shop.

"It would have been right around here," Wendy said.

Her eyes landed on a tree near the corner. It was older than the other trees on the street. Almost inconveniently big for the downtown. Sean was surprised it hadn't been taken down.

Wendy wandered toward it. She studied it for a long moment, then called Sean over.

There were a series of numbers carved into the tree. 730. 814. 1020. Each number had a check mark carved next to it.

Sean said, "I've seen something like this before. The way the bark's dented outward around the letters. On a tree outside the old Beyond Academy. You know that Sophie Porter girl who disappeared? It was about her. Or to her. Or maybe from her. The chief has people looking into it."

He ran his hand over the bark. Just like the tree he had seen near the Beyond Academy, it looked almost as if the numbers had been carved from the *inside* of the tree.

"What do you suppose the numbers mean?" Wendy asked.

Sean glanced back and noticed the boy who'd been leaning against the wall was gone.

"I don't know. Maybe it's some kind of signal. Maybe someone's leaving messages."

Wendy's hand moved over the carvings again. "These check marks were carved with a different knife. See how the numbers bulge outward? The check mark's more like a normal carving. Like the bark was cut away."

He rubbed his chin. "So maybe the number's the message and the check mark means 'message received'. What's the date today?"

"The twentieth."

"October twentieth." He tapped the *1020* carved into the tree.

Wendy nodded slowly. "You think they're dates."

Sean shrugged. "It's a theory." He reached into his pocket and pulled out a Swiss Army knife.

"My boy scout," she said. "What are you gonna do?"

He grinned. "On my honor, I will do my best. I don't remember any more of it." He flipped open the knife. "I'm gonna leave a little message of my own and see if anyone responds. I think I'll try 1029." He bent down and brought the blade to the face of the tree.

"Don't!" someone behind him screamed.

Sean spun and saw a teenage boy, maybe fourteen years old. The boy's fists were clenched and he was shaking with anger. "You don't know what you're doing. Don't touch that tree."

He stood up and made a show of closing his knife. "Okay. Why don't you go ahead and tell me."

The kid shook his head. Sean noticed the broken clock tattoo on his hand. The smaller boy, the one who'd been leaning against the building when they arrived, stood beside him.

"Alright. Why don't you tell me what you know about this tree?"

The kid's voice shook when he spoke. "I know if you cut a single line in that tree, bad things will happen to you. Things that'll make a brick through your windshield look like nothing."

Wendy put a hand on Sean's shoulder. He brushed it off and stepped forward. "You trying to scare me, son?"

The kid's face was beet red now. "You think we're just a bunch of kids, don't you? You have no idea. There are more people loyal to the Regulations than you would believe. You think because the feds showed up, this is over? It's just getting started."

"Grant," Wendy said. "You know me, right? Ms. Caulfield? I'm sure you've seen me around school."

He nodded.

"You want to be careful now. I understand you're upset. If you don't want us to cut the tree, we won't. But Officer Lee isn't your enemy."

"The way I heard it, he's everybody's enemy. Everybody who cares about Rook Mountain, anyway." With that, Grant grabbed the younger kid by the arm and dragged him into the pawn shop.

"Seems like a nice kid," Sean said.

"A lot of them are like that these days. You still want to carve up the tree?"

He shrugged. "No point now. I wanted to see if they'd respond, but they'll know it was me now. Seems pretty clear the Zed Heads are the ones doing this."

Wendy paused for a moment. "But why? There are a million ways to communicate. This hardly seems like the most efficient."

"Maybe they're communicating with someone else."

Her head snapped around suddenly. "Like someone who went through a mirror?"

His brow creased. "Come on. You don't actually think they're talking to Zed, do you?"

She didn't answer. She kept staring at the tree. "I've seen something like this before, too."

He smiled. "You gonna take me there or what?"

* * *

3. Sanctuary

Jake sat in a large wooden chair in the living room of his home. The chair had a high back and was a bit taller than any of the others in the room, giving it a throne-like appearance. Sophie sat on the couch next to the chair. She felt like a kid in the principal's office.

Logan and Baldwin stood near the couch. They'd each finished sharing their versions of what had happened earlier in the night. It was still dark outside, but ten or so people Sophie had never met were gathered in the living room with them. Sophie was starting to realize the nocturnal nature of the society she was now living in.

"Maybe Frasier should be answering for this," Baldwin said. "He's the one who said she was ready."

Jake frowned. "He's a little busy tending to Carver. Anything else, Baldwin?"

The big man shook his head. "I'm ready."

Jake raised an eyebrow. "Ready for what?"

"You're kidding right?" He paused, but Jake said nothing. After a moment, Baldwin leaned closer to Jake. "I'm ready to hear your sentence."

"Oh come on," Logan said. "It was an accident."

They'd left Carver with Frasier. Apparently he served as the doctor here as well as the orienter of newbies.

Frasier had made it clear how serious the situation was. He'd said he wasn't sure whether he'd be able to save the arm. Sophie felt sick when she heard those words. It hurt Sophie's brain to even consider it; the idea was just too big. She'd caused this. It felt like a swarm of bees buzzing around in her head. She couldn't think straight. So she listened and did what she was told.

Logan had yelled at Sophie plenty on the long walk back to the house. She'd told her they needed to explain the situation to Jake, and she'd warned her to expect the worst. But then Logan surprised her. When telling the story to Jake, Logan defended Sophie at every turn. She told the truth, but it was a version of the truth that painted Sophie in the best possible light. Baldwin fumed through the telling, and then told his version, a version that probably erased all the benefit of the doubt Logan had built.

Baldwin shook his head. "It wasn't an accident. She disobeyed a direct order, and Carver might lose his arm because of it. That fits the definition of hurting someone. Hence she broke the rules. Hence she should be banished."

"Are you kidding me?" Logan responded. "Was it a stupid move? Yes. I'd like to beat the shit out of her right now. If it wasn't against the rules for me to do so, she'd be a walking bruise by sun-up."

So much for the good will, Sophie thought.

Logan continued. "But it was in no way malicious. She didn't know what she was doing."

Jake turned to Sophie. She'd been quiet until now. "You got anything to add?"

"Just that I'm sorry. I know that doesn't count for much, but it's true."

"You're right," a voice from the back of the room said. "It doesn't mean much." Murmurs of approval swept through the room.

I'm off to a great start here, Sophie thought.

"She loves the Larvae so much, maybe she should stay with them for good," someone else said.

"You're all forgetting something." As soon as the man spoke, ice clutched Sophie's chest. She recognized that voice,

117

though the last time she'd heard it had been years ago in a courtroom. It was Taylor. Sophie hadn't known he was here.

"May I, Jake?"

Jake nodded. "Of course. Have your say."

"You're all forgetting the other part of the story. If what Logan and Baldwin are saying is true, she killed two of the Larvae. Not scared them off. Killed them dead. Think of what that means."

Sophie was frozen, almost unable to move as she watched Taylor. The man moved like a snake. He put his mammoth hand on Sophie's shoulder. It was all she could do to not vomit. Or break down in tears. Or grab his hand and break every finger. But she knew that wouldn't go over well at this exact moment. Not now. But soon.

"It's a damn tragedy," Taylor continued. "No one here would argue with that. But let's not condemn this woman. Today she brought us tears. But tomorrow..."

"Tomorrow what?" Baldwin asked.

Taylor shrugged. "If she can do it again, if she can kill the Larvae and teach the rest of us to kill them, how many lives has she saved in the long run?"

"How about it, Sophie?" Jake asked. "Did you get lucky, or can you do it again?"

"I can do it again," she said softly.

The room was silent now. Every eye was on her. A tension hung in the air, but it wasn't the agitated tension that had been there a few moments ago.

Taylor took his hand off her shoulder, and Sophie felt a wave of relief. She hadn't realized how tightly she'd been gritting her teeth.

After a long silence, Jake pointed at Sophie. "You learned a terrible lesson tonight about leaving the trail. Even in the dead of night. I take it you won't do any such thing again?"

Sophie gave her head a quick shake.

"And you'll listen to your walk leaders like their voices are the voice of God?"

She nodded.

"Good." He turned to the group. "As far as I'm concerned, her mistake tonight counts as part of her past. That means it's off limits. Don't discuss it. Don't hold a grudge. I know I'm asking the impossible, but the impossible is what we do here. Right?"

Sophie saw a few hesitant nods around the room.

"Good." Jake pushed himself to his feet. Then he spoke softly in a voice meant only for her. "I'll stop by the Welcome Wagon this afternoon. We need to talk."

He marched into his office and shut the door.

4. Rook Mountain

Getting the key to the Beyond Academy hadn't been simple, but nothing worthwhile ever was. Zed had told them that in one of their assemblies, and Colt believed it. The more difficult the challenges, the bigger the chance to prove yourself.

Colt's mom had been branded as a Regulation 10 breaker back when he was eleven years old. She had been hoarding food. Hoarding wasn't exactly the right term. Colt's father was terribly allergic to shellfish. However, Colt's mom had been taking her full, allowed ration of seafood and selling or trading the shellfish to friends. This had been going on since almost Regulation Day, and it probably would have continued until the end of the Zed era, if not for Clara Summers. Mrs. Summers was caught for an infraction of Regulation 6 and tried to avoid punishment by squealing about Colt's mother's black market fish operation. The police showed up at Colt's door a couple hours later, and Colt's mom was branded with the number 10 on her cheek right there in the living room. Colt, his father, and his sister had been spared because his mom swore they had no knowledge of the situation.

Colt had felt an odd combination of feelings watching as the branding iron pressed against his mom's cheek, hearing the flesh sizzle, and seeing the smoke roll off her skin. Of course, he didn't enjoy seeing his mother hurt. Her screams made him feel sick. But there was also another feeling. Relief. For years, he had felt a constant sense of dread, a persistent nag of worry. Everything he was being taught about the Regulations at school was being defied right here at home. His own mom, who helped him memorize the Regulations for school, was the one breaking them. So as he watched her being punished, he felt relief. Something wrong in the world had been made right. He no longer needed to feel the discord of criminal behavior in his own home. Justice had won the day.

When Colt got a little older, he decided to look into Officer Benson, the man who had branded Colt's mother and, in effect, made things right in Colt's world. Thing is, Colt noticed something interesting. Benson had doled out punishment for plenty of Regulation infractions, but every Regulation Breaker Benson punished, at least every one Colt could find, was a woman. Then Colt thought back to that day in his living room and the look of barely masked glee in Benson's eyes as he applied the branding iron.

And Colt realized something. Officer Benson enjoyed hurting women.

So Colt wrote a proposal for a magazine article. This was in the days shortly after the so-called Deregulation, and all the magazines and websites were dying for Rook Mountain stories. They were willing to pay very good money for it, too. Colt knew his compositional skills were above average, and he knew the article about his personal experience watching his mother be scarred for life by a sadistic, woman-hating cop would find a semi-prestigious home.

However, before submitting it to any magazines, he sent the proposal to Officer Benson. He made it clear he was willing to rethink writing the article if Benson was willing to compensate him with a few small favors.

By noon the following day, a key to the Beyond Academy had made its way from the police station into Colt's pocket, along with a handful of favors to be named later.

Since that day in May, this new generation of Zed Heads had met in the Beyond Academy two to three times per week. But events such as the one tonight had only happened twice before. Tonight was special. They'd received another message on the tree downtown. A message with today's date. Tonight, Zed would be attending the meeting.

Colt stood by the door, greeting each person as they arrived, giving them a hearty hand-shake and a sincere welcome. He tried to run this group the same way he imagined Zed would have. He was positive but not unrealistic. He was gentle when possible and heartless when necessary.

All eighteen full members were required to attend tonight. Not that they would have missed it. There were more than eighteen young people who called themselves Zed Heads, but only the core group, the ones who'd been dedicated enough to get the broken clock symbol permanently inked onto their hands, were invited tonight.

Still, he did worry some members would get cold feet, so he kept count. When his count reached eighteen, he locked the door and went to join the others who were waiting in the auditorium. He nodded toward Grant who was standing near the stage.

"Everything ready?" Colt asked.

Grant nodded. He held up a red shoe box. "Good to go."

Colt took a deep breath and then trotted up the steps to the stage. The kids went silent. Every eye was on him, but Colt didn't rush. He paused, enjoying the moment. He always felt an odd combination of feelings while standing up here, the very stage where Zed had stood and delivered the speeches that opened and closed the school year. Now he stood on the same stage, preparing to address many of the same students. He felt unworthy, but he also felt proud to have the opportunity. He didn't have Zed's gift for eloquence —who did—but he'd do his best.

"Hello, my fellow Zed Heads." He paused there, waiting to see if there would be a response, like the pastor greeting his congregation on Sunday, but there was none. "As you know, this is a special night. We're expecting a guest one or two of you might be familiar with."

A stir went through the crowd. Some laughing. Some shifting in their seats. But all were smiling.

"With that comes another opportunity. The greatest honor our group has to give. I'd ask for volunteers, but you all remember what happened last time." During the last special session, Colt had been touched and surprised when every one of the eighteen members had volunteered. "So instead, I'll do this the other way. Is there anyone who would like their name taken out of consideration?"

He waited a long moment. It was so quiet a single footstep would have echoed through the room. "Speak up now if you want out. There's no shame in it." Of course there was, but he had to say it. It made the volunteers feel braver.

Colt waited a full minute, and then nodded. "Good. I want you to know I am proud of you. No matter who gets selected, I am proud of each and every one of you. Any questions before we do this?"

"Will it be like last time?" The voice came from Grant. Colt silently cursed him. The two of them had spent all afternoon preparing. He couldn't have asked his question then? The last thing this group needed at this already tense moment was to be reminded of what happened last time.

"Honestly, Grant, I don't know." He let the uncomfortable silence linger for a moment before continuing. "But let's look at the evidence. In most ways, Zed's arrival was better last time than the time before that. Zed's getting stronger. So I can't say for sure what will happen and I can't say how long it'll last, but I do think we'll see an improvement. Anyone else?"

Thankfully, no one else asked a question. Colt motioned for Grant to bring him the shoe box. Colt took the box and held it aloft so it was clear he couldn't see into it. In reality, it didn't matter. Grant and Colt had prepared the box alone. They could have stuffed it with any names they wanted. They could have rigged this thing a dozen different ways. They wouldn't do that, though, and their friends knew it. Colt trusted the process, and his friends trusted him. Trust was still a must.

Colt thrust his hand into the box and stirred it around, feeling the slips of paper brush against the tattoo on the back of his hand. He ran his fingers through the paper like it was a lover's hair. He was waiting for something, though he didn't know what. He wanted to feel some indication of which piece of paper he should choose. He didn't believe it was actually him making the choice, and he didn't want to get in the way of the process.

Then he felt it. A tiny twinge as his index finger rested on one particular slip. And he knew. This was the paper he was meant to draw. He wrapped his fingers around it and pulled it out of the box with a flourish. As he did so, relief washed over him, a relief not unlike the one he had felt while his mother was being branded a Regulation Breaker. The paper had been selected. All was right with the world.

He unfolded the slip and read the name aloud. "Sam Graverton."

Sam made a strange sound that was half laugh and half gasp. Every eye was on him, but no one spoke. The Zed Heads all looked at him with compassion. No judgments would be given, no matter his reaction. Every person in this auditorium understood Sam Graverton must be experiencing an almost unfathomably complex combination of emotions. They all understood, because it could have been any of them. They'd all imagined the moment their names would be called, and they all had experienced a tiny pretend version of what Sam must be feeling.

Colt let the moment play out. After a few moments, Sam stood on wobbly legs and shuffled toward the stage, as Colt knew he would. If Sam tried to flee, the others would grab him. There was no going back once your name was selected. But Colt knew it wouldn't come to that. Sam was a good man. A strong man. He was faithful to the core.

Sam was one of the older boys in the group. He was Colt's age, and he and Colt had gone to school together their whole lives. While they hadn't always been friends, they'd been acquaintances who liked each other well enough. And last March, fighting the Unfeathered together, they had become something more. They'd become brothers. Colt couldn't help but feel a little sad that it was Sam's name that had practically leapt into his hand. A little jealous, too.

Sam hesitated at the bottom of the steps. Colt's heart went out to him. It must have taken a tremendous act of will to make it this far. The mind and the heart might know the good and the honor in what was happening, but the flesh was programmed with a fierce survival instinct that wasn't easily overcome.

Colt held out his hand to Sam. Sam looked up at him, and Colt saw the water in his eyes. Colt smiled, trying to pass a bit of resolve to the other man, and gave him the slightest nod of encouragement. Sam reached out and took Colt's hand. Sam's hand was cold and sweaty. Colt gripped it tightly and pulled ever so gently, encouraging his friend.

As if his legs had been unfrozen, Sam stepped forward. He climbed the steps and moved to the center of the stage with long confident strides.

Colt breathed a sigh of relief. Sam had passed through his moment of crisis and made it to the other side.

Sam took his place at the center of the stage. Colt put a hand on his shoulder.

"Anything to say before it begins?"

"Just...when the coming happens, know I'm with you in spirit."

Colt nodded. As far as last words went, those seemed mighty fine. "Well said. Let's begin."

This was their third time, and Colt still had no idea how it worked. Was Zed listening somehow? How did he know when they were ready? Whatever the method, as soon as Colt called for the change to begin, it did.

It started with Sam's feet. It was like he was shrinking or

crouching down until you noticed the puddle of goo
spreading out under him. The melting process worked its way
up the body. Since Sam wore long pants, it didn't look as bad
as it had on Brent, the lottery winner last time —he'd been
wearing shorts.

Sam's mouth was a thin white line. He clenched his fists as
his lower half liquefied and spread out on the stage. The
process reached his torso. The skin dripped off his arms and
hands. The bones were exposed for a moment before they
too melted and dripped into the growing puddle.

This was the bad part, but Colt forced himself not to look
away. If Sam could endure it for the cause, Colt could sure as
hell bear witness. The skin of Sam's lower jaw melted,
exposing muscle and bone and his bottom teeth. As the jaw
melted, his teeth fell into the puddle with tiny plops before
melting and joining the rainbow colored liquid. Watching the
eyes melt was always the worst. Colt saw a final flash of panic
in Sam's eyes, eyes that seemed to stay alive even as they
liquefied and ran down his face.

A moment later, it was over. All that was left of Sam was a
thick puddle of liquid.

The Zed Heads waited in silence. Then it happened.

The surface of the liquid quivered. A round thing like a
bubble appeared in the middle of the pool, and, like a man
rising from the water, Zed appeared. His skin glistened for a
moment, and then the wetness fell away like scales. All that
had ever been of Sam was gone, and Zed stood in its place.

Zed spread his arms wide like he wanted to embrace them
all in a giant hug. He looked solid, but Colt knew from
personal experience he wasn't. The first time Zed had
appeared two months ago, Colt had been overwhelmed with
emotion and ran to Zed to hug him. His arms had passed

through Zed like the man was made of smoke. Colt had been embarrassed by the incident, but at the time he hadn't been able to control his actions. It all happened without a single conscious decision.

"My friends," Zed began. There was a crackle in his voice, as if he was speaking on a radio station that was not quite in range. Colt was instantly relieved though. Last time the Zed Heads had only been able to discern every third word. "Thank you for your continued faith and perseverance. I wish I could be here with you more, but as you know the cost is high. Who was it who paid the price this time?"

"Sam," Colt answered.

Zed squeezed his eyes shut as if he were in pain. "Ah, Sam. I always enjoyed his jokes. And his bravado. I hope someone will make sure his collection of Unfeathered feet goes to a worthy home."

Colt hadn't thought of that. During the fighting in March, many of the Beyond Academy students had collected the feet of their enemies. But Sam had been the most zealous. Not only did he collect the feet of his own kills, he took the feet of Unfeathered killed by students who weren't collectors, people like that traitor Trevor Hinkle. Before long, Sam was even talking people who *did* want the feet out of their well deserved prizes. He kept the feet hidden from the media and the government even though he certainly could have traded them for a boatload of cash and attention.

It was too soon to think about such things. The memories brought a lump into Colt's throat.

"Let's not let Sam's sacrifice be in vain," Zed said. "Tell me the latest."

Colt cleared his throat. "We have a lead on one of the Tools."

127

Zed cocked an eyebrow. "Really? Which one?"

"The compass."

A smile crept onto Zed's face. "Okay. Tell me more."

"Tim Rodgers. He was a guard at the prison."

"I remember him. He was a believer, but too much of a loose cannon to be of much use. I notice you're referring to him in the past tense."

"Yes," Colt said. "Turns out he had the compass. Priscilla Nettles heard him mouthing off about it in a bar one night. How it always pointed to City Hall where you disappeared rather than North. She told us about it. Anyway, we were planning our strategy to take it from him. Thing is, he offed himself, and we can't figure out what he did with it. We think maybe this cop Sean Lee took it, but we're not sure." Colt paused, feeling another lump rise in his throat. Why did he always feel so emotional around Zed? It's like all of his feelings intensified. "I apologize. And I take full responsibility. If we'd only acted faster—"

Zed waved his words away. "Nonsense. I taught you to be cautious. Keep looking for it. In the meantime, we have something else to discuss. I need something different from you now."

"What do we have to do?" a voice from the crowd asked. Colt looked up and saw it was Megan. At fourteen, she was one of the youngest members of the Zed Heads, but she'd already proven herself resourceful and dependable.

Zed smiled. "Great question. And I'm happy to see you taking a more active role, Megan. I have big plans for you, if I haven't mentioned it already. Something big's coming soon, my friends. We need to remind the people of Rook Mountain about what happens when the Regulations aren't upheld."

Colt looked out over the faces in the auditorium, and he

couldn't help but feel pride at what he saw. Every face was alight. Everybody was leaning forward. These kids wanted to please Zed like a thirsty man wants water.

They listened in rapt silence while Zed explained what was required of them.

"There's a tree somewhere in this town with a certain message carved into it. I need you to find it."

5. Sanctuary

Jake showed up at exactly three o'clock. Sophie knew by the cheap digital watch Frasier had issued her a few days ago. In her old life, her Sophie Porter life, she'd never worn a watch. She'd considered them old fashioned. But in this new world of no cell phones, a watch turned out to be pretty important. The one she'd been given wasn't fancy, but it did say it was water resistant up to fifty meters, so that was something.

She was waiting on the porch when Jake arrived. He waved her towards him by way of greeting. "Let's go for a walk," he said, and he pointed down the trail leading into the woods.

She cocked an eyebrow. "In the daytime?"

Jake smiled a crooked smile. "There's no rule against it. It's just stupid. And today I'm not feeling all that smart."

She hesitated, and then nodded and followed him toward the cover of the trees.

"You got your knife?" he asked.

She patted the blade dangling from her belt. "You know it."

"Then I'm not worried."

The silence hung heavily in the air. Finally, Sophie broke it. "I am sorry about Carver."

"I know you are. That's why I sided with you in the meeting. And, Taylor isn't wrong. Having you show us how to kill the Larvae will be a huge boon."

Her eyes scanned the forest floor for the black round creatures. Come to think of it, the ones she'd seen last night had been sleeping. Who knew where they hung out during the day? They might be up in the trees waiting to fall on her. Or hiding in a tree's shadow, waiting to attack her from behind after she passed. She suddenly felt much less at ease. "Is that why you brought me out here? So I could show you how to kill them?"

"No. I mean, if we see one and we have the opportunity, sure. But I brought you here to discuss something else. I've been debating whether or not to bring this up. I'm not sure if it's fair to ask while you're working on cutting ties with the past and starting a new life. On the other hand…I really need to know."

Her heart sank deeper into her stomach. This guy was basically the patriarch of this entire society, the society she was forced to live in, at least for the time being. And he was about to ask her something he was clearly uncomfortable bringing up. If this place turned out to be a sex cult, she was gonna be pissed. "Okay," she said tentatively.

"I'm sure Frasier told you it's considered rude to ask about a person's past here. I'd like your permission to be rude."

She cocked her head, bemused at the request. "You don't need to ask my permission."

"That's where you're wrong." he said. "I do need your permission. What I'm asking is no small thing." He rubbed his chin for a moment before continuing. "The past is like a shadow. It follows us everywhere. For good or for bad, it's attached to us. And too often we're defined by our pasts. By the things we have done or the things we didn't do. When I started bringing people here, I knew that the types of people who would knowingly accept a life sentence in this weird forest would be the types of people who would need a clean break from the past. In normal life, that's almost impossible, but I knew I could offer it. Here there's no past. This is a place without shadows. So, you understand when I ask you to discuss your old life, even for one conversation, I don't do it lightly."

She nodded slowly. Much of what Jake was saying made sense. To escape her past and the horrors that lived there was a long-time fantasy of hers. And Jake seemed to have truly accomplished that here. But a complete break with the past for someone like Taylor? That was something she simply couldn't abide. But what else could she say but yes? "I understand. You have my permission."

A wide smile broke out on his face. "Good. Thank you. And, the offer goes both ways. You know those things they used to do where minor celebrities would go on the Internet and answer any question from random fans?"

Sophie smiled. This was a topic she knew a little about. "Ask Me Anythings?"

"Exactly. Consider this my 'Ask Me Anything'. But I'll start if you don't mind."

"Fire away."

He cleared his throat. He was obviously nervous. It was actually kind of cute. "Based on the tree we found you under, I assume you're from Rook Mountain."

She paused, momentarily confused by the question. How did the tree they found her under reveal where she was from? "No, sorry. I live in Nashville."

Jake's smile disappeared.

"But I, um, got here by way of Rook Mountain. That's where I almost died and said Sanctuary and all that."

His smile returned with a vengeance. "Excellent. I was hoping you could tell me a little bit about what's been happening in the town lately."

Sophie suddenly wished for a Larva to leap out at her neck. "Well, geez, I don't really know where to start. Some seriously weird stuff went down in Rook Mountain last March."

"Yeah, I know. I was there for that. Part of it anyway. I'm looking for information on what happened after. June through...what month was it when you left?"

"October. Wait, you couldn't have been there in March. Frasier says you've been running this place more than ten years."

His smile looked forced all of a sudden. He resembled a starving man who is being asked to instruct some slow child before being given bread. "Time works differently here. Very differently."

This was some Harry Potter-level weirdness. If she went back home now, how long would have passed? A week? A month? Her stomach turned at her the thought of her parents left wondering about her fate for all that time. There was no time to think about that now. She had to concentrate on getting back to them. "Okay, let's see, June through September...I'm not sure. Rook Mountain's been in the news a lot, but I haven't followed it super closely. Shame my mom isn't here. She reads all the tabloids."

He smirked. "They're writing about Rook Mountain in the tabloids?"

"It's a different theory every week. Strange metal found in Rook Mountain. Scientist claims he built a machine that sent Rook Mountain outside of time. New study reveals Rook Mountain Incident was all an elaborate hoax. That kind of thing. You know things have gotten weird when the tabloids are arguing the weird stuff *didn't* happen."

"Hmm. I was hoping for a little bit more specific information."

She kicked a rock out of the path. "Well, I wasn't in town long, so I doubt I'll be of much help. But try me."

He took a deep breath. "I was hoping for news about my wife and son. Christine Hinkle and Trevor Hinkle. Those names mean anything to you?"

She shook her head.

"Wait, her name's Osmond now. I almost forgot. Christine Osmond."

She shook her head again. "Sorry man. Like I said, I was only there for a day."

Jake sighed. "Okay. Thanks anyway."

"Listen, it's none of my business but…"

He spread his hands. "Ask me anything, remember?"

She grinned. "Yeah. Okay. If you want to find out about your wife and kid, maybe man up and go visit them. I'm sure they would appreciate it."

He squinted at her. "Sophie, don't you understand? There's no leaving. Not for any of us. Not ever."

She looked into his eyes, and she suddenly knew it was true. There would be no leaving here. No seeing here family again. Or her friends. Or anyone other than the couple dozen weirdos here at Sanctuary. There would be no taking Taylor to justice.

"Damn," she said softly, hoping he didn't notice the tears standing in her eyes. "I was really hoping that was just an act you pulled for the newbies."

"Guess we're both disappointed, then," he said.

She looked off into the trees. No fuzzy ball-of-death monsters in sight. "You asked me a favor before. Can I ask you one in return?"

"Of course."

"I want you to tell me what's going on here. Don't be cryptic or cute. Tell me straight up like a human being. What the hell's going on here? How are you bringing people here? And why can't we leave?"

He nodded slowly. "I don't know what the media and the government said about Rook Mountain, but the truth is it was taken out of time. I didn't find that out until I was here, but that's what happened. This place, Sanctuary, is kind of like that. Except instead of being outside of time, it's outside of place."

"What the hell does that mean?"

"This place wasn't always like this. It was used up somehow." He put his hands on his hips and stared up into the sky. Whether he was looking for Larvae or just trying to collect his thoughts, Sophie didn't know. Eventually, he said, "I came here trying to find help for my family. We'd exhausted our resources and we were almost out of hope. There was this mirror, and all I knew about it was it would send me far away. Maybe I would be able to find help for my family and maybe it would be a one-way trip. I rolled the dice and came here."

"Guess that was a bad roll."

Jake moved his head back and forth as if considering. "Yes and no. It did cut me off from my family, which was my greatest fear realized. On the other hand, it might have saved the world."

She sighed. "What did I say about being cryptic?"

He held out his hands. "Hear me out. When I first got here, I found a book. It was a special book. Using it, I could look into a few select places. Rook Mountain was one of them. There's a small town in western Wisconsin called King's Crossing. One in Texas. One in Florida. A few others. I found I could bring things through the book. I brought food, clothing, furniture. Fuel for the generators. I could also bring things from this place's distant past into the present. Like the house I live in, for instance. But I spent the first few years watching. I watched everything that happened in Rook Mountain. And it was both wonderful and torturous. I could see my family anytime I missed them, and I could even take things from their world and bring them here to ours. But I couldn't send anything back the other way. I had no way to communicate with them. Eventually I watched my wife remarry. As difficult as that was, I couldn't blame her."

"Damn, that's pretty big of you."

"Not really. It was the right thing to do. It protected her and our son. Besides, I can never go back there and she deserves to be happy. Eventually, I had to stop watching them. It was too painful for me, and it wasn't fair to them to have me constantly spying." He paused for a moment before continuing. "After a while, I tried to bring a person through. It didn't work. It turns out, unlike inanimate objects, humans can resist being brought through. For it to work, they have to want it."

"So everyone here came from one of those special towns you can see in the book?"

He nodded. "There are fifteen towns in the book. All the people here are from one of them."

"And the trees…You said you knew I was from Rook Mountain because of the tree they found me under."

"Yeah. I can pull inanimate objects through the book. It doesn't work that way with people. It's more like I'm opening a door. They appear somewhere in this forest. There are some trees that seem to be connected to the towns somehow. I can usually guess which town folks came from based on the tree they appeared under. Usually." His face darkened. "You ever heard of Zed?"

"Sure. The Rook Mountain boogeyman. Or scapegoat. Depends who you ask. A lot of the folks from Rook Mountain blame what happened to the town on him. But, conveniently, no one outside the town has ever seen him."

"He's real enough. Trust me on that. I believe the towns in the book all have something special. Something Zed desperately wants. That special something is the reason for what happened in Rook Mountain. Which gets us back to the saving the world thing."

"I was wondering when we'd get back to that."

Jake took a deep breath before continuing. "Zed was trying to do something in Rook Mountain. He had an endgame. I don't know what it was exactly, but my wife, my brother, and some of my friends stopped him before he could finish. Thing is, he's gonna try again."

"How do you know?" she asked.

"Because Rook Mountain wasn't his first time. Whatever he was trying to do in Rook Mountain, he did it successfully here first." He waved his hand at the forest around him. "He somehow used this place up. And now it's a sick thing. It's like a nuclear test site. It's radioactive."

Sophie took a step closer toward the center of the trail.

"Not literally. It's a different kind of sickness. Spiritual maybe. Or metaphysical. I don't know. But those things that grow here, the Larvae, they feed off the sickness."

"Geez, man. Thanks a lot for bringing everyone here."

He grimaced. "I wouldn't have done it if it wasn't important. Leaving my family was the most painful thing I've ever done. Watching my wife remarry and move on was a close second. The third was bringing all the people here. But I can honestly say it was worth it."

"Because of the saving the world thing?" Sophie found she could actually say it with a straight face now.

"Yes. The sickness here is hungry. It wants to spread. And where do you think it's gonna spread to first?"

"Those fifteen towns the trees are connected to?"

Jake nodded.

"So when you say this place is hungry—"

"I mean it's literally hungry. It wants more land in order to grow its trees and develop the Larvae."

"So that's the problem. How do we go about stopping it?"

His brow suddenly tightened. "The book I found? I can use it to fight the sickness. A little bit anyway. What the sickness wants above all else is chaos. It's constantly changing the land, rearranging it. Flowing it back and forth like water. But using the book, I can insert tiny bits of order into the chaos. Your job, and the job of everyone at Sanctuary, is to help keep the order intact."

"You're talking about the trails."

He nodded. "When I create the trail, it's a tiny thing, barely even noticeable. But as more people walk the trail more often, it grows larger. If we don't walk it, it starts to fade."

She thought that over for a moment. "So you think if you make enough of these trails, you can destroy the sickness?"

He shook his head. "I don't know. That might be too ambitious. But we can fight it back. Keep it from growing."

Sophie looked around at the thick trees surrounding her. They were nearly countless. Above her head, the branches tangled so thick they blocked out the sun. "No offense, but that seems like a pretty shitty plan. It's like you're trimming the weeds instead of using weed killer."

His eyes shone with emotion. "Weed killer's in short supply these days. You got a better suggestion?"

She silently cursed herself. Here she was, her second day on the job and she was already criticizing the way the boss did things. And her first day on the job she had caused an injury that could cost a man his arm. "Look, I'm sorry. I didn't mean it like it came out."

"No, no. I wasn't being sarcastic. I really want to know if you have a better idea."

"Sorry, man. I really don't." Sophie bit her lip and thought. "You said Zed caused all this, right? Any idea where he is?"

He shook his head.

"Maybe he's dead."

He chuckled. "I highly doubt that. I have it on good authority the man's unkillable."

She decided to let that slide for now. "Best guess?"

Jake shrugged. "He didn't finish his work in Rook Mountain, so he's likely hiding out in one of the other towns waiting to make his next move. I'd say the only place we could rule out is here. He's already squeezed all the juice out of this place."

"Do you know what it was before it was 'out of place' or whatever you said?"

"No. These trees are a side effect of what Zed did. They've wiped out everything else. Nothing remains of whatever was here before."

He turned and started walking down the path. She followed.

She saw something out of the corner of her eye, and she froze. It was another message carved into a tree with that same odd technique that caused the bark to bend outward.

The tree was close enough to the trail that she could read it without stepping off. Once again, it seemed to have been written specifically for her.

He lies. Ask him about the banishments.

She paused, took one last look at the strange message, and then hurried to catch up to Jake.

"So…I can still ask you anything, right?"

He didn't turn to face her, but even from behind she could tell he was nodding.

"If you knew where I came from based on the tree I appeared under, I'm guessing you also know where Taylor's from." She paused to see if he'd respond. He didn't, so she continued. "Since we've got this whole pause on the 'no talking about the past' thing, there's some stuff you should know about him."

He shook his head briskly. "I gave permission to discuss my past, and you gave permission to discuss yours. It's not our place to talk about someone else's."

She felt her pulse quickening. Screw Jake and screw his rules and screw Sanctuary. "He's a killer."

Jake spun on his heels. His teeth shone in the light of the forest. "Didn't Frasier tell you what would happen if you broke the rules? I swear to God, Sophie, if you hurt another person here or breathe a word about Taylor's past again, I will banish you. Understand?"

She managed to nod.

"Tell me about the banishments," Sophie said. "What happens when you banish someone?"

"I'm not ready to tell you about that yet. After you've been here a while, we'll discuss it." He sighed. "Look, I'm sorry I yelled. I appreciate your help today. I badly needed an update on Rook Mountain."

"Why didn't you ask your buddy Taylor?"

Jake paused, as if unsure whether to answer. "I did. I made him the same offer I made you. I asked if he'd be willing to discuss the past."

"And?"

"He declined."

Sophie laughed. "If that's not a red flag, I don't know what is. You don't know what it's like—"

"I do know," Jake said. "Back in Rook Mountain, Zed has these…let's call them disciples. When he took power, they got elected into office. They became the selectmen that ran the town's government. They enforced Zed's rules. They hurt people I cared about."

"Yeah, I read about that," Sophie said. She didn't see the connection.

"A while back, I brought someone here. I didn't know who it was. Just another person yelling Sanctuary, asking for my help. Turns out, it was one of the selectmen."

She squinted at Jake. "What'd you do about it?"

Jake shrugged. "I welcomed that person to Sanctuary. We both pretended like we didn't know each other, and over time we've even become friends."

"If you think Taylor and I are gonna be friends, you are out of your mind. You don't know what you're asking."

Jake put his hand on her shoulder. "Please Sophie, listen to what I'm telling you. Follow the rules. If you have a problem with Taylor, stay away from him. If you lay a hand on him, I'll pass judgment on you. Even if you are special."

She tilted her head at him. That was the first time in a long time anyone had called her special. "How am I special? Because I killed the Larvae?"

Jake smiled. "I knew before that. See, the book lets me

140

know in advance when someone's gonna request Sanctuary. Sometimes I let them through. Sometimes I don't. But you were different. I never got any warning. You just showed up in the middle of the night."

"So what the hell does that mean?" she asked.

"It means I didn't open the door to let you in. It means someone else did."

IN THE WOODS (PART FOUR)

Frank followed Mason down the thin line of dirt that had probably once been a wide trail. Today it was nothing more than a faint sketch in the woods. Frank had trouble seeing it at times in the dim beam of his flashlight.

Mason, on the other hand, was having no such trouble. He wove his way down the trail like a much younger man. There was a spring in his step and every time he looked back to see if Frank was keeping up, the look on his face spoke of sheer delight. Frank was reminded of the Tolkien character, Tom Bombadil, the man of indeterminate age who was so quick he could go out in the rain without getting wet.

The beam of their flashlights bounced on the trees and roots ahead of them. Frank wiped the sweat off his brow with his free hand. They'd only been going for about twenty minutes, but their pace was such that Frank didn't know how much longer he'd be able to keep this up. Part of it was the heavy lockbox that dangled from his right hand. The box had a durable handle built into the top, and it fit Frank's hand like an old baseball glove. He'd hauled a box like this one down to the river and over mountains and God only knew where else. It had been his near-constant companion for a few years when he was a kid. It sure felt heavier now than he remembered.

Mason rounded a curve and stopped. He bounced back and forth from foot to foot, too excited to stand still. "This is it. Right up here."

Frank shined his flashlight where Mason pointed, but he couldn't make out much more than the vague shade of the cabin.

Mason continued on without waiting for a reply.

The shape of the cabin grew more distinct as they approached, and before long he could see a hole, blacker than the rest of the structure, that could only be an open door. When they were ten feet away, a figure emerged from the darkness.

Even though he couldn't see more than a silhouette, and even that was only faintly visible, he knew. His senses were suddenly a bit sharper. The tang of the forest burned in his nose and the dark figure's every footfall rang like a gong in his ears. His hands were cold and clammy.

Frank reached down with a shaking left hand and clicked the Cassandra lock into place on the latch of the box.

The shadowy figure raised something to chest-level. Frank heard a click and the object illuminated, covering a twenty-foot radius with light. He blinked against the harsh illumination of the lantern. It was a moment or two before his vision adjusted enough for him to clearly see the man standing before him.

Zed said, "Hello, Mason. I see you've brought company."

Mason practically danced forward. Zed squinted in Frank's direction, his eyes apparently adjusting to the light the same as Frank's. Maybe the man was human after all.

"Why, if I didn't know better, I'd say that was Frank

Hinkle."

Frank stood frozen on the spot. He didn't know what to say, what to do. He wanted to lunge at Zed, gouge at his eyes, but he knew such a gesture would be worthless. The man wouldn't die and couldn't be hurt. Or, was that still true now that he no longer had his beloved pocket watch? He certainly seemed to have healed from the incident on the top of city hall.

While Frank was still mulling over how best to test Zed's vulnerabilities, Mason spoke. "He did it, Zed! Just like you said he would. He found a lock box in my dad's office. And he brought it with him."

As Mason spoke, Frank bent down as far as he dared and dropped the lock box onto the ground. He hoped Zed had been too focused on Mason to notice the move.

"Please, Mason, let's not jump right to business. I know you grew up in the woods, but that's no reason to forget your manners." Zed took three long steps forward, encircling them all in the light of his lantern, and extended his hand. "Frank. Last time I saw you, you looked a bit worse for the wear. But the mirror and its time shifting ways are peculiar. I'm not sure if the last time I saw you was the last time you saw me."

Frank stared at the hand like it was made of vile, rotting meat. Then he looked Zed up and down. The man looked exactly like he had the day he sent Frank Away, right down to the wide smile and the brightly colored tee-shirt. Not bad for fifty-some years later.

Zed slowly lowered his hand. "Well then. It's going to be like that, is it?"

Frank still held his tongue. There were things he wanted to say to this man, but everything that came to mind seemed so inadequate to express the utter despair he felt. In the last few hours, he'd learned that the man he'd given up everything to save was long dead, and the only man in the world he truly wished was dead was alive and well and standing in front of him.

Zed sighed. "I felt you arrive, you know. I'm pretty tuned into this place, and I felt a," he paused, as if looking for the right word, "crackle. It crackled when you arrived. The time you spent in the Away marked you, and the woods sensed it. As soon as I realized it was you, I began hoping things could be different between us this time."

Mason said, "I found him down by the creek. One of the Larvae was locked in on him. I put it down and brought him here."

"Fine, fine," Zed said, his eyes never leaving Frank. "It can happen, Frank. We can work together. I know it seems unlikely, but alliances do change."

He waited, his eyes wide and hopeful. Frank said nothing.

Zed waved a dismissive hand at him. "Okay then. Let's forgo the howdys and the fat chewing and get to it. Where's this lock box?"

Frank met Zed's eyes. He tried to put all his hatred into that look. "Zed, Mason's crazy as all hell. After a couple hours with him, I'm getting nostalgic for the Ones Who Sing."

Zed met his gaze. The smile never left his face, but his eyes were ice. "That can be arranged. But, really, is that any way to talk about family?"

Frank's heart sank. Until that moment, he had been open to the possibility that Mason was a crazy person. But even though he had no reason to trust Zed and many reasons not to trust him, something about hearing him say it made it more real to Frank.

He glanced at Mason and saw the hurt look on the man's

145

face. He felt bad for the guy. It wasn't Mason's fault he'd been raised by the worst foster father in history. He hadn't picked his circumstances. Still, choice or not, that didn't make him any less dangerous to Frank. Who knew what sick ideas and programming Zed had put into his head?

"How long have you been here, Zed? I came through the mirror a couple months after you did, but from what Mason tells me you've been here much longer."

Zed smiled, neither confirming nor denying. "How are things back in Rook Mountain? You all keeping the place warm for me?"

Frank suppressed a laugh. "You think you're going back there, is that it?"

"I left once before, if you remember. After you opened the box."

Frank shook his head. "I don't buy it. Seems to me you would have gone back already if you were able. Besides, you don't have your toy anymore. The pocket watch."

Zed's smile wavered for only an instant. "I'm not going to lie. Losing that hurt. I've had it a long time. Longer than you could imagine. There are other Tools. The mirror. The lighter. The knife. Perhaps you've even seen the coin. Little silver thing. You'd know it if you saw it."

Now it was Frank's turn to smile. "I did see it. Right before I came through the mirror, in fact." He paused to take in the hungry look on Zed's face. "I stuck the knife through the coin. It made the worst sound when it shattered."

Zed drew a sharp breath, making a noise that could almost have been described as a gasp. "You're lying."

"Not at all. We also destroyed the lighter. And the key. And the cane." He counted them off on his fingers as he listed them. "And Christine was going to destroy the mirror as soon as I came through it. Hope you weren't counting on that to get back."

Zed's lips curled, making his smile look like it was painted on his face. "But she wouldn't have been able to destroy the knife, would she? I think when I get back to Rook Mountain, the first thing I'll do is pay the Osmonds a visit. Then I'll show them how that knife really works. Oh, the things that can be done with that knife. If I'd had that from the get go, I wouldn't have sent you Away at all. I would have made things so much more painful."

Mason looked back and forth between the two men, as if he were trying to figure out the rules of a sport he had never played. "Uncle Frank's brought us the hidden box. That's what you wanted, right?"

Zed nodded. "It is. But your uncle has the strange talent of being able to hide things. Even from me. And he doesn't seem to want to tell me where the box is. Frank, I believe there is a book in the lockbox you found. I can use the book to get us out of here. You may have noticed that this forest is not well. It's used up. The animals have died out. Even the Larvae are sluggish. This place is dying, and we will die with it unless you give me the box."

Frank said nothing. No way was he going to put his trust in Zed to save them. Wasn't that how the Regulations had been passed into law to begin with?

Mason's breath quickened. He said in a soft voice, "Uncle Frank, please give Zed the box. You don't want to make him angry."

"It's okay, Mason," Frank said, though he knew it wasn't.

"Yes," Zed said. "It's fine." He turned toward Mason. "Use the compass."

Mason's face lit up. "Of course." He pulled the Tool out of

his pocket and squeezed his eyes shut. When he opened them, his face fell. "The compass can't find it either."

"Impressive," Zed said.

"There's something else," Mason said, his voice suddenly urgent. "Frank saw someone in the woods."

Zed's eyes narrowed.

"The man with the beard."

Frank had seen Zed in some extreme situations. When he was attacked by the Unfeathered in Rook Mountain. At the end of the battle on top of city hall when Zed knew he had lost. But Frank had never seen Zed truly afraid. Not until now.

When Zed spoke, his voice was slow and quiet. "We need to move quickly." He turned to Mason. "Frank has the box. We have to make him give it to us. He has to reveal it of his own free will. I can't dig it out of his head unless he lets me."

"Okay," Mason said. "How do we do that?"

"We're going to have to hurt him."

Frank took a short step backwards. He knew he should run now. He should run into these woods and hide. But Mason and Zed had lived here for years. He didn't think he could evade them for long. And then there were those creatures. The Larvae.

"Do you understand what I'm saying?" Zed asked.

Mason nodded.

"It may not be quick," Zed continued. "Frank doesn't break easily. I know from experience. But we need that box if we're ever going to learn your father's secrets. We might have a long night ahead of us, and I need to know you're with me all the way."

Mason pulled a rusty knife from his belt. His voice sounded tired when he spoke. "I'm with you."

"Good." Zed rubbed his chin as if deep in thought. "We'll start with the feet. It's amazing how much pain can enter the body through the bottom of the feet." He looked at Frank. "Unless you want to give us the box. We can look through it together."

Frank felt his heart speed up. He slipped his hands into his pockets, hoping to find something, anything, to help, to buy him a little time. He was surprised when his hand closed around something metal. The thing his brother had asked him to bring. The Cassandra lock. He'd forgotten he had two of them now. The one he'd brought with him and the one he'd found on the lockbox in Jake's office.

Something Zed had said moments earlier now came rushing back to him. *Your uncle has the strange talent of being able to hide things.* And it was true. The locks Frank made could render objects invisible to prying eyes. It was how Will and Christine had hidden the Tools from Zed for so long.

"Sounds like you've got a fun evening planned," Frank said, "but I've gotta run."

The fingers of Frank's right hand snapped the Cassandra lock shut. As it closed, he concentrated with all his might and imagined the thing it was locking was *him*. He squeezed it tightly in his fist and willed himself locked away from Zed and Mason.

Zed's jaw fell open.

"Where is he?" Mason asked. "Where'd he go?"

Frank bent down and carefully picked up the lock box. He backed away slowly. He knew he was invisible to their eyes, but he wasn't sure if the lock would also mask his sounds.

As Zed and Mason searched for him, Frank slipped into the forest.

CHAPTER FIVE: THE PRICE

1. Sanctuary

Sophie watched the Larva as it gathered itself into a tiny ball and prepared to launch into the air.

"On its lower left side," she said. "Do you see it?"

Logan gritted her teeth. "Where? Be more specific. What am I looking for?"

"It's a little bump. You don't see that?"

Logan glared at her. "If I saw it, you think I would have asked the question? The thing's covered with hair. How am I supposed to see a bump?"

"Fair point. Okay, you see that spot with slightly less hair?"

Logan squinted at the creature. "I really don't."

The thing began to quiver.

Sophie stepped toward it, her knife extended.

"Come on!" Logan yelled, but by that point, Sophie's knife was already buried to the hilt in the Larva.

Sophie flicked the resulting sludge off her knife and looked back at Logan. The woman was beyond frustrated.

"You said you wouldn't do that again!" Logan bellowed.

"It was about to leap at you. What was I supposed to do?"

"Maybe let me learn the hard way."

They were entering their third hour of this. In that time, Sophie had killed a dozen of the Larvae while trying to show Logan their weak spot. The plan was for Sophie to teach Logan and then for Logan to teach the rest of Sanctuary, but the plan wasn't playing out too well so far. Maybe if she could have pointed out the spot on a dead or immobile Larva, it would have been easier. But the way the things melted when killed wasn't conducive to a proper learning environment. Whenever Sophie got near a live one, it pounced at her and she was forced to put it down.

"It's not your fault," Logan said. "Sorry I snapped. Let's find the next one."

They were walking one of the thinner, less well-kept trails and it was the middle of the day, so the Larvae were plentiful. Between the events of the last few days, switching day shift to night shift and back again, and the stress of trying to teach Logan, Sophie was exhausted. But from what she knew of Logan, the woman wouldn't agree to stop until she'd mastered the strange art of Larva killing.

As they walked, Logan said, "You been to see Carver yet?"

Sophie shook her head. "Not yet. I wasn't sure if he'd want to see me."

"Good call. He's a little torn up right now. Send him a note and then wait a day or two before you go."

That wasn't the advice Sophie had expected, but she was quickly learning she never knew what to expect with Logan. Even though the hazing was only a week ago, Sophie found herself starting to like the woman. Given time, they might become good friends.

Frasier had removed Carver's arm that morning. An amputation was a terrible thing in the best of circumstances; Sophie couldn't imagine how horrible it must have been in this under-equipped location. Apparently, all talking about the past aside, Frasier was a man who knew his way around traumatic injuries. Carver was expected to pull through.

As a weird side effect of the injury, Sophie had gotten her own cabin. Carver was recovering at the Welcome Wagon, and so she and all her possessions, scant as they might have been, were moved into a vacant cabin. It just so happened to be the one next to Logan's.

Sophie had laid in bed last night for hours, unable to sleep in spite of her tiredness. She'd stared at the compass with one thought in her mind. *Taylor.*

Now that she knew she would never see her family or friends again, the idea of dealing with Taylor had grown in her mind from simply something that should be done into something that *had* to be done. Coming here—putting her parents through losing another child, forfeiting whatever shot at a normal future she might have—it had to mean something. It couldn't just be a random, freakishly strange series of occurrences. Something good had to come of it.

And the more she thought about it, the more she came to realize that carrying out Taylor's punishment was the only positive outcome possible. Maybe all of it, Heather dying, Taylor escaping, had happened to put her in this very place at this very time. Maybe she was the only one who could do what needed to be done. She couldn't get squeamish now.

As she watched the compass, she had seen his position moving throughout the night. It wasn't surprising considering he was working the night shift, but there was something satisfying about constantly tracking his position. It made her feel like she had one up on him.

One aspect of the compass troubled her. Whenever she wasn't thinking of something specific she wanted the compass to find, its needle pointed at her. Just like Rodgers had said.

She'd been using the compass for other things, too. She'd found that by thinking of something and pressing the broken clock symbol, the compass would point her to it. It came in handy for everything from finding her way around the strange, shifting landscape of Sanctuary to finding a missing sock.

She could have used the compass to point them to the nearest Larva, but she had no intention of revealing it, not even to Logan. If she had been willing to share the compass, this could have been over with much more quickly. Logan could have held it and seen the Larva's kill spot as quickly as Sophie had. But it was Sophie's secret, her edge, and she wasn't ready to share it with anyone.

"How long you been in Sanctuary?" Sophie asked. Then she quickly added, "That's an okay question to ask, right?"

Logan revealed a rare smile. "Yeah, it's fine. Some people are touchier than others about the whole past thing. Me? I couldn't care less. I'd tell you my story, how I got here, but I wouldn't want to bore you to death. It's like I said to you during the hazing. Life starts the moment you arrive here. The rest isn't really worth talking about. At least not for me."

Sophie thought about her mundane life in Nashville. The woman did have a point. This was certainly more exciting.

"Nine years," Logan said.

"Wow," Sophie said. "And Mason's what? Eight?"

Logan scowled. "Yes. Jake and I got right to it. Don't get judgy."

Sophie held up her hands in mock horror. "Trust me, I'm the last person who should be judging anyone."

Their eyes scanned the trail for Larvae, but they came up

empty.

"How many people were at Sanctuary when you got here?" Sophie asked.

"Four, including Jake."

"That's all? Who hazed you? Anyone I know?"

Logan shook her head. "No one you know."

Sophie gave her an indignant look. "Oh come on. That's all I get? I want to hear about it. You got to haze me. The least you can do is let me hear about yours."

Logan slowed to a halt. "Things were different then. Very different. We didn't have hazings. We didn't even have the rules."

"Really? So I take it there was an incident or something?"

She nodded. "There was an incident. Two of the people didn't like the way Jake kept the book to himself. They thought we should all share it. When he wouldn't hand it over, they attacked him. Almost killed him. They did kill one man, a guy named Davis. Thankfully, they underestimated me."

Sophie couldn't imagine anyone underestimating Logan. One look at her told you she was a badass.

As if reading her mind, Logan said, "I was different then, too. I've come out of my shell a lot since those days. Anyway, we eventually overpowered those two. Their names were Rosenberg and Harris. They were the first two banished. It was just me and Jake here for a while after that."

"The Adam and Eve of Sanctuary," Sophie said.

"More like Hatfield and McCoy. Jake and I didn't always get along so well. Still don't, I guess. We butted heads on a lot of things. I guess that's why we're not together now. That and the fact that he never fully got over the wife he left back home."

"Wow. So you've been here through it all. Longer than anybody."

"Almost everybody. Don't forget Rosenberg and Harris. They're still out there somewhere." She looked around, scanning the trees, whether for Rosenberg and Harris or Larvae, Sophie didn't know.

"How many have been banished in all?"

Logan shrugged. "A dozen. Maybe a little more."

"But they're still out there, right?"

Logan nodded.

"You ever worry they'll come back? Like for revenge or something?"

"No." Logan looked away. "They won't come back. They never come back."

"But if they did—"

"They won't come back," Logan repeated.

A whiny hum cut off the conversation. Sophie spun and saw the Larva near the edge of the trail, less than two feet from Logan's foot.

"Logan," Sophie began, but the other woman cut her off.

"I got it." There was something strange in her voice. If it had been anyone else, Sophie would have characterized it as a laugh. "I do. I think I've actually got it. Near the top. It's like a small protrusion."

"That's what I said."

Logan drew her knife. "You said bump. It's definitely a protrusion." With that, she thrust the knife into the Larva. She looked at Sophie. She was positively glowing. "Holy hell. I just killed a Larva."

Sophie smiled at her. "That you did. About time, too. I was starting to think you were unteachable."

"It's a poor teacher who blames her student."

155

Sophie couldn't help it. She grabbed Logan and gave her a hug. And, to Sophie's surprise, Logan hugged her back.

Sophie stepped back and watched the liquefied Larva run off Logan's knife. "So, what do we do now?"

"First, we kill another one or ten to make sure I've got the hang of this," Logan said. "Then we start teaching the others."

2. Rook Mountain

Sean frowned at the tree and the message carved in it: *Use the Tool and the book and you can bring him home.*

It was raining lightly, coming down just hard enough to moisten the skin but not enough to soak through clothes. Rare for eastern Tennessee. Normally, the sky suddenly went dark and the precipitation was a hard angry rain that started without warning, and ended as quickly.

"By *Tool*, do you think they're talking about the, you know, Tools?" Sean asked.

Wendy nodded. "Yep."

"And the *him* in *bring him home* is Zed?"

"Yep."

"Huh. And when did you see this?"

They were standing in front of a tree in a front yard on the far west side of town. It would be inaccurate to say Rook Mountain had a bad part of town. The rough elements were mixed in with all the rest like someone had dumped everyone into the town at random and given it a rough shake. That said, the west side had a higher percentage of late night police calls and drug deals than the rest of town.

"Day before yesterday. I swung over to the library after school and noticed it on my way home. I saw it through the window of my car. I didn't think much of it at the time. But after what we saw earlier…"

"Yeah," he said. He noticed the way the bark around the letters bulged outward again. Truly strange. After everything they'd seen and heard over the last eight plus years, it was always tempting to jump to a supernatural conclusion when seeing something out of the ordinary. Sean was careful to avoid that trap. Most things, even in Rook Mountain, had a perfectly logical explanation. There was no call to assume the letters had been carved from inside the tree or by someone in the great beyond or something.

"Hey, we've got a fan." Wendy nodded toward the window of the house where a curtain was fluttering as if it had been hastily moved back into place.

Sean grunted. He wasn't in uniform. A couple of strangers in the yard staring at a tree—they had probably freaked out some little old lady or something.

"I'm gonna go knock on the door," Sean said.

"Why?"

"I want to let her know we aren't casing her house. Besides, maybe she knows something about all this. You coming?"

Wendy hesitated, then nodded.

He rapped on the door and waited for what seemed like an eternity. He concentrated on acting non-threatening.

"What's that look on your face?" Wendy asked quietly.

"What do you mean? It's my non-creepy smile."

She shook her head. "It isn't working."

He dropped the smile.

"If it's a woman, you better let me do the talking," Wendy said.

The door opened the tiniest of cracks.

"Help you?" The voice was distinctly female.

Wendy took a slight step forward. "Sorry to bother you

ma'am, but we're investigating some vandalism going on around town, and we happened to notice your tree."

The door opened a smidge wider, enough for Sean to see a sliver of a pale face and a single blue eye. "Investigation, huh? Investigation for who? You some of those federals?"

Sean shook his head. He didn't want to get into whether or not they were here on official police business. "No, ma'am. I'm Rook Mountain PD."

She relaxed visibly at that and swung the door wide enough for Sean to see both of her eyes and even some of her dirty blonde hair. The woman was short and thin and probably under thirty. "That so? I guess you'd better come in then."

She pulled the door open the rest of the way, and Sean followed Wendy into a living room cluttered with toys, partially folded laundry, and a dozen short stacks of paperback novels.

"You're a reader," Wendy said with a smile, like she'd found one of her own tribe.

The woman nodded. "Mysteries, mostly. I like the ones that keep me guessing. You'd think after reading all these I'd have sense enough not to let strangers in without asking for ID even if they claim to be cops. Especially if they claim to be cops."

"I don't have my badge, but maybe this'll do." Sean pulled a business card out of his wallet and handed it over.

She took the card and looked at it for a long moment. "Nice to meet you, Officer Sean Lee. I'm Christy Havert." She looked at Wendy. "You got a card?"

"I'm not a cop," Wendy said.

"Huh. Amateur sleuth then."

Wendy turned on her best smile, and Sean had to admit it was very non-creepy. "Isn't that the best kind?"

The woman let a smile of her own slip out. "I'm partial to Nick Stefanos. You ever read any of George Pelecanos' books?"

Wendy shook her head.

"Shame." Christy set down Sean's card on a bookshelf near the front door. "You wanted to know about the carving in the tree?"

"Yeah, anything you could tell us would help," Sean said. "Do you know who did it?"

"I don't. My husband noticed it about three days ago. He saw it first thing in the morning. Though I can't say for certain it happened during the night."

"How about the message itself?" Wendy asked. "Any idea what it means?"

Christy let out a mirthless chuckle. Sean noticed there were tears in her eyes.

"What is it?" Wendy asked.

"This damn town. It makes me so tired. I'm sick to death of watching my mouth and not knowing who to trust. It was bad with the Regulations, but this is almost worse in some ways. Nobody shows their true colors."

"Maybe it's time to take a chance," Wendy said.

Christy paused for a long moment, as if considering. Then she said, "I'm glad it was you who showed up here. I was afraid it might be someone else. Maybe those kids with the tattoos on their hands."

"Why would they come here?" Sean asked.

"There's something I've been living with for a long time. A burden, you might say."

Sean opened his mouth to speak, but then he caught the look Wendy was giving him and closed it.

There was a new light in Christy's eyes as if an idea had

occurred to her.

"Would you take it, Officer? Would you take my burden from me?"

Sean was about to ask her what the hell she was talking about when Wendy said, "Of course, honey. We'll take it for you."

She nodded excitedly and ran out of the room.

Sean whispered to Wendy, "What the hell's going on?"

"I have no idea. But if she has some crazy secret, I wasn't about to tell her not to show it to us."

Christy ran back into the living room, clutching something wrapped in cloth. "My husband's gonna kill me." She glanced at Sean. "Not literally. He wouldn't hurt a fly. He's gonna be fuming mad though. Kept this thing hidden for years. But now, with somebody carving that message, I know they're on to us. It's even more dangerous than it was before."

She held out the cloth to Sean. He took it, and the unexpected weight of the thing almost made it slip from his hand. It was an object wrapped in a tee-shirt. He opened it.

"My husband found it at a construction site. He brought it home and kept it in his tool box all these years."

It was a ball peen hammer. On the head of the hammer was the broken clock symbol.

"It's something, isn't it?" Christy asked. "Just think, that thing could have got us killed during the Zed years. You ever seen anything like it?"

Sean wasn't sure how to answer, so he just smiled his best non-creepy smile.

3. Sanctuary

On her twentieth day in Sanctuary, Sophie tried to kill Taylor.

Life had fallen into a comfortable rhythm. Logan had asked Sophie to join her team of walkers full time. She was rebuilding the team from the ground up. Carver was going to be out of commission for a good long while, and Baldwin refused to work on a team with Sophie. He'd given Logan an ultimatum: pick Sophie for her team or pick Baldwin. Logan hadn't hesitated before selecting Sophie. Leonard, who along with Baldwin had carried Sophie that first night, volunteered to take his place. Since there were no newbies to mentor now that Sophie had moved to her own cabin, Frasier also joined the team.

They walked the trail every night. Usually, it took about four hours, but sometimes they completed the loop in fifteen minutes. Sometimes they hustled to make it home before dawn. There were very few encounters with the Larvae. Apparently they slept through the night as long as someone wasn't sticking her hand into their nests.

As they walked, Sophie kept her eyes on the trees. She looked for more of the strange carved messages, but she didn't see any.

Sophie and Logan had spent a few days teaching the rest of Sanctuary how to kill the Larvae. It turned out Logan was a much better teacher than Sophie, and it went faster than they could have hoped. Every adult in Sanctuary was now able to find the weak spot and kill them.

Sophie didn't sleep much during the day, though she tried. Knowing Taylor was so close by certainly didn't help, nor did the switch to sleeping in the day and working at night. But the main cause of her insomnia was the weighty sense of uncertainty that hung over her. She'd long fantasized that, through some unlikely twist of fate, she'd be the one to turn on the lethal drip when he received his final injection. Now

161

she had been given something even better. Not only did she have the opportunity to be Taylor's executioner, she'd also be the one to select his means of execution.

Yet, still she waited.

Sometimes she spent hours thinking about how she'd do it. There was no end to the methods and techniques of death and torture that went through her head in vivid color and detail. Sometimes the level of creativity she was able to come up with frightened her. But, while she had no trouble envisioning his death, it was imagining the moments after his final breath that caused her trouble. What would she do? Escape into the woods? Turn herself in to Jake and throw herself on his mercy?

None of the options seemed perfect. Ideally, she'd cover up the crime, but she knew that would be difficult in Sanctuary. There were only thirty-five residents, but it seemed like someone was always nearby. There was almost no privacy. Even sneaking into Taylor's cabin during the day while most of the community slept would be risky. She hadn't ruled it out, but it didn't seem like the ideal option.

And then there was Jake.

Half of what he had told her in the woods sounded like the fantasies of a madman. Or a cult leader. Telling your disciples they could never leave and building circular trails that all led back to the same place seemed like a nice technique for keeping them loyal. But Sophie had seen too much to deny that his explanation made a strange kind of sense. She'd been transported here in an impossible way. She'd seen the Larvae and heard their other-worldly voices. She'd walked the trails that changed lengths night after night.

What was the real extent of Jake's power? Had he been honest with her in the woods? Would she even have a chance at covering up her actions, or would he be able to see what happened using that book of his?

And who was leaving her those messages?

None of that mattered in the hour before dawn when she saw Taylor standing on a tall ladder.

The majority of the residents in Sanctuary spent their working hours walking the trails, but there were exceptions. There was Yang, who made wonderful dinners for the town and served them each day before dawn. There was Nate, who handled logistics and kept the schedules. Jake spent most of his time locked away in his office.

And then there was Taylor. He served as sort of a handyman, taking care of repairs and upkeep on the grounds and the cabins.

"His disposition is best served by working alone," Logan had told Sophie. Sophie had bit her lip to stop the flood of automatic responses to that observation.

Sophie didn't know what he was doing up on the ladder, but he was leaning against a third story window of Jake's house. She didn't think. She turned on her heels and marched toward the ladder.

She was almost there when Taylor saw her. He looked down, and his eyes widened. The knowing, terrified look on his face gave her a feeling of deep satisfaction. He didn't move; he just stared down at her.

The ladder drew her like a magnet. She felt calm, no anger or adrenaline rushed through her. She was doing what needed to be done. She was almost there now. She reached out her hand, and her fingers brushed against the cool aluminum.

"Sophie!"

The voice startled her, and she snapped her head around to see Logan behind her, a troubled look on the woman's face.

Sophie froze, her fingers still resting on the ladder.

Logan looked up. "You too, Taylor. Get down here."

Taylor looked at Sophie, a slow grin spreading across his face. There was a moment where Sophie almost did it anyway, damn the consequences, just to wipe away that smug look. But she managed to control her hands, and she took a step back as he scurried down to the ground.

Logan looked back and forth between them. "We have a problem."

Sophie's heart was racing.

"Baldwin's dead," Logan said. "Vance attacked him. Apparently they were arguing. My guess is it was about Abby, although we haven't been able to confirm that yet. Anyway, things got heated and Vance picked up a brick and used it on Baldwin. Abby saw the whole thing, but Baldwin was dead before she could get help."

Sophie's mind was spinning, trying to catch up with this new information.

"That's all the info I have at the moment," Logan said. "Vance will be banished tonight. Be at the main trail head at sundown." With that, she spun on her heels and marched away, and Sophie was left standing alone next to Taylor.

After a long quiet moment, Taylor said, "Strange thing about this place. They hate violence unless it's the official kind dished out by the authorities. Then everybody shows up to watch."

Sophie clenched her fists. That voice grated on her like gravel across her face.

"I remember you," he continued.

Without looking at him, Sophie said, "We're not supposed to talk about the past."

He shrugged. "I won't tell if you don't. Besides, that's not true. We aren't supposed to ask about others' pasts. I'm talking about my own. Sharing some memories."

She glared at him. She'd forgotten how short he was. She stood five foot five, and he wasn't much taller. His face was a lumpy thing with thick lips and eyes that always looked swollen. His hair was the color of dirt, and his skin had the pink complexion of a slight sunburn.

"When my verdict was read, there was a lot of cheering in that courtroom. But, I'll never forget, there was one voice that jumped out at me. The first cheer came from a girl. And, again, when I was sentenced to death, that same girl was the first one cheering. So, I gotta ask, what made you so blood thirsty?"

An image passed through Sophie's mind: a coroner's photograph of the back of Heather's head, a smashed in, ruined thing. Sophie wasn't supposed to see it, but she had snuck a peek and spent the next ten years wishing she hadn't.

"You did." The words came out of Sophie's mouth as little more than a whisper.

Taylor grunted. "I'm a patient man. I sat in that hellhole in Rook Mountain for eighteen years, including while the town was outside of time or whatever. I never hurt a single person while I was there, not until the time I hit the guard. But I did think about that girl and the way she cheered. I thought about it a lot."

Sophie noticed her legs were shaking.

"I waited a long time, until the moment felt perfect, and then I took my shot at Sanctuary." He spread his hands in front of him. "Worked out pretty well. So I don't mind being patient again."

"Go to hell." She choked out the words.

Taylor looked her in the eye for the first time. "You're

gonna learn something tonight. You can't touch me here. No matter how much you miss that sister of yours or how much you wish you could see me bleed. After tonight, you'll understand."

"I'm patient too."

Taylor curled his lips in an attempt at a smile. It looked unnatural, and it only served to accentuate the misshapen nature of his face. "Something tells me that ain't the case."

She felt venom rising inside her, a poisonous anger she'd worked so hard and so long to suppress. It had seeped out anyway, souring so many things in her life: relationships, jobs, friendships. But standing there, she realized she didn't have to hold it back anymore. It had a direction now. It could be useful to her, helpful even. It would keep her pointed toward her goal, the one and only goal that mattered. She'd spent the last few weeks worried about consequences. But consequences came after the action, and the action was the important part. There was an ache in her chest, a fury and a shame that made her wish she ignored Logan's voice and knocked over the ladder.

"My sister died without understanding what was happening or why," she said. "It won't be like that for you. You'll know who's responsible. And you'll know why."

The quasi-smile melted off Taylor's face. "Killing ain't as easy as you think. It takes strength. Maybe tonight we'll find out if you're really as bloodthirsty as you pretend to be."

He gave her a parting wink and headed toward the front door of Jake's house. Sophie watched him go, her legs still shaking.

4. Sanctuary

Banishments were rare in Sanctuary, but not rare enough

for Nate's liking. It reminded him too much of the years he'd spend serving Zed.

Time was, back in Rook Mountain when he'd been one of Zed's selectmen, he'd relished the opportunity to witness a Regulation Breaker get the justice that was coming to him. These days, things were different. It was partly due to the bizarre, stomach-turning nature of the punishments in Sanctuary, sure, but holding a branding iron to a kid's face was pretty stomach-turning, too. The bigger difference was the leaders of each community. Zed had feigned concern and regret at the punishments, but in truth he was indifferent. And, every once in a while, it almost seemed like he enjoyed it.

But Jake never enjoyed the banishments. He showed no emotion whatsoever, but Nate knew each banishment weighed on him.

It had only happened four times since Nate had arrived. He'd never forget the first one he'd witnessed. It was a woman named Suzanne who'd broken into Jake's office and tried to steal the book. Dumb move. Jake caught her and did what needed to be done.

The residents of Sanctuary weren't required to attend the banishment, but everyone did anyway, even the few who had kids. Some enjoyed it. Some came to say their goodbyes to the convicted. Some just felt it was their responsibility.

To Nate, the banishment represented an organizational nightmare. It fell to him to find a fairly empty place in the woods where the ceremony could take place. It couldn't be in the Sanctuary itself and it couldn't be so far away that the Larvae would be drawn to attack them. With the ever-changing landscape of the woods, this was no easy task, especially since it had to be done during daylight hours. The ceremony would take place at sundown, and there were a hundred little things to get ready before that.

The other difficult part was getting everyone to leave after the ceremony was over. People tended to linger, as if they didn't want to depart from the final meeting they would have with their banished brother or sister. It was essential life get back to normal as quickly as possible, and it was up to Nate to politely but firmly send people away and get them back on their nightly routines. He generally gave them ten minutes or so to disperse naturally before he took action.

Today, he'd gotten lucky on a location. The forest had shifted last night and there was a nice big clearing only twenty yards from Jake's house. It would be the perfect spot, and there was plenty of room for the thirty-four spectators who would gather tonight. It was as if the woods had known what was coming and done Nate's job for him. Almost as if the forest was hungry for the banishment.

Nate stood for a moment, arms crossed, looking at the spot. It was almost anticlimactic the way the solution had been so easy this time. His eyes combed the area for any flaw that would make the spot unusable. He found none.

Nate decided not to look a gift horse in the mouth. This was the spot for Vance's banishment. He trotted the short distance back to Jake's house.

Jake's office door was closed as usual, so Nate knocked, rapping with his knuckles quickly and softly, in the distinctive cadence he always used to let Jake know it was him at the door.

"Come in," a voice called through the heavy wood.

Nate entered and found Jake sitting at his desk, his eyes closed and his head resting against his peaked fingers. The book was sitting beside him, haphazardly pushed aside. Nate felt the familiar pang of concern. Jake had been using the book to prepare for the banishment, and that always took a lot out of him. He wouldn't be himself for days after tonight. These ceremonies were hard on Jake. Too hard.

Nate knew himself well enough to realize he wasn't a leader, but he did have one skill that was a rare commodity. He'd discovered it during the years he'd worked for Zed, and he'd honed the skill here working with Jake these last few years. Nate had the ability to sense what a leader needed and provide it before the leader even asked.

"Hey boss," Nate said. "I've got the location set. It's out in front of the house."

Jake sighed. "So I'm gonna have to look at it for the next however long it is until the forest shifts again?"

Nate didn't take it personally. Sometimes a leader needed to vent. He allowed himself a small smile. "You could always close the curtains."

Jake chuckled and eased his eyes open. "So, tell me, should I be concerned? Was this thing with Vance an isolated incident?"

Nate paused. He hadn't anticipated that question. "It's been, what, six months since the last banishment? I don't think we're looking at an epidemic of violence or anything."

Jake leaned back in his chair. "I don't know. There's something in the air lately. A sort of...discontent. Have you felt it?"

Nate nodded. Taking the pulse of the community was his bread and butter. Of course he'd felt it. But he hadn't thought Jake was perceptive enough to sense it.

"I wouldn't worry about it. It's probably one of those cyclical things. Maybe the banishment will let out some of the tension."

Jake looked up. The dark circles under his eyes stood out in the harsh light of the desk lamp. "Is that what we are now? We need our fix of violence every now and then or people start getting antsy?"

"Is that so bad?"

"Yes."

Nate tapped his foot. "Listen, I know you don't want to hear this, but people need a purpose. Maybe if you clued them in on what it is you're actually trying to accomplish here —"

"They have a purpose. They know they're protecting the world from the forest. Saving the world isn't a big enough goal?"

"Maybe it's a little too big." Nate took a breath and reminded himself to proceed with caution. Jake didn't like discussing this, but Nate knew Jake needed him to bring it up from time to time, if only to play the devil's advocate. "Look, boss, the people care about you. They'll fight for you if you let them. If they realized what they're doing is for you, they'd have something more tangible to hold on to."

Jake grimaced. "Do you have any idea how it would go if I told them? Everyone would have an opinion on how we should proceed. You of all people should know that. You lead the scheduling meetings."

Nate couldn't argue there. It took forty-five minutes of discussion to get the group to agree to a single route adjustment on the trail-walking schedule. "I know committees aren't always the most efficient way to run things—"

"Then we agree." Jake's tone said this topic of conversation was closed. He glanced at the book on the desk and a look of weariness passed over his face.

Nate knew Jake had hours of work left before tonight. He

left without saying another word. He knew when the boss needed silence.

5. Sanctuary

Sophie joined the rest of them in the small clearing outside Jake's house. She stood between Frasier and Logan. The little boy, Mason, stood in front of his mother. She had her arms around him, pressing his back against her. She leaned down and whispered something in his ear, but Sophie couldn't hear what it was.

Frasier leaned over to Sophie. "If you start feeling dizzy or sick in the middle feel free to hold my hand. I won't take it the wrong way."

Sophie frowned. "Is there a chance I'm gonna get sick?"

Frasier nodded. "There's always a chance. Especially the first time."

Sophie shifted her feet and crossed her arms. What the hell kind of thing was this going to be? "And if I am sick, how exactly is holding your hand gonna help?"

Frasier winked. "I don't know. But it'll make me feel better. Holding a pretty lady's hand always does."

Sophie rolled her eyes, but she had to suppress a smile.

She looked around. Everyone was here. Even the kids. Besides Mason, there was a four-year-old boy and a baby girl. The only one missing was Jake himself.

"Is this ceremony long?" Sophie asked.

"Not long at all," Frasier said.

"Feels plenty long, though," Logan muttered.

Vance stood alone in the center of the clearing, his face pale and his eyes wide. Sophie had never spoken with the man, but she couldn't help feeling the tiniest bit sorry for him.

On the other hand, he'd killed Baldwin. She hadn't exactly liked Baldwin, but murder was murder. He deserved what was coming to him.

"If this whatever-it-is is so bad, why doesn't he run?"

Frasier shook his head. "Wouldn't matter. He'd still be banished. Better to do it here where he has a clear view of the sky."

Sophie let that go. She knew he enjoyed being cryptic. It was an annoying habit, but over the time she'd spent with him, first in the Welcome Wagon and later walking the trails with Logan's out team, she'd grown used to it.

She scanned the crowd again, and her eyes stopped on something, caught like cotton on a barb. It was Taylor. He was the only one who wasn't facing Vance. He stared at Sophie, a slight smile on his face.

She wasn't the type to let a creep leer at her without saying anything. She started to take a step forward, but, before she could, Jake walked through the crowd toward the clearing. He held a book in his hand. The book had a crudely drawn image on the cover: a globe. There was a crack running through it, just like the crack on the clock etched into the compass.

Jake didn't look like the same man she'd walked through the woods with a few weeks ago. This man had circles under his eyes. His hair hung in wet ropes and his face was covered with sweat.

Sophie turned to Logan. "Is he okay?"

She nodded quickly. "It takes a lot out of him. He'll recover in a few days."

The response troubled Sophie, but she didn't push for more information. Not now. She glanced over at Taylor. He was still staring at her.

Jake reached the center of the clearing. He leaned toward

Vance and put a hand on the man's shoulder. He spoke to him for a few moments and Vance seemed to relax a little.

Sophie felt a shift in the crowd with Jake's arrival. Before, there had been tension, anticipation, and anger. Now that was gone. It felt calmer. As she looked around, all she saw was sympathy on the faces around her. She had some experience being in the courtroom when a killer was convicted—she supposed Taylor did as well. This felt completely different.

This felt like the man standing in front of them had already paid his debt. Like he was forgiven.

Jake gave Vance one more pat on the shoulder and then took three large steps back. He didn't turn or address the crowd in any way. He just opened his book.

He held the book in one hand, and his other hand moved across the pages. His index finger moved in a fast scribble as if he were tracing a picture.

A hand grabbed Sophie's. She looked over at Frasier, but he didn't meet her gaze. His eyes were on the clearing.

She felt a slight rumble. At first she thought it was her imagination. Maybe her nerves were playing with her. But the feeling grew stronger until she was certain the ground was quaking beneath her feet.

"Stay still," Frasier whispered. "It'll be over soon."

Sophie's head whipped around as she tried to fight the panic rising within her. She looked behind her and saw Jake's house was shaking. She turned back and saw the trees quiver. She squeezed Frasier's hand.

The trees shook faster and faster, so quickly they seemed to be moving, trading places. The ground heaved and bucked as if it was trying to throw them.

The only place of stillness was the center of the clearing where Vance and Jake stood. Vance drew a deep breath, and then looked down at his fingers. He stared at them with wide eyes, as if seeing them for the first time.

Then Sophie saw it too. His fingers were lengthening.

But it wasn't just his fingers—it was all of him. He was stretching. His skin seemed to be drying out in front of her eyes. Hardening. Cracking. Changing into something else.

He let out a piercing scream. As he held the scream, it became lower, more throaty. Almost hollow. His open mouth lengthened slowly, stretching to an impossible tallness. A dark liquid filled the hole of his mouth, and a single drip spilled over and hung on his lip. The substance hardened into dark amber.

Sophie realized she was craning her neck now, looking up —how far?—twenty feet to his face. It hardly resembled a human face at all now. It was something else. Something older. Harder.

There was a pop-pop as his sneakers burst, first one and then the other. His clothes were tearing, falling away from him in shreds. His legs were pressing together as they grew, melding into something else, something familiar.

A trunk, Sophie realized.

His arms were stretching, dividing, splitting, growing, into hundreds of branches.

The tree-thing gave a final, very human shake, and then it straightened with an audible *snap* and was still.

Where Vance had been only moments before there now stood a tall, twisted tree.

Sophie had no words. Even taking a breath was challenging.

The crowd parted in front of Jake. He trudged silently back to his house.

"He's a real orator," Logan said under her breath.

The crowd stood silently for what felt like an hour, staring at the forest's newest tree. Then, Nate stepped forward.

"Okay, that's enough," he said. "I appreciate you bearing witness. Time to get back to work."

The crowd dissipated slowly, each member drifting off in their own time.

Taylor approached her, and he said quietly, "Now you understand. You might want revenge, girl, but you can't take it. Not in Sanctuary." As he passed, he bumped his shoulder against hers.

A shudder ran through her. What was this place, this horrible place, she had come to? Who were these people? Who was Jake, what was Jake, to do that to someone?

Soon, she was the only one left. She felt a hand on her shoulder. She looked away from the tree, Vance, whatever, and saw Nate standing next to her.

"You want to talk about it?" he asked. "You have any questions?"

She shook her head.

"Okay. You will later. God knows I did." His eyes drifted up to the tree, about where Vance's face had been, and he quickly looked away. "Anyway, you should go."

"Yeah."

"It's hard not to judge him. Jake, I mean. Doing something like that to someone."

She grunted noncommittally.

"But you gotta understand, he does it for a purpose. He doesn't have time to police this place, and we don't have the manpower for a full-time sheriff." He paused. "I read this book once, *The Savages*. It's about these drug dealers. You heard of it?"

She shook her head.

"Well, there's this one line that always stuck with me. *If you*

175

let people think you're weak, sooner or later you're going to have to kill them. That struck me as true. We don't have time for games. The work we're doing here's too important."

"Yeah. Saving the world. I heard."

"Okay. Well. You should get to work. Logan's team will be leaving soon."

Sophie's eyes scanned the trees. Something inside, the same part of her mind that tingled when she used the compass, told her there was something else to see here. And then she saw it. Something carved into a tree directly across from her. Another message.

Use the Tool and the book and you can bring him home.

IN THE WOODS (PART FIVE)

Frank watched Zed in the glow of the man's own lantern. The man moved slower, more carefully, and his smile was a bit thinner than usual. Zed knew Frank was out here, and he crept through the undergrowth like a man who knew he was being watched.

Frank considered his options. The idea of picking up one of the many pieces of downed redwood and taking a swing at Zed's head—or, hell, using the lockbox—was mighty appealing. Zed wouldn't see it coming. But, again, Frank didn't know the extent of Zed's current powers. If he was still as invulnerable as he'd been in Rook Mountain, Frank would be doing nothing but giving away his position.

Still, it might be worth it to hear the satisfying thud of the wood hitting Zed's skull.

Frank held his position, his back pressed up against a tree so large it would have taken ten men to wrap their arms around it. He was frozen with indecision.

Zed stopped, fifteen feet past the tree. "I don't know if you can hear me. I'll be honest and admit I have no idea where you are. That's why I've said this ten times over the last two hours I've spent searching for you."

Frank tried to counter the thunderous beating of his heart by taking the shallowest breaths he could manage.

Zed's voice was gentle. "Frank, we've been through a lot, you and me. I want this to end. Your prospects here are grim. This is my place. I know it like you'd know your childhood bedroom. I've spent a long time here, even by my standards. But you're alone, and without shelter or food. And daylight's coming. It's so close I can feel it."

He twisted in a circle as he spoke. "Show yourself, and I promise you I'll treat you fairly. I truly respect you, and I can show you things. I can show you how to use your abilities in ways you've never imagined."

Frank squeezed his eyes shut and concentrated on the sharp bark pressing into his back. He was so cold. His tongue was thick with thirst. Only inertia and indecision kept him from falling for Zed's appeal.

After a long moment, Zed turned in one more circle, his flashlight and his eyes scanning for any sign of Frank, and then he moved on.

Frank waited a full minute before allowing himself to move. He took a deep breath and staggered forward, placing his hands on his knees.

He stood like that for a while before dropping to the forest floor. He sat with his back against the tree and put his head in his hands.

It wasn't just his thirst and the cold that had made him briefly consider Zed's offer. The man was right. Other than running, he had no idea what he was doing out here. He had no plan, no goal other than to avoid capture. He needed shelter. He needed water. After that, he'd need food.

His best bet would be to pick a direction and start walking. But, it was dark, and, even if it hadn't been, he had no compass. He'd read somewhere that most people lost in the woods end up walking in circles in the direction of their dominant hand, all the while thinking they were going in a straight line. Maybe he'd compensate by veering slightly to the left? But how far?

He sighed and rubbed his temples. He didn't buy what Mason said about this place being inescapable. The man had been raised by Zed, after all. Who knew what kind of crazy his head had been filled with? That said, this forest must be pretty vast if Mason had never reached the edge of it in his wanderings.

And, if it was possible to walk out, what was Zed still doing here?

Frank sat like that for a long time, until he saw the faint glow of light over the horizon. At least he knew which direction was east. Assuming the sun rose in the east in this weird place.

Even with the sun rising, he felt no great desire to move. He'd lost all sense of direction. If he started walking now, he'd be just as likely walking toward Mason's cabin as away from it. Maybe that would be a good thing. Maybe he should take advantage of his invisible state, head there, and grab some supplies.

As the sun rose, Frank noticed a sound rising with it. It was a strange sound, a cross between a hum and a chirp. It was a rapid sound and it came from multiple directions.

He knew what made that sound, but he wasn't afraid. He clutched the Cassandra lock tight in his hand and visualized himself locked away from the Larvae.

He sat silent as the hum to his left grew louder. He concentrated on remaining quiet. A small black sphere inched into sight. It crawled out of the undergrowth less than three feet from his left foot.

The way the creature moved reminded him of a snail. It compressed its body toward its forward-most end and then expanded forward. This method of movement was painfully slow, and Frank sat transfixed watching the thing's persistent, methodical movement.

When it was almost past him, the creature paused. Frank watched it, wondering what it would do next. The Larva shivered and its long strands of thick fur rippled. Then, though it made no perceivable movement, Frank sensed it turning. He was sure it was looking at him.

The creature compressed and stretched, inching forward. But it wasn't moving past Frank now. It was creeping toward him.

Frank's pulse quickened. He tried to reassure himself he was safe, that the Larva couldn't possibly have seen him, that something else had triggered its sudden change in direction.

As he watched, the creature's fur gradually straightened outward, until its body was covered in spike-like appendages.

He staggered to his feet, cursing himself. He'd waited too long. Sure, it was moving slowly now, but, from what Mason had said at the stream, they had the ability to move much more quickly.

Why had he assumed his lock would protect him from these creatures? How could he assume anything in this bizarre land? Zed had called it his own place, after all.

Frank could almost see the wide smile that would be on Zed's face when he found Frank's bones, the flesh stripped away by the Larvae.

Or would he stay invisible, the Cassandra lock clutched in his hand as his remains turned to dust over the centuries?

Frank didn't want to think about it.

What he did next came from habit. He did what he'd always done in the Away when he needed to distract the Ones Who Sing. He whistled, long and loud, the tune that summoned the Unfeathered.

The reaction was instantaneous. The Larva began to shake, but not like it had before. There was a fury in its movement. It had moved slowly and deliberately before; now it began to roll haphazardly this way and then that way. It changed directions suddenly and launched itself toward Frank's face. It whirled through the air like a buzz saw.

He had just enough time to throw his arm up to protect his face before the creature reached him, burying its long spiky appendages into his arm.

CHAPTER SIX: THE BROKEN WORLD

1. Rook Mountain

Sean was driving home from a movie in Elizabethton when he decided to swing by Christy Havert's house. Something about the message on the tree called to him. It was stuck in his mind. Maybe the *Tool* it referenced was the hammer, and maybe the *him* it referenced was Zed. But what was *the book*? Was it the notebook he'd found in the Beyond Academy? Or was it something else?

He felt like if he could see it again, maybe it would make more sense. Besides, the Haverts' house was only a few blocks out of his way.

The movie had been a dud, filled with giant robots, explosions, and action scenes that cut so fast it made his head hurt. Maybe he'd gotten old over the last eight years. This was his first time seeing a movie at the theater since the Deregulation, and he had a feeling it might be his last for a while.

Wendy had some PTA function, so he flew solo. He was hoping she'd call him when she was finished and maybe they could get together for a late night drink or something.

He slowed to a roll as he reached the house. There it was.

The tree with the words carved into it. Even in the dim glow of the streetlight, he could make them out a little. Not well enough to read them though.

Had it said, *Use the Tool and the book to bring him home*, or, *Use the book and the Tool to bring him home?* It probably didn't matter, but he thought he might as well check since he was already here.

Something about this whole thing bothered him. He needed to talk it out with someone he could trust. He texted Wendy: *Can you stop by my house when you're done? I want to chat about the tree.*

He got out of the car and walked toward the tree, but something else caught his eye before he reached it: the front door to the house was open. And it was dark inside.

He felt a buzzing in his pocket. His cell phone was ringing.

He looked at the illuminated screen, so bright on this dark night the people across the street could probably read the words 'Private Caller'. He stabbed the answer button and held the phone to his ear.

Before he had a chance to say hello, the voice on the other end of the phone said, "Officer Lee! What brings you to the Havert residence this fine evening?"

He squeezed his eyes shut. He'd known who it would be the moment he saw the blocked call.

"You watching the house, Colt?" As he asked, he spun around, looking for a parked car the kid could be hiding in. Of course, he could easily be inside the house.

"This is actually super convenient. I was planning to have to go hunting for you, and here you are."

"Here I am," Sean said, still turning in a circle. "And where are you?"

Colt chuckled. "We found your card in the house. Mrs.

Havert was a little reluctant to talk about you. We had to ask both her and her husband quite a lot of times. Thankfully, we didn't have to resort to asking the kid. They're here with me now. Want to talk to them?"

"Colt, stop for a second. Think about this. You're holding an entire family against their will. This is a whole lot worse than throwing a brick through a car window."

"Officer, we're talking about Regulation Breakers here. Not regular people. But you know all about that, don't you? She told us about the hammer."

"Think really hard before you do something you can't take back."

There was a long pause. "I have thought hard. That's why I'm doing this. I'm not a sheep who follows whatever government happens along. Not like you."

Sean gripped the phone. Best to let the kid think he was in control here. Which, if Sean was being honest, he'd have to admit was totally the case. "So what do we do?"

He could almost hear the kid's smile when he spoke. "In just a minute, a car's gonna swing by. You get in the car and tell the driver where to go to get the hammer. We already searched your house."

Sean's mind was spinning fast. What was his best chance to help the Haverts? Should he get in the car? Or should he run and get help?

"After you get the hammer, you'll bring it to me. When it's in my hand, I'll let them go."

Sean took a deep breath and thought about the woman who lived in this house. "Okay. I'll take you to the hammer. But how do I know you'll let the Haverts go? You gotta give me something here."

"Give you something?" Colt sounded genuinely surprised.

"I'm giving you the Haverts. I'm letting them go. Do you understand how much I'm *giving* you by doing that? They're Regulation Breakers, and they deserve to die."

Sean tried to think of something else to say to buy a little time, but a car rolled to a stop in front of the house.

"Looks like you're ride's here," Colt said. "I'll see you soon."

Sean heard Colt hang up. He took a deep breath and got in the car.

2. Sanctuary

Sophie stood in front of the door, the key in her hand. Once she opened the door and crossed the threshold, she'd be breaking one of Sanctuary's rules. She'd be subject to possible banishment. And she sure as hell didn't want to spend the next thousand years as a tree.

But in spite of the risks, she knew she had to continue.

It had been a week since the banishment. A week since she'd borne witness to Vance's terrible transformation. A week since the message on the tree had changed everything.

Use the Tool and the book and you can bring him home.

The message had been simple enough to figure out. The *Tool* referred to the compass. Rodgers had told her that's what the objects with the broken clock symbol were called. And the *book* could only be the one Jake kept locked in his office. And *him*...that was no doubt in her mind that referred to Taylor.

She wasn't a killer, as much as she tried to convince herself she was. But maybe she could take Taylor back to justice like the message said. Maybe she could get home and see Taylor punished.

She'd known what she needed to do almost immediately,

but it took her a few days to work up the nerve.

When she overcame her internal resistance, she took the compass, feeling its cold weight in her hand. She pressed the broken clock symbol on the back of it and thought as hard and as loud as she could, *Spare key to Jake's office.*

It had taken a minute. At first the needle only quivered a little. But Sophie thought harder, so hard she felt a sharp pain behind her eyes, and even then she didn't stop.

The needle had swung suddenly and stuck on a spot. Sophie followed the needle into Jake's home, and, after confirming he was in his office, upstairs to his bedroom. The spare key was hidden in the bed frame under the box spring.

Next she had to wait for the opportunity. She couldn't hang out at Jake's house, watching his office door all day without arousing suspicion. Thankfully, she had another plan: she'd watch Logan instead.

Sophie wasn't the keenest observer of human nature, but she certainly wasn't oblivious to it. Either Jake and Logan's undercover affair was something everyone pretended not to notice or they were all too wrapped up in their own drama to see the obvious.

But Sophie had noticed. She'd seen the way they were careful not to look at each other. The way they sat as far away from each other as possible at every group event. The way Logan disappeared and made overly elaborate excuses for her absence.

Sophie certainly didn't begrudge them their secrets. It seemed odd that they were keeping it under wraps, especially since they had a child together. But maybe they craved the excitement of an illicit affair. Sophie didn't know the reason, but she was glad for it. It would give her the chance she needed.

She'd watched Logan's cabin, hoping to see her leave at an odd time. Today, it finally happened. Nate showed up and took Mason somewhere, and Logan had left. Right in the middle of the day.

Sophie headed to Jake's five minutes later and lurked in the woods near the house. Ten minutes after that, Jake walked out the door, and Sophie knew this was her chance.

She took a deep breath and slid the key into the lock, doing it slowly, feeling the key slide past each pin. When it clicked home, she turned the lock and stepped into the unknown.

She shut the door behind her, locked it, and breathed a sigh of relief. She'd done it. She was inside.

She looked around the sparse office space. A large desk made of dark-stained oak dominated the room. The desktop was clear. It was odd seeing an office without a computer. But what use would it be here anyway? It's not like there was Internet access. Two large filing cabinets stood along the back wall. A small bookshelf sat in the corner, a few paperbacks lining its shelves.

Enough messing around. She needed to find the book, and she needed to do it quickly. She briefly considered searching the drawers, but why not automate the process? She pulled the compass out of her pocket, pressed its back, and thought *book*.

The needle spun immediately this time. She didn't know if it was because she was closer to the object she was seeking or if it was because she was getting better at using the compass.

The needle pointed at a rusty old lockbox under the desk.

She approached the desk, her heart feeling suddenly larger in her chest. This was still the first step, granted, but if she had the book she might have a real shot at making things right. There was a way to get the book to take her home, she knew there was. Maybe Jake couldn't figure it out himself, or maybe he didn't want the rest of them to know about it.

Besides, Jake didn't have the compass.

She pulled up the lid on the box. It came open with a loud squeak. And there it was. The book.

The cover was a dark earthy brown. She ran her hand across the leather.

She picked up the book with her free hand. Suddenly the compass came alive. The needle spun with a speed and fury she hadn't seen before. She hadn't even pushed the button.

She'd intended to stuff the book under her shirt and wait until she was safely back in her cabin before opening it, but the needle made her more curious. Was she imagining it, or was the needle in the back of her mind telling her to open the book? It felt the same as when she thought at the compass, but the other way around; it was as if the compass was thinking at *her*.

Before she even realized what she was doing, she set the book down on the desk. She put the compass next to it so both her hands would be free. She lifted the cover and opened the book.

There was a poem on the first page.

Upward, outward, always spinning,
Always singing, faceless grinning.
As they open, time will close
In a place without shadows.

The writing on the next page was small and the language was one Sophie had never seen. It was handwritten in a strange, slanted hand. The pages were thicker than they looked, almost as heavy as card stock, but they turned easily. On the next page, there was a pencil drawing of some sort of strange bird creature.

As she flipped through the pages, she noticed the needle of the compass slowing. She flipped a bit farther. When she was about a third of the way through the book, the needle stopped altogether.

The two page spread was filled with drawings. Drawings of trees.

Sophie picked up the compass and moved it near the page. The needle shifted as she moved the compass back and forth, and she realized it was pointing to one particular tree.

The drawing looked no different than any of the others to her, but it was clear the needle was fixed to that specific tree. It hadn't steered her wrong so far.

She felt that tug again in the back of her head. It was like a voice she couldn't hear, a song she couldn't hum, but it was there. She knew what to do.

She saw a shape in her mind. The top of the shape was the letter z and the bottom of it was a circle.

Sophie reached out and touched her index finger to the drawing of the tree. She felt a small shock, like static electricity. Touching the paper ever-so-lightly, she traced the shape from her mind onto the paper.

3. Sanctuary

It was daytime, so no one from Sanctuary was there to see it happen. The only witnesses were the trees, and the Larvae.

Near the center of the forest, if the forest had such a thing, stood an especially tall tree. A tree Jake visited once a week.

All the trees in this forest occasionally shifted locations, but this tree often seemed to move deeper into the wilderness, like it was trying to get farther away from the little gathering of people who called themselves Sanctuary.

Most of the trees in the forest had counterparts, reflections, in other places. Places like Rook Mountain, Tennessee, King's Crossing, Wisconsin, and Bald Crop, Colorado. These trees were something more than trees. They drew their water, their food, their lives, from multiple places at once. And multiple times. Their root systems stretched across the ages.

This tree was different. It stood in only one place. It didn't span time nor space. But it too was something more than a tree. Or perhaps something less.

The change started with the branches at the top of the tree, the ones so high the Larvae on the ground couldn't see them. They began to recede, draw in on themselves. It was like a time-lapse video of a tree growing in reverse.

Soon most of the branches were gone, drawn into the trunk, and the trunk too began to shrink. It compressed in quick, jerky motions, seemingly withering away. The rough, cracked bark softened and puffed outward.

When the tree had shrunk down to no more than ten feet tall, the trunk began to split, developing what were clearly arms and legs.

And then it was over. The Larvae on the ground looked on, frozen with what might have been horror or shock or awe. And there he stood, naked and shivering but a wide smile on his face.

Zed had returned to human form.

4. Sanctuary

Nate was on the ground, playing with Mason when it happened. They were building castles in the mud near the Welcome Wagon. Logan would probably kill Nate when her son came home covered in dirt. He smiled at the thought.

Served her right, leaving him to play babysitter.

Truth was, he liked spending time with Mason. He felt sorry for the kid. No one his own age to play with. No playgrounds or swing sets. No G.I. Joes or Thundercats or whatever toys kids played with these days. The boy lived his whole life on the thirty acres or so that made up the Sanctuary. His parents rarely allowed him on the trails, even at night.

His mother tried her best, and she was a good mom in her own way. His dad was nice enough, but distant, his head always on the mammoth tasks he felt were his duty.

So, when Nate saw the mud puddle, it occurred to him that the boy had never had the opportunity to build a sandcastle. He'd decided that needed to be rectified immediately, even if it meant using alternate building materials.

The mud here was odd. It was sticky and thick and smelled strongly of decomposition. Nate didn't mind, and he didn't think the kid did either. The stuff packed wonderfully. They were building a castle that stood taller and had more structural integrity than anything Nate had built at the beach.

Mason had taken to it immediately. He was more focused than Nate had never seen him. He took over as the leader of the project without any discussion, planning each spire and moat, and directing—and occasionally correcting—Nate's efforts. And, Nate had to admit, the castle looked pretty good for something made of mud.

"Hey," Nate said. He waited until the kid broke his focus away from the mud castle before continuing. "What do you want to be when you grow up?"

Mason's face scrunched up and he tilted his head. "What do you mean? I'll be a man."

Nate felt a sudden sinking feeling in his chest. The kid had no idea what Nate was asking. He'd never been exposed to the concept of a career. Nate instantly regretted the question. It was a dumb question anyway, such old-world, pre-Zed, pre-Sanctuary thinking. *What do you want to be?* Like people's jobs define them.

"Agreed, you'll be a man. What I meant was, what job do you think you'll want? Do you want to be a chef? Or lead an out team like your mom? Or run the whole show here like your dad?"

"My dad will still be running the show. My mom will still be leading out teams. And we already have a chef." He paused for a moment, his brow furrowed in thought. "Frasier is old as a goat, my mom always says. Maybe he'll die and I'll run the Welcome Wagon." He turned back to his castle of mud.

The one thing Nate didn't enjoy about hanging out with Mason was that the kid's age made him think too hard about the future. Sanctuary was great for now. Jake had done an admirable job building the place from nothing. Not to mention the lives he'd saved. Every person here would be dead if it weren't for Jake and his book bringing them here in their hour of need. But long term...that's where things got dicey. Would they still be here fifty years from now, a new leader using the book and a whole new generation walking these trails?

Nate was one of the few, maybe the only one, who knew the scope of Jake's plan, who knew there might actually be an endgame here, that they might not be stuck here for all of time. He knew their chances were slim, and hope was a frail thing. He mostly tried to put the distant future out of his mind.

He didn't know how the rest of them, the ones without even that sliver of hope, coped. Maybe they were more optimistic than he was. Maybe they embraced the fact that they'd been saved from certain death and given a new life. Even if that new life could be tedious at times.

Mason's eyes were focused on the in-progress tower that would serve as the castle's prison. Without looking up, he said, "Leonard wants to talk to you."

Nate twisted around and, sure enough, saw Leonard a ways down the trail.

In that glace, he knew something was terribly wrong. Leonard was likely the most easy-going person in Sanctuary, a gift that made him both a blessing and a curse to the community. He could be infuriatingly slow about things— things such as showing up for his shift on time. But his laid back attitude meant he was a nice guy to have around in a crisis.

Two things about what Nate saw now disturbed him: Leonard was pale as a ghost, and he was sprinting down the path toward them.

Nate struggled to his feet.

Leonard stumbled to a stop in front of Nate. "Oh, thank God."

"What is it?" Nate asked. He tried to mask the concern in his voice, but he knew he had failed. His first thought was that another rule had been broken. Someone was hurt or even dead. His mind reeled in panic at the thought. There had never been two banishments this close together. He didn't know if Jake could physically do it. It seemed to take him a longer to recover from each banishment now, and this one had hit him harder than most.

Leonard opened his mouth. No words came out, and Nate stood there for what felt like a minute staring into the thin man's black gaping maw.

"Come on, out with it."

Leonard shook his head. "I can't...I don't know how to say it. Let me show you."

Nate nodded briskly, and then glanced back at Mason. "Is it safe to bring the kid?"

"I'm not sure...I'm sorry, I really don't know."

Nate groaned. "Mason, come on. We have to go."

Mason didn't look up. "I'm building my castle."

"You can build it later!" The timbre of his voice surprised him. It was sharper than he'd intended. He sounded just like his own father had when he'd been angry.

Mason sighed and reluctantly got to his feet. He made a great show of brushing the mud off his hands. Nate put a hand on his back to guide him.

"Where we going?" Nate asked Leonard.

"Jake's house."

Nate kept Mason in front of him, and close. He had no idea what they were walking into and he wanted to be able to grab the kid if the need arose. Plus, Mason had a tendency to wander, and Nate didn't want to keep looking back to see if he was still there.

Nate decided to try an alternate approach with Leonard. "So you were there? You were outside Jake's house when it happened?"

"Yeah." His voice was hollow. Nate realized the man was terrified. "I was walking and I saw him."

"Him who?"

But Leonard would say no more. They passed the next two minutes in silence. Nate took a deep breath before rounding the curve that would bring Jake's house into sight. He didn't know what he'd see, but if it had spooked Leonard, it wasn't likely to be pretty.

At first glance, he noticed nothing amiss. He'd expected something disturbing on a grand scale. Blood splattered everywhere or someone chopping up other people with an ax or something. But nothing seemed out of the ordinary.

Then he saw a pale figure crouched by the side of the house.

He pulled Mason toward him and spun him around, looking him in the eyes. "Wait here. Got it?"

Mason nodded.

"I'm serious. Stay right here and don't wander off no matter what happens."

The kid nodded again.

Nate wasn't sure of the man's identity, but two things were very clear: the man was naked, and he was digging in the dirt. The man's body was smeared with mud, and he was facing the house, giving Nate a clearer rear view than he appreciated.

Nate crept forward. When he was ten yards away, he said, "Excuse me."

A low mumbling came from the naked man.

Nate took a step forward. "I didn't catch that." When there was no reply, he said, "What are you doing? You're digging up the boss's yard."

This time he did hear the response. The voice was low and throaty, and it had a gurgle to it as if the man were drinking a glass of water while speaking. "I left something. Under the ground. In the dirt."

Nate took another step forward. Was it possible Jake had brought this man over and forgotten to tell anyone? That could explain the confusion. "Okay. Maybe I can help. What did you leave?"

A strange, bubbling laugh came from the man. "There was so much of me down there. I was everywhere. I felt so much at once. All the bugs and creepy, crawly things. Some of them were bitey. And the water! I could pull the water right out of the dirt."

The voice sounded suddenly familiar.

The man turned and smiled at Nate, revealing teeth caked with dirt. "I can't do that anymore. I tried, I sucked the dirt as hard as I could, but it didn't work."

That was a smile Nate had seen before. The naked man was Vance.

Nate staggered backwards. "Vance, what happened?"

But Vance had turned his attention back to the black soil in his hands.

Nate marched back to Leonard. "What happened? Tell me everything."

Leonard shook his head. "I- I don't know. He just came out of the woods. I tried to talk to him, but he brushed past me. He dropped to the ground. He stuck his face into the dirt and started chewing."

Nate's head was spinning. How was this possible? No one had ever come back from banishment before. It was a one-way trip. What the hell was he supposed to do now? And where was Jake?

He took a deep breath. "Okay, listen. I need to find the boss. I want you to stay here with Vance."

Leonard's eyes widened. "You want me to what?"

Nate put a hand on his shoulder. "It's okay. Let him do...whatever he's doing. And don't get too close. Keep him in sight. Copy?"

Leonard nodded, eyes on his naked former friend.

Nate froze. What he saw drained the color from his face. Another naked, dirt-covered person was staggering out of the woods. This one Nate recognized immediately. It was Helen.

Helen, who had been banished over a year ago.

"No," Nate whispered. "No, no, no. This isn't good."

Leonard saw her too now. "Holy shit, Nate. What do we do?"

Nate didn't answer. If these two were out, it stood to reason the others might be too. And if they were all out, that meant....

He grabbed Mason's hand and sprinted down the trail.

5. Rook Mountain

Sean felt the cold metal of the kid's gun pressing against his back. He took the hammer out of his closet, the same closet he'd kept the coin in for all those years. The door had one of Frank's locks on it, so the Zed Heads wouldn't even have known the closet was there when they searched the house.

Grant said, "Hold it up so I can see it."

Sean held up the hammer, turning it so they could clearly make out the broken clock symbol.

A wide smile broke out on the other kid's face. He was taller than Grant. Sean didn't know his name and couldn't remember ever having seen him before tonight. He supposed the kid had seen him, though. He'd surely been one of the creeps standing on Sean's sidewalk that night when Colt came to talk. He might even have been the one who threw the brick through the windshield for all Sean knew. But, if Sean had to guess, he'd have said Colt probably reserved that honor for himself.

Grant took a step back, pulling the gun away from Sean's spine. "Okay, we're gonna walk to my car now. You first, me following. Go slow. If you don't feel my gun on your back, that means you're walking too fast. And if you're walking too fast, I'm gonna shoot you."

Sean glanced at the hoodie on the recliner. He'd left his Swiss Army knife in the pocket. Not much of a weapon, but better than nothing. "Mind if I grab my sweatshirt?"

The gun jammed into his back. "Yeah, I do. Start walking."

Sean made his way out to the car, walking slowly and making sure his back didn't lose contact with the gun.

The car was a newish four-door sedan. Sean wondered if this was Grant's parents' car, and, if so, how they would feel about it being used to abduct a police officer.

Grant opened the back seat door and waved him in. The tall boy slid in next to him, and Grant got in the driver's seat.

"It won't be long now," Grant said. His voice sounded high and childlike. Sean wondered if he was trying to comfort Sean or himself. He actually felt bad for the kid for a moment, the way he was in so deep over his head. But only for a moment.

As they drove, Sean glanced back as casually as he was able, looking for headlights behind him. He saw none.

The car rolled to a stop on a darkened street in downtown Rook Mountain. A single streetlight illuminated a tree. The tree where he and Wendy had found the writing. A group of at least twenty teenagers stood on the sidewalk near the tree, waiting in the dark.

It suddenly occurred to Sean that he'd spent nine years successfully concealing his involvement in the Unregulated from Zed only to be brought down by a bunch of teenagers. Like a damn Scooby Doo villain.

Grant shut off the car. The tall boy got out, pulling Sean after him. Sean walked forward, the hammer in his hand, and made his way to the tree where Colt stood waiting for him.

Colt said, "What we're doing here tonight will be

remembered. They'll write songs about it. I know you aren't too psyched to be here, but soon you'll understand you're being given a great honor. A great privilege."

Sean frowned. "Where are the Haverts?"

Colt ignored the question. "You spent nine years defending the Regulations. By all accounts, you did a good job. You weren't a sadist like some of them, but you didn't shirk from your duty either."

Images flashed through Sean's mind of the Regulations he'd enforced. Things he'd never told anyone, would never tell anyone. The things he'd done to protect the coin from Zed.

"It must have been tough for you too," Colt continued, "going back to a pre-Regulation society. Throwing aside the world you'd been working so hard to build and pretending it never happened. In some ways, I think it was harder on you adults than it was on us. You have so much social pressure to conform."

Sean looked at the kids standing around the tree. "I'm the one conforming, huh?"

"The point is, we don't blame you. We know it's not your fault, everything that's happened. The media, the government, all the people who weren't here, they'll never understand what we went through."

Sean sighed. He'd had enough of this. He was tempted to take a swing at the kid, but there were at least eight guns pointed at him, and those were just the ones he could make out in the darkness. "You want the hammer or not?"

Colt nodded toward the darkened pawn shop.

The door to the shop opened with a ding, and Christy Havert, her husband, and her little daughter staggered out. Two kids with guns came out right behind them.

Colt said, "Go. Don't look back. Forget this ever happened."

Mr. Havert nodded vigorously and led his family quickly down the street into the night.

The Zed Heads watched them go in silence. Then Grant said, "What if they go straight to the police?"

Colt snorted. "You think it matters at this point? By the time the police get here, it'll be over." He looked at Sean. "See? I keep my promises."

Sean leaned toward the young man standing before him, hoping to find some humanity in him. "Let's talk about what you want with this hammer. I know you think what you're doing is right. You barely remember life before Zed."

"Yes!" he said. "That's what makes us strong. The good news is we have a chance to fix things, to put things back the way they should be. Right here. Tonight. We've been talking to Zed."

Sean squinted at the kid. "What do you mean?"

"He's trapped in another place. In a world inside a mirror or something. But we can communicate with him using this tree."

"I saw the messages you carved."

"Those are meeting times. But we didn't carve them."

Sean raised an eyebrow. "What meetings?"

Colt smiled. "You think something like a weak-ass mirror world can hold Zed? He can get out every once in a while, a little bit of him can anyway. He's been coming to us. Giving us instructions."

Sean wasn't sure whether the kid was crazy or lying. But then he remembered the strange way the numbers had been carved on the tree, like they had been carved from within.

"Why you?" Sean asked. "Why not the selectmen? A

couple of them are still alive."

Colt shook his head. "Their time's over. They failed him. It's our time now. And we proved it to him. He told us there was a tree in this town with a message about a Tool carved into it, and he told us that's where we'd find the hammer. We combed the city for days, but we finally found it. Bit of a shame that you found it first. The timing couldn't have been better, though."

He gestured toward the tree next to him. "We have someone watching this at all times, looking for new messages from Zed. I believe you met Grant's little brother the other day while he was on duty. Helps the younger kids feel involved. Anyway, a few hours ago that message appeared."

Sean crouched and looked at the tree. The same dates as before were there, but now something new was below them:

The time is now—Open the door.

Colt's voice was alive with excitement. "We've been waiting for this moment for so long. I never lost hope."

The night air had a sudden chill, and goose bumps covered Sean's arms. "What's it mean? What door?"

Colt giggled. "It's the tree! The tree is the door."

Sean nodded toward the hammer. "Wild guess, but you use that to open the door?"

Colt shook his head. His smile seemed a foot wide. "No, silly. You do."

Sean looked at the Tool in his hand. It suddenly felt heavier. "Seriously? After all that, you don't want to be the one to do it? Or, one of your friends here?"

Colt scratched his head with the barrel of his gun. "Ideally, of course. But, well, to be honest it was Zed's idea. We don't know exactly what will happen. You could get sucked into the door. Or the process could kill you. And Zed needs each and every one of us now. So few have been faithful. He can't spare a single one of us in the fight that's coming."

Colt turned to the group. "Guys, as you know I'm not big on speeches. I wish I could talk like Zed, but I can't. Thing is, tonight you don't need me to."

As Colt spoke, Sean's eyes scanned the street. He saw something—no, someone—peeking around the corner, watching. He gritted his teeth. Dark as it was, he knew that silhouette.

It was Wendy.

Sean didn't know how she'd found them, but he hoped she would stay hidden while whatever was about to happen here went down.

Colt continued. "You all know what's at stake here. You know how hard we've worked. And you don't need me to praise you. Soon enough, in a few minutes, you'll be hearing the thanks of Zed himself."

A rush of excitement so tangible it was like electricity shot through the crowd.

Colt pointed the gun at Sean. "Officer Lee, I need you to press the broken clock symbol and hit the tree with that hammer."

Sean took a deep breath. He could act the hero and refuse. But that would only serve to get him shot. They would grab someone else to do it. Maybe it would even be Wendy. No, he wanted to play this out, see how it ended.

There was one thing Sean knew that these kids didn't. Zed wasn't the only one in that mirror world. There were allies there. Friends. Jake and Frank. If this would release Zed, maybe it would release them too. His finger found the broken clock symbol.

He pulled back the hammer and swung it forward hard,

hitting the trunk of the tree with all his might.

The tree split with a deafening crash. A jagged crack appeared in the trunk, not unlike the crack depicted on the broken clock symbol, and brilliant white light poured through.

Sean blinked hard to clear his vision and then squinted into the crack.

"Get back," Colt shouted, pushing Sean out of the way. The boy crouched in front of the crack and leaned close. "Zed," he called. "We've done it! Come home!"

There was a moment of silence as the group waited. Then a small round creature sprang through the opening. It whirled through the air and collided with Colt's face with a thick, wet thud.

6. Sanctuary

Mason clutched Nate's big hand and struggled to make his short legs move fast enough to keep up. He didn't understand where they were going and he didn't understand why. It was always like that. No one ever explained anything.

Today had started out okay. Breakfast with mom. She'd seemed especially happy. She'd even laughed at his knock-knock jokes, the ones Frasier had taught him, and that rarely happened. Then she'd taken him over to Nate's and dumped him off like she did every week or so.

There was nothing wrong with Nate. He was nice and a little funny, although Mason didn't think he was trying to be. The best part was he actually liked playing with Mason. He taught Mason games like hide-and-seek and tag, and Mason taught him some of the games he'd thought up himself like stomp-the-Larva and pick-a-tree. So it wasn't like he *hated* hanging out with Nate. He always had a good time. But it wasn't as good as hanging out with Mom. Or Dad. Dad was busy, Mason knew, and he spent time with Mason as often as he could, but Mason couldn't help but wish it happened more often.

Now here he was being dragged off to somewhere else.

Nate started down the short path that led to the cabin Mason shared with his mother.

"Are you taking me home?"

Nate's face looked different than Mason had ever seen it. More focused somehow, more intense. "I don't know, kid. I'm trying to find your mom."

Mason's face brightened at that. Though he realized a moment later he had no idea where his mom was, and Nate didn't seem to either. Certainly she wasn't at home or she would have kept him with her.

Nate pounded on the front door of the cabin for three minutes, but no one answered. He sighed and looked around. His face was sweaty, as if he'd been exercising or something. His eyes settled on the next cabin over. "Come on."

He led Mason toward the cabin, once again setting such a brisk pace the boy felt like he was being dragged. This time when Nate knocked on the door there was an immediate rustling from inside.

"Come on, come on," Nate muttered. When there was no answer, Nate pounded again, louder this time.

He was in the middle of his third round of banging on the door when it opened. And there she was.

Mason had seen Sophie a few times before. At the banishment, of course, and at a few gatherings at Dad's house. He'd never forgotten the first time he saw her. Walking the trails with Mom. A rare treat, even if it was only at the edge of the woods. It had felt like the day couldn't get any better, and he'd rounded the corner and seen her sitting on the porch of the Welcome Wagon next to Frasier. She was the most beautiful woman he'd ever laid eyes on. She practically glowed. He felt inexplicably drawn to her. He wanted to touch her cheek and run his fingers through her hair.

Her face was red now, like she was angry and she wore a jagged scowl. To Mason, it made her even more beautiful. She glanced down at him, and he thought his heart might burst.

She looked back at Nate. "Any reason you're trying to bust in my door with your bare hands?"

"I need your help. Something's happened, something bad, and I need to deal with it."

"Care to be a little more specific?"

"No. I'm in a bit of a hurry here. I need you to watch Mason for a while."

Mason didn't dare breathe. Could this really be happening?

Sophie's face drained of color, as if maybe she wasn't quite as excited about the possibility. "What? No, you have to find someone else."

Nate slammed his hand into the door frame. "You're not listening. There's no time to find someone else. I need to deal with this *now*."

Sophie shook her head. "I never babysat. I didn't have any little brothers or sisters. I wouldn't—"

"Sophie! I don't have time to discuss this. Take the kid, and I'll send his mother to collect him as soon as I see her. In the meantime, give him a snack and play with him a little. I think you can manage."

Without waiting for an answer, Nate stormed off, leaving Mason standing on the porch with Sophie. She rubbed her eyes with the backs of her hands and let out a noise that sounded like a carefully concealed scream.

She gave Mason a barely passable fake smile. "Hey, look, I'm sorry about that. It's not that I don't want to hang out. I was a little busy."

Mason said nothing. He was afraid he might start to cry if he spoke. And if he started, he would be so humiliated he might not be able to stop.

Sophie stepped aside, clearing the doorway. "You want to come—"

He brushed past her and went inside before she could finish.

The inside of the cabin was a bit of a disappointment. The open main area was bare except for a small kitchen table, a couch, a rocking chair, and a few lamps. He'd expected something more...girly. Abby watched him sometimes, and her house was all frills and fancy things. On the other hand, Sophie hadn't been here long. And there was something kind of nice about the minimal setup.

And the place smelled like her.

He heard footsteps behind him and the click of a door shutting.

"You know what's got Nate so worked up?" she asked.

Mason nodded. He was suddenly excited to have something to talk to her about. And this wasn't some lame kid's stuff either. This was an adult conversation.

"You know Vance? The one who got banished the other day?"

Sophie nodded.

Mason paused, drawing out the moment before he revealed all. "He came back."

She frowned. "What do you mean?"

"He wandered into my dad's yard like he'd never been

banished. He was naked and dirty, like he'd been crawling around in the mud, and he acted like he'd lost his marbles. He was eating dirt."

Sophie bent down and grabbed his arms. He felt the heat of her hands through his shirt. "Mason, has this ever happened before?"

He shook his head. "That's why Nate was freaking out, I guess. Once you're banished, you can never come back. My dad told me that."

Sophie stood up. She wandered over to the counter as if deep in thought, and slammed her hand against it. She grabbed a small bag off the counter. She marched to the couch and pulled something out from under a cushion. Mason only caught a glimpse of it, but it looked like his dad's book.

"What's that?" he asked.

She didn't answer. Instead, she slung the bag over her shoulder, crouched down next to him, and touched his arm again. All thoughts of the book melted away.

"Mason, we need to go somewhere."

He nodded slowly.

"It's in the woods."

He looked at her questioningly. No way would his mom go for this. She very rarely let him walk in the woods, but only in the night when the Larvae were asleep. She didn't even go in the woods during the day herself.

"I know it's dangerous, but did you hear how I can kill the Larvae?"

He nodded. It had made him fall in love with her even harder.

"Then you know I'll protect you."

He paused for a moment. Going into the woods in the

daytime frightened him, terrified him actually, but no way was he going to chicken out in front of Sophie. In an act of unparalleled bravery, he reached up and took her hand. His heart soared when she didn't pull away. Even better, she squeeze his hand.

After this, a walk in the woods would be cake.

She led him out the door, and they walked down the steps hand in hand. She stopped at the trailhead and pulled a round, gold object out her pocket. She held it tighten in her free hand while she squeezed her eyes shut. He heard her mutter, "The message. Take me to the tree with the message on it." Then she opened her eyes.

She groaned and shook the object in her hand. "Come on. What's wrong with you?" She shook the object, squinted at it, and groaned again. "What the hell? Okay, take me to the Rook Mountain tree."

She looked at the object and smiled.

"What is that thing?" Mason asked.

She paused for a moment and then brought the object down so he could see it. "It's a compass. Ever seen one?"

He shook his head.

"You see that little needle? It tells you which way north is. On most compasses, anyway."

Mason had never heard the term *north*, but he decided to let that go for now.

They walked the trail in silence. To Mason's surprise, the walk went without incident. He'd imagined the woods during the day would be teeming with Larvae, so many you couldn't take five steps without being swarmed by the creatures. But they'd been walking more than five minutes and hadn't seen a single one.

No sooner had the thought entered his mind than he saw a

black shape in the center of the trail. His body tensed and his feet refused to move.

"It's okay," Sophie said. "Stay here."

She pulled her hand out of his cold, sweaty grip and took a large knife from her bag. Then she approached the creature casually, as if going for a morning stroll in Sanctuary. She wasn't hurrying, but there was also zero hesitation in her walk.

When she was almost to it, the creature compressed, and Mason drew a sharp, terrified breath. His mom had taught him the behaviors of the Larvae. He knew they compressed like that before they attacked.

But it was Sophie who sprang into action. She lunged with her knife, diving at the thing on the ground and plunging her weapon into it. The creature melted into a puddle of black goo.

She wiped her blade on a nearby fern and dropped the knife in her bag. She nodded at Mason. "It's safe now. Let's go."

Mason felt himself move toward her, his body on autopilot, his mind enthralled with what he'd seen. He'd heard what she'd done, but seeing it with his own eyes was something different. No one had been able to figure out how to kill the Larvae before Sophie came here. Not even Dad.

"That was amazing," he said.

She took his hand and continued down the trail.

A few minutes later, they rounded a corner and Sophie put out a hand to stop Mason.

They stood at the base of a large tree with an especially tangled root structure. Sophie stepped off the trail, and Mason let out a soft, involuntary, "Eep!"

She wandered all the way around the tree, muttering a

string of curse-words, some of which the boy had heard before and others he thought she might be making up.

As Sophie rounded the tree and came back into sight, Mason saw her face was pale and her eyes were filled with tears.

"What is it?" he asked. "Was this what we were looking for?"

"It's gone," she said, her voice hoarse with emotion. "The message is gone."

IN THE WOODS (PART SIX)

1.

Mason crept through the undergrowth, his eyes scanning the ground for Larvae and his ears alert for any sounds of movement that might give away his uncle's position.

The frustration was like a cold ball of steel in his gut. He'd been waiting and preparing for this day ever since he was eight years old, and it wasn't going well.

At first it had played out exactly as Zed had scripted it. He met his uncle and earned his trust like Zed asked him to. He genuinely bonded with the man. Yeah, maybe he told a lie here and there, but most of it had been true. The stuff that mattered. And then, at Dad's house, something amazing happened.

It had always been the plan to enlist Frank's help to find the book. Zed knew the Hinkles had a way of hiding things from him—he'd told Mason about how they kept the Tools from him, probably for years—and he was hoping Frank would be able to use that same technique to find the book. They planned on slowly introducing the idea and enlisting his help over the course of weeks. They discussed the possibility that the search could take years.

But all it took was a single glance.

How had Frank located it so quickly? Even though Mason was delighted, he was also annoyed his uncle did something in mere moments he hadn't been able to do in years of trying.

Still, mission accomplished.

He led Frank back to his cabin, knowing full well Zed would be waiting for them. He felt a little bit of sadness that Frank had to die, that he'd only gotten to know his uncle briefly. But there was nothing to be done about that. None of it was his fault. He was standing at the end of a long line of dominoes, watching them fall. None of this would have happened if it weren't for the mistakes of his father. And his mother. And especially that woman, Sophie.

He remembered the crush he'd had on her and how she'd been the first to take him into the woods in the daytime. And he remembered the sharp, bitter pain in his heart when he learned she'd killed Dad. When he realized she'd betrayed them all.

And now Uncle Frank, the first blood relation he'd seen in over fifty years, had to die in order for Zed to make things right.

But they hadn't considered the possibility Uncle Frank would be able to hide not only physical objects, but *himself*, too. Impossibly, he even managed to hide from Mason's compass. The needle spun and wobbled with uncertainty when Mason tried to make it locate Uncle Frank.

The compass had never failed him before and its inability to locate Frank had his stomach in knots.

He looked up toward the tree to his right, the one he thought of as the King's Crossing tree, and the one ahead of him, the Bluff Haven tree. These trees had been in the same position for days now. Things weren't moving around as quickly as they used to. Not nearly as quickly as they had when he was a boy.

He glanced down at the compass. Almost there.

He walked fifty more feet to the base of the Bluff Haven tree. He pushed aside the ferns and opened the chest. He had similar caches hidden throughout the woods. With Larvae, you could never be too careful. He made sure he always knew the location of the closest chest.

He looked at the contents of the chest and considered his options. He'd need the .38. He strapped the pistol to his side.

With his gear in place and some extra ammo in his pocket, he closed the chest.

He was ready.

He didn't like what he had to do. He'd rather have gotten to know Frank a little more. There were so many things he would have loved to ask him. But Zed needed Mason to do his duty.

Frank was blood, but Zed was family.

A scream rang out through the forest, and Mason knew it was Uncle Frank. He turned and ran in the direction of the noise.

2.

Frank screamed as the creature buried itself in the flesh of his forearm. It hit hard and stuck there like a dart thrown into a dartboard. He reeled, and his back slammed into the broad trunk of the tree behind him. He let out a groan as the creature squirmed, digging its quills deeper into him.

He shook his arm hard, trying to dislodge the Larva, but he only succeeded in increasing the pain tenfold. Waves of agony raced up his arm. He forced himself to be still, and he took a deep breath. Then, twisting it so the creature was against the ground, he slammed his foot against the Larva and pulled his arm away hard. It detached with a wet sound.

Frank yelled in frustration as blood poured from his arm. The creature compressed itself, preparing to launch back at him. He staggered to his right, hoping to duck around the tree.

A figure raced out of the undergrowth toward him. Mason.

The man held a pistol in his hand. Ignoring Frank, he stopped three feet from the creature, took a moment to aim, and fired. The gunshot echoed off the trees and bounced around in Frank's head. The Larva deflated and dissolved into sludge.

"You have no idea how difficult that shot was." Mason grinned at Frank. "That's two you owe me."

Frank was no longer holding the Cassandra lock. He cursed silently. He must have dropped it during the struggle. His eyes scanned the ground and he saw a flash of metal near Mason's right foot.

Mason squinted at Frank's arm. "Geez, it got you pretty good. I've got medical supplies back at the cabin. Had to learn to patch myself up. I'm not bad at it, if I do say so."

Frank cradled his injured left arm. The amount of blood pouring out of it was alarming. Both his hands were slick with the stuff now.

"I don't think that's a good idea, Mason. Not the way you've taken up with Zed."

Anger flashed across Mason's face. "You're mad I took up with Zed? Does that offend your delicate sensibilities? I was a child. He took care of me. What would you have done?"

Frank took a step back. He didn't like the way Mason was waving that gun around.

"I don't blame you," Frank said. "You did what you needed

to do to survive. But things are different now. I'm gonna find us a way out of here."

Mason chuckled. "I met you like twelve hours ago. I've lived here my whole life and you think you can just find a way out? If it was possible, I would have found it. Or Zed would have."

"I found the box. How long were you looking for that?" He let the question hang in the air a moment before continuing. "Look, I get it. I'm just some guy you met a few hours ago. But I'm asking for your trust. Family's important to me. That's why I came here in the first place. And I'm good at finding my way out of these situations. I've done it before."

Mason shook his head. "You've never been here before."

"No, but I was in the Away. Zed sent me there. And he said it was impossible to escape. But I did it."

Mason paused for a moment and then shook his head "No. You don't know what it's like here."

Frank smiled weakly and held up his shredded arm. "I'm learning pretty quickly. Look, Mason, I need your help here. Turn around and walk away. You never saw me. I promise I won't leave this place without you. I'll find a way out, and I'll come get you. We'll leave together."

A scene flashed though Frank's mind: introducing Mason to the family back in Rook Mountain. *Christine, this is your sixty-year-old stepson.* He didn't even want to figure out what Mason's relation to Will would be.

"That won't work," Mason said. "Zed wants you dead, but listen. I think I can talk him out of it. Let me take you back to the cabin. I'll see to your arm and we'll talk about Zed."

"I'm not going back there, Mason. That man wants to torture me, and I've experienced his brand of torture before.

I didn't much like it."

Mason raised his gun. "Then I have to kill you."

Frank grimaced. "How do you think Zed's gonna feel when he finds out you killed me before you found out where I hid the box?"

"Fine. I won't kill you yet. I'll shoot you somewhere painful. Like the kneecap."

"And then what? Carry me back to the cabin? See, the only way you can get me there is if I come willingly. And that ain't happening."

Mason sighed. "You're starting to remind me more of my dad."

Frank nodded toward the gun, still pointed at him. "So are you. He was a stubborn son of a bitch, wasn't he?"

Looking at Mason, with his cold eyes and his ragged clothes, Frank couldn't help but feel sorry for him. If what he'd said was true, he'd grown up alone except for occasional visits from a madman. What must that have been like? Frank had experienced a taste of something similar when he'd been in the Away with the Unfeathered and the Ones Who Sing, but at least he'd been an adult. To experience all that isolation, the constant threat of violence, as a child must have been horrible. And to have lost his family, too? Mason surely knew more about fear and grief than Frank ever would.

A stab of pain shot through Frank's arm and he cried out.

Mason shook his head, his face drawn with what looked like genuine concern. "Please. Let me help you."

"You heard what Zed said earlier about torture. The best way to help me now is to leave."

Mason's face hardened. "Fine. Then we wait."

"For what?"

"For Zed to arrive. Or for you to bleed out. Whichever

happens first."

"Really? And how's Zed gonna find us?"

"This is his place. He won't have much trouble in that regard." He looked at his compass and smiled. "It won't be long now. I asked the compass to locate him for us. The needle ain't moving, so he's either standing still or heading straight for us. And Zed doesn't stand still. Not when there's work to do."

While Mason was speaking, Frank noticed a dark shape on a branch behind Mason. It was one of the Larvae.

Frank ran a hand through his hair, considering the risk involved. He didn't want anyone to die. He fully intended to keep his promise to find a way out of here, and he intended to take Mason with him. But that couldn't happen if he was being slowly sliced and diced by Zed, or, worse yet, sent back to the Away. He had to get out of here, risk or no. For his sake and for Mason's.

Frank took a deep breath and began to whistle.

Just like before, the Larva reacted to the whistle like it was being zapped with a kiloton of electricity.

"What the hell?" Mason asked. The creature contracted one final time, and launched itself into the air. It rose in a high arch unlike anything Frank had seen the creatures do before. Mason glanced at Frank, then turned his gaze upward toward the creature. His eyes grew wide. As it descended, he flung himself backwards.

But it wasn't enough. The Larva buried itself in his shoulder. Mason released a guttural howl of pain, but he didn't stop moving. He pulled a hunting knife out of his belt and brought it up hard, stabbing the creature.

It may have been Frank's imagination, but he could have sworn he heard a tiny squeal as the knife pierced the Larva.

It all happened fast, but it was enough time for Frank to act. He dove at the ground and scooped up the Cassandra lock. He squeezed it in his hand and willed himself invisible to Mason.

Mason yanked out the knife and the remains of the creature dripped off his shoulder. "Uncle Frank! Don't do this!"

Frank couldn't wait any longer. He planted his feet and delivered an uppercut that had all his weight behind it.

Mason careened backwards and fell to the ground.

Frank put his foot on his nephew's chest, pushing his body flat. Then he leaned down and yanked the gun away. He paused for a moment, then took the compass out of the stunned man's other hand.

Mason screamed in frustration.

Frank picked up the lock box.

"You'll never survive," Mason said. "Do you have any idea how hard it is to do what I just did? You'll never figure out exactly where to hit them."

Frank backed away, resisting the urge to respond.

"I tried to help you." Mason's voice came in a breathy moan. "Whatever happens next, don't forget I tried to help you!"

Frank staggered away, deeper into the forest. He didn't dare stop for fear of the Larvae, but he stuck the gun in his belt and the compass in his pocket and pulled off his shirt. He wrapped it around his injured arm as tightly as he could, hoping it would be enough to stop the bleeding.

When he was confident he'd secured the shirt, he pulled out the compass. He gripped tightly, pressed the broken clock symbol, and thought, *Safety. Take me to safety.*

To his relief the needle spun immediately.

He followed the direction of the compass for ten minutes until he reached a cabin. The exterior was almost hidden with ferns and moss. It looked a lot like Mason's except for the foliage.

He cleared the overgrowth away from the door and went inside.

It was musty and dim in there, but it was empty. He carefully searched the house until he was confident there were no Larvae inside. Then he found a spot where plenty of light was coming through a window. He took the lock off the box and pulled out the book.

His heart sank when he saw the text in the book was written in a strange language he couldn't identify, an odd combination of hieroglyphics and tiny slanted scribbles.

There has to be something in here that can tell me about this place, he thought. The compass was still in his other hand, and the needle spun wildly at the thought.

He looked at the compass for a moment, and then began turning pages. He was nearly to the end before the needle began to slow and finally stopped.

The words on the page were handwritten in a sloppy, hurried cursive. But it was English. And it was legible.

Frank began to read.

CHAPTER SEVEN: ALWAYS SPINNING

1. Sanctuary

Sophie gripped Mason's small hand in her own and stormed down the trail, so angry she could hardly see straight. The message on the Rook Mountain tree—*Don't trust them Sophie*—was gone. As if it had never been there.

The moment she saw the pristine, unmarred bark of the Rook Mountain tree, she'd known she'd been incredibly stupid, and that her stupidity and the return of a recently banished person to Rook Mountain were not unrelated.

All the messages. They'd been, what? Tricks? A way to make a naive woman follow orders?

All this time, she'd considered herself so smart. She'd thought she knew what was best. But now she knew the truth. She'd been used.

And below anger there was something else. The sinking feeling that not only had she been tricked, but that the trickery had resulted in something awful. That her actions had brought about consequences she didn't want to think about.

Mason was quiet, his wide eyes fixed on her face. For that, she was grateful. She needed to think. The path back to Jake's house was blissfully free of Larvae but also cruelly short.

They rounded the bend into the clearing and nearly collided with Logan. She dropped to her knees when she saw Mason, her face awash with relief. She pulled him into a tight hug, and the boy let out a surprised squeak.

Logan looked up at Sophie. "Thank you. I was so worried." Sophie nodded. "Where's Jake? I need to talk to him."

Logan nodded toward the house. "There's a bunch of them up there. Planning what to do. This is jacked up, Sophie. I don't know what caused this, but I've never seen Jake this scared. He's all panicked. I think we have to prepare for the worst."

"What's the worst?" Sophie asked.

"Mommy," Mason interrupted. "Sophie took me into the woods. She killed a Larva right in front of me. It was so cool!"

Logan eyes narrowed. "You took my son into the woods? During the day?"

Sophie withered under Logan's accusatory gaze. It was almost more than she could handle right now. Besides, she didn't have time for this.

"I'm really sorry," Sophie said. "I need to see Jake now."

"Wait," Logan yelled as Sophie brushed past her, but Sophie ignored her and kept moving.

There were eight of them in the living room when Sophie arrived. Jake and Nate were huddled close together in the corner, deep in conversation while the rest of the group chatted nervously among themselves. There was Leonard. And Frasier. And Gail and Evan, who Sophie thought might be a couple, but she'd never gotten around to asking. And another man who's name she couldn't remember. And Taylor. Of course, Taylor would be there.

Sophie scurried through the group towards Jake.

"Hey, we need to talk," she said.

He glanced up at her. "Good. Glad you're here. Most of us haven't actually killed Larva. We're gonna need you."

"Yeah, before that though, there's something we need to discuss."

Jake smiled a nervous smile. "I agree. That's why we're all here." He looked at the group. "I know some of you have seen some scary things in the past couple hours. And those of you who haven't have at least heard about them."

"Is it true Vance came back?" Gail asked.

"Yes it is. And not just him. All of them. All the banished."

A terrible moan rolled through the group. Even though some of them had seen it, it hadn't been real until they heard their leader confirm it in his own voice. Sophie felt a cold lump in her stomach. This was all her doing.

"They were wandering around Sanctuary," Jake continued. "They seemed confused. Then, a few minutes ago, they wandered back into the woods."

The door opened, and Sophie saw Logan and Mason squeeze into the room.

"There are still a lot of questions," Jake continued. "Let me tell you what we know. In the last few hours, someone broke into my office and stole the book. Then this person used it to reverse all the banishments."

"Why would someone do that?" Evan asked.

"That's a good question," Jake said. "A better one is *how* they did it. They would have had to find a way into my locked office. But it's even more troubling that they knew how to use the book. It took me years to figure out how it worked. And they released all those people in one fell swoop. That isn't an easy task. It would take a deep understanding of the book."

Logan's voice came from the doorway. "Look, I don't want

to minimize anything, but what are we talking about here? Twelve people? And from what I hear, they aren't armed. They're wandering around the woods naked. Let's round them up."

A murmur of approval ran through the group.

"Two things about that," Jake said. "First, and less importantly, these people didn't come back right. Nate saw Vance eating handfuls of dirt. We don't know what they're capable of. We have to be cautious."

Logan said, "Seems to me their craziness could be a help rather than a hindrance. If they're eating dirt, it should be easy to outsmart them."

"There is a bigger problem," Jake said. "I banished one person most of you don't know about. To fully understand how dangerous he is and how careful we need to be, I need to do something I probably should have done a long time ago. I need to tell you about my past."

So he did. He told them about Rook Mountain, and about the Tools. He told them about the Unfeathered and about the mirror. But mostly he told them about Zed. About the man who couldn't be killed and wouldn't be stopped. The man who always wore a smile as he twisted minds and manipulated people into hurting each other.

To Sophie, some of it was familiar. She'd read the reports along with everyone else when Rook Mountain had changed that day in March. But some of it was new. Like his explanation of the Tools. Sophie felt the metal of the compass growing colder in her pocket as Jake talked about the powerful objects with the broken clock symbol and about the terrible things Zed had done to acquire them.

"Zed arrived here at Sanctuary about a year and a half after I did. I'd spent that time living alone. I'd learned enough about the book that I was able to pull the items I needed through the trees. Things like food and clothing. The book was slowly revealing its secrets to me. The first time I opened it, it all looked like nonsense, but the words were gradually changing to English, as if the book was learning to trust me. By the time I had fully understood one section, a new section would reveal itself. It was a long, slow process, but it seemed like the book always gave me exactly what I needed to survive."

He paced as he talked. The group had withered back from him now, giving him room to expose his past. "I had just read the section on how to develop the forest by transforming a person into a tree. Then Zed appeared. It was sheer luck that I found him the way I did. He was confused and angry. And he was injured. I didn't wait. I didn't try to talk to him. Instead, I went right to work. And it was a good thing I did. By the time the banishment was underway, his head was already clearing, and he was speaking coherently. He told me how this was his place. How he'd made it and he couldn't be defeated here. He tried to take the book from me. He said it was his. But by that time, it was too late. He was already transforming."

Jake stopped pacing and looked out over the group. "And that was that. He was just another tree in the middle of the forest."

The room was silent for a long time. Then Nate spoke up. "You gonna tell them the rest?"

Jake paused for a long moment and then nodded.

"My goal was always to find help for my family. To save them from Zed. Now that I'd trapped Zed, I wanted to get back to them as soon as possible. And before long, the book showed me how."

He marched to the window and pointed at the forest. "Many of those trees are more than what they seem to be. Many of them are doorways. They lead to all sorts of different places and different times. Using the book, I can open the doors and pull people through, which is how all of you came to be here. But it doesn't work the other way. I can't send anything from here to there.

"I could watch my family using the book. I could see every breath they took, the food they ate, every kiss they exchanged. But I couldn't send them a simple note. I couldn't touch them or be with them or even let them know I was still alive. I had given up. I decided to stop torturing myself and vowed to stop watching them. The book showed me another way. Using the book, I could open the doors the rest of the way and it could be used both ways. But there was a catch."

"There always is," Logan muttered.

"It was an all or nothing type deal. To open one door, I would have to open all of them. And that would release the banished. It would mean Zed would be free, and he'd be able to travel to any of the hundreds of times and places the trees led to. Including Rook Mountain. I couldn't afford to take that risk."

"Is that what happened today?" Sophie asked in a shaky voice. "Someone opened doors the rest of the way?"

"I don't think so," Jake said. "They reversed the banishments, but the doors are still closed. For now anyway. Who knows what they have planned next."

"So when you figured out about the door, that's when you decided to stay here?" Logan asked, her voice an impatient rush. "Forever?"

Nate and Jake exchanged a glance.

"It started out like that," Jake said. "I intended to live out my life here in the woods. But then, once again, the book showed me something new. It taught me about the trails."

"They weren't here when you got here?" It was Taylor who asked that question.

"They weren't. It was my greatest frustration, the way the forest was always shifting. The book taught me how to cut trails that would limit the movement of the trees. But there was a problem."

"The trails had to be walked," Logan said.

"Exactly. And there was something else. The book suggested that if the trails were deep enough, they might allow me to isolate certain parts of the forest and open some doors without opening all of them. So I cut a trail that would, if it were deep enough, allow me to open a door to Rook Mountain without freeing Zed."

"Wait." There was more than a hint of anger in Logan's voice. "You're telling us you brought us here as slave labor? So we could walk your trails and help you escape?"

Jake looked her in the eye. "Yes."

The group was stone silent.

"Of course," Logan said. Her voice was venom. "You always intended to go back. To hell with the rest of us. As long as we did your work for you."

"You know it's not like that," Jake said.

Nate said, "Listen, we'd all be dead if it weren't for Jake. We all came here voluntarily. We all said the word. He didn't pull in anyone who didn't say the word."

"Wait a minute," Sophie said. "If you couldn't get anything back, not even a message, how did the Sanctuary legend start exactly?"

"I didn't create it. It already existed."

Sophie scratched her head. "The story I heard was that the

legend never existed before Rook Mountain went out of time and came back."

"I don't know anything about that," Jake said. "Look, the reason I am telling you about this is that Zed's out there now. He's free. And he's gonna be pissed. He wants the book, and he'll kill all of us to get it."

Sophie thought for a long moment, her backpack clutched to her chest, before speaking. "Is there any way to stop him?"

Jake sighed. "Maybe if I had the book. But even then, we don't know how to find him. He's got every advantage. He'll try to destroy us."

Sophie slowly unzipped the backpack, feeling each tooth of the zipper release as she went. She wasn't looking forward to this, but it was something she had to do.

She pulled out the book and the room gasped. She held the book out to Jake. "I'm sorry. I was looking for a way out of here. And one of the trees had writing on it, and it seemed like it was talking to me."

Jake took the book, his face pale.

"She broke into your office. She put us all in danger." Sophie didn't even have to look up to recognize her friend's voice. It was Logan. "She has to be banished."

"There's more," Sophie said.

She held up the compass, its back facing out so Jake and Nate could see the broken clock symbol.

"Good Lord," Nate groaned.

"Damn it, Sophie, where'd you get that?" Jake asked.

"It came over with me. It belonged to this guy who pushed me off a building. That's how I got here, by saying Sanctuary while I fell. He had this compass. I grabbed it from him while we were falling."

Jake's jaw was set like stone. "We have to hide it. We have

to hide both these things. Who knows the damage Zed could do with one of them, let alone both."

A murmur of agreement rolled through the group.

"Okay, here's what we do," Logan said. "We all hunker down here at the house and defend our position."

Nate shook his head. "I don't think you understand Zed. Assuming he has all his powers back, he could materialize in the middle of this house at will. If we try to hide this stuff, he'll torture the information out of us. Or, even easier, he'll read our minds."

"Then let's not wait here," Sophie said.

Logan scoffed. "No one wants to hear from you, traitor."

"No, I'm serious." She held up the compass again. "We can use this to find him. It can find anything. And we have the book. Jake, you can turn him back into a tree."

All eyes were on Jake now.

"Maybe." He spoke slowly, his eyes distant. "But, look, it's not as easy as you make it sound. The book's getting harder and harder for me to use. It's like it's wearing me down."

"You got any better ideas?" Sophie asked.

Logan frowned at her across the room. "Kinda mouthy for someone who may have gotten us all killed."

It was quiet in the room for a long moment. Finally, Jake said, "Sophie, come with me. Nate, go warn the others. Logan, you're in charge of the defense here."

"Wait, you can't go off with her," Logan said. "We can't trust her after what she did."

"All the more reason to keep her with me."

"Then let me come with you. You need someone to watch your back."

Jake put a hand on her shoulder. "Our son needs you here. I'll be okay. If all goes well, we'll be back in no time."

Logan reluctantly agreed.

Jake dropped to one knee and gave Mason a tight hug. Then he stood and headed for the door. He didn't look back. He didn't need to; Sophie was right on his heels.

Sophie followed him, working her way through the group. When she was almost at the door, she felt a shoulder bump against her. She looked up and saw Taylor.

She froze, returning his gaze with an icy one of her own. From a certain perspective, all this trouble was *his* fault. She'd done it all, all the stupid mistakes and missteps, so she could bring him to justice. If she'd succeeded, at least she'd have something to show for this mess she'd made. And here he was, scowling at her, alive and free.

But maybe it didn't have to be that way. Maybe she'd been over-complicating this all along. He was standing right there, his shoulder touching hers. And there was a knife hanging from her belt. A knife she was not unskilled in using. She could finish this right here and now.

He squinted at her as if reading her thoughts. "Don't you think you've caused enough trouble already?"

"Sophie!"

She looked up and saw Jake at the door, glaring back at her. "Let's move."

She nodded and followed Jake, not daring to look back at Taylor, afraid she wouldn't be able to control her knife if she did. She marched toward the door.

They were about to exit the building when the attack started.

2. Rook Mountain

At first, Wendy hadn't understood what she was seeing when she spotted the three men.

229

She'd gone to Sean's house, just as his text had asked. She'd parked across the street and gotten out of her car. Then she saw three men come out of his house. In the darkness, she only recognized one of them. Sean. He was carrying the hammer. The other two appeared to be teenagers. They were leading Sean down sidewalk at gunpoint.

It had to be the Zed Heads.

She slipped quietly back into her car and fished her cell phone out of her purse. She dialed 911 and told the operator Officer Lee had been taken hostage and that she was following the perpetrators. The operator had urged her to stay calm and to keep her distance.

Wendy followed the car when it left Sean's house, staying on the line with the 911 operator the whole time. When they reached downtown and pulled over, Wendy knew exactly why they had picked this location. She politely relayed the address and hung up the phone over the operator's protests.

She didn't care. She wanted to get closer. She needed to know what was happening. So she exited her vehicle and trotted around the block to the closest corner to the Zed Heads, where she'd be able to see them and even hear some of what they said while still being able to hide when the need arose.

She watched them, peeking out around the corner as far as she dared. At one point, she was almost certain Sean saw her, but she didn't think the rest of them did. She tapped her foot nervously as she waited. The police would be arriving any minute, but would it be soon enough?

Then Sean hit the tree with the hammer, and a beam of white light poured out of it. And the next thing she knew, Colt was screaming.

She couldn't help it. The responsible adult in her, the part that had been a school teacher for fifteen years, the part that held her genetic wiring to protect children, was too strong. She ran around the corner toward the scream.

Grant raised his gun and fired at the creature attached to his friend's face. The bullet ricocheted off the thing, and Wendy gasped. Whatever the creature was, it was apparently bulletproof.

Wendy's eyes frantically scanned each of the kids, making sure the bullet hadn't hit anyone. Everyone but Colt appeared unharmed.

She stopped five feet away from Colt, halted by the gruesome sight. A strange black ball covered with two-inch spikes was embedded in the upper half of his face. His mouth was uncovered, leaving his scream of pain and terror unmuffled. The upper half of his face, including his eyes and nose, had to be ruined. The strange ball was wedged too deeply and too much blood poured out around it.

The ball gave a quick shudder and let out a tiny squeak. Wendy had the nauseating realization this thing was alive.

Colt reached up and grabbed the thing with both hands and pulled, trying to get it off. It didn't budge, but Wendy could see from the way the muscles on Colt's arms stood out that he was pulling hard. Suddenly, the spikes covering the creature grew an inch longer. Colt's screams started anew as the spikes impaled his hands and, Wendy had to assume, dug deeper into his face.

The group of teenagers was frozen with horror and revulsion. Sean took a hesitant step toward the boy, his hand raised. What exactly he intended to do, Wendy didn't know.

As he was still reaching out, a sudden noise filled the air, and the hairs on the back of Wendy's neck stood on end. Her first thought was, *the Unfeathered*, but this was something else.

This song came from a dozen places at once. This song had words.

"Why have you brought the little one to this place? This bad, bad place."

"What the hell is that?" Sean whispered.

She followed his gaze up the street, hoping to see police cars. Instead, she saw a large black mass swirling through the sky. She squinted at it, trying to make out some form in its ever-changing mass. Her breath caught in her throat as she saw it was moving toward them.

The mass suddenly jumped fifty feet backwards in a second. It paused and began moving toward them once again.

"This is a bad place," the many voices repeated. Somehow they seemed like they were coming from everywhere at once. *"You shouldn't have brought the little ones here."*

Colt's screams had mellowed into a series of agonized moans. Two of the Zed Heads ran over to help him. The rest of them had their eyes on the black shape.

"Little ones?" Sean asked. "What are they talking about?"

"I don't know," Wendy said. "But I think we need to get out of here, like right now." There was a tickle in the back of her mind, as if she were missing something. The voices had said 'little one' the first time. The second time they'd said 'little ones'.

Suddenly, it clicked. She looked down and had to suppress a scream. One of the round creatures was on the ground near Sean's feet. It was quivering and drawing in on itself, making itself smaller.

"Sean, look out!" she yelled.

He turned in the direction she was pointing and then yelped and jumped back. But he wasn't fast enough. The creature launched into the air, its spikes extending as it went, spinning in a crazy spiral toward Sean's face.

He swung the hammer wildly, and somehow managed to hit the creature mid-air. Wendy had no idea how he did it. He must have been operating on pure instinct. When he connected, a loud snapping sound split the air.

The creature fell to the ground and lay still.

Wendy squinted at it. "Sean, look. You cracked it."

A long jagged crack zigzagged down the side of it. As they watched, the crack grew wider, then wider still.

"You don't think—" Sean said, but he never got to finish the thought. The creature cracked in half like an egg. Something slipped out of the shell and glided into the air. It was like a shadow, and its form shifted and flowed like water as it moved skyward.

"What the hell is that thing?" one of Zed Heads asked.

Wendy shot the kid a look. "You idiots brought us out here. You tell us."

The shadow creature spun around them haphazardly.

"*A new voice for the song!*" The black swarm moving toward them was going faster now, and there was excitement in their voices.

The shadow creature made a tentative, soft try of its voice. "*Hurts...time hurts.*"

The other voices answered quickly. "*Do not try to speak alone, little one. Join the song. Join and we will take you to a place with no time. A good place that does not hurt.*"

Still the solo shadow spun and wobbled through the air.

Wendy realized Colt was still whimpering. He'd fallen to his knees now. His hands were still impaled on the creature's spikes. The tattoo on the back of his right hand had a spike sticking through the middle of it. His friends looked on helplessly.

Wendy said, "Sean. Use the hammer."

A crooked smile grew on Sean's face. "I've wanted to hit that kid with a hammer for a while now."

He swung and connected dead center. Colt let out his loudest scream yet, and Wendy felt a twinge of sympathy. That couldn't have felt good. The creature split down the middle, and Colt groaned as the shadow creature wormed its way out.

"*Hurts,*" the new arrival said. "*It all hurts.*"

The two halves of the shell fell off Colt's face. Wendy had to look away from the mess of puncture wounds and oozing liquids that had once been his eyes and nose. The boy fell to the ground, moaning.

Suddenly, another sound split the air. A sound that made Wendy's heart soar. Sirens.

Two police cars skidded around the corner five blocks away and sped toward them. Wendy wasn't exactly sure why the sight made her so happy. After all, what exactly were a few cops going to do against the abominations that were circling overhead? Or the mass of black shapes coming out of the hole in the tree?

She didn't know. But the normalcy of police answering the call, of officers of truth and justice coming to her aid, made her feel better. Of course, she'd had an officer of the law here with her the whole time, and he was doing a mighty nice job with that hammer.

But the police cars weren't the only ones racing toward them. The dark mass of clouds had almost reached them now. "*We can help, little ones. We will stop the pain.*"

"Officer Lee!" one of the Zed Heads shouted, pointing at the door in the tree.

Wendy glanced down. Three more of the creatures had

slipped through onto the pavement while they had been distracted.

"Damn it!" Sean shouted. He swung his hammer, striking the three creatures in quick succession. Soon three more moaning shadow creatures were slipping out of their shells and rising up to join their brothers.

The black mass was circling now, and the voices were still singing. *"We will help you. We will stop the pain."*

The discordant newborn shadow creatures were singing too. *"It hurts. The seconds hurt. They bite as they pass."*

Then Wendy noticed something even stranger than the creatures above her. The pitch of the police sirens was lowering. She stared at the police cars, and she could have sworn they were traveling much slower than before. Barely moving, actually.

The breath caught in her throat. "They're stopping time. These creatures are taking us back out of time."

"No, no, no," Sean said. Four more of the round creatures had passed through the gate. Sean went at them one by one. The sky over their heads darkened as the number of shadow creatures grew, blotting out the moon and the stars.

One of the shadow creatures brushed past his hand as it escaped its shell, and Sean cried out and dropped the hammer. Blood began to seep from a large cut between his knuckles.

The creatures overhead spun faster and faster. *"Time hurts, little ones. It kills all things. But we are not of time. It is not our master."*

Wendy reached down and scooped up the hammer. The creatures were coming through the gate faster now.

"You have to press the broken clock symbol when you hit them," Sean said. He gripped his hand, applying pressure to the wound.

Wendy nodded. She pressed the symbol and swung the hammer. It landed with a satisfying thud, and a crack ran across the creature. She found another creature and swung again. And again. They were passing through the gate in the tree almost nonstop now. She could keep going forever, and she wasn't sure if they would ever stop.

One of the Zed Heads, Wendy thought it was Megan Hassle, ran forward and kicked one of the round creatures, then cried out in pain as she got a foot full of spikes.

At least she was trying, Wendy thought. The rest of the Zed Heads stood dumbly, looks of terror on their faces.

Something new caught Wendy's ear. Something she hadn't heard in months but would always recognize. The song of the Unfeathered. At the same moment, she realized she no longer heard the police sirens. She glanced over and saw them standing still, less than a block away.

"There, little ones. Your pain is over. You are home."

Wendy looked at Sean, and she saw her own terror reflected in his eyes.

The shadow creatures had done it. Time had once again stopped in Rook Mountain.

3. Sanctuary

The window next to the door shattered, and a Larva flew through the air, spinning and sending a stream of glass shards in front of it.

Sophie had been observing the Larvae for weeks now. She'd killed dozens of them, most of them during the daytime when they were at their most active. But she'd never seen any of them move like this. Usually the creatures spun through the air at a fairly slow rate, using the unpredictability of their flight patterns to cause confusion. But this one was moving like a fastball right down the middle. There was no curving or twisting as it sped toward its target, which appeared to be Nate.

He dove to his left, sliding face first onto the floor. His desperate dive worked, and the creature sped past him. The victory didn't last long, though. The creature turned a quick button hook before reaching the wall. It again headed straight for Nate, who was now defenseless on the floor.

The one dodge had given Logan the time she needed to regain her battle sense. She had her hunting knife in her hand, and as the Larva careened past her, she stabbed at it, landing a deadly-accurate blow in just the right spot.

The creature deflated, and tar-black sludge oozed down Logan's knife. She flicked her blade, sending the thick liquid splattering to the floor.

"How many of you are armed?" Logan asked.

Only Leonard and Sophie raised their hands.

Logan glared at Sophie. "Yeah, you would be."

The words hurt, but Sophie tried to let them roll off her back.

Logan turned to Jake. "I doubt that will be the last. We need weapons."

Jake nodded and pulled a key out of his pocket. It looked exactly like the one Sophie had in her own pocket. He unlocked his office and threw the door open. "There are knives, guns and a few other things in the cabinet on the left. Take whatever you need. Sophie? Let's go."

The others looked at each other, shocked at the invitation.

"You aren't gonna...banish us if we go in there?" Leonard stammered.

Jake smiled weakly. "Not today."

Logan nodded toward the office. "You heard the man. Get your asses in there."

The men hustled to the office.

There was a crash as another Larva smashed through a window. This one buzzed toward Sophie. She cleared her mind, forgot about Taylor, Logan, Jake and all of it, and acted on instinct. When the creature was almost to her, at the last possible moment, she dropped to the floor. As it whizzed over her head, she stabbed upward.

The blade sank to the hilt, and a stream of black sludge hit Sophie in the face. She spat and wiped her face with the back of her hand.

Logan didn't even try to suppress her smile.

The group emerged from the office. Each person carried a pistol and knife. Taylor held an ax.

Nate handed a pistol to Logan, then said to Leonard, "You come with me. We'll round up the others."

Logan said, "The rest of you, let's circle up and figure out a defense strategy."

Another creature buzzed through the broken window next to the door. It headed for Logan, but Jake turned without waiting around to see how she dispatched it.

"Sophie, let's go," he said.

She gave a quick nod and spat again. Her mouth tasted like an oil refinery.

Jake hustled to the door. Sophie slipped her backpack on and quickly followed. Jake threw the door open and then froze, causing Sophie to slam into his back. She leaned to the side to see what had stopped him.

A naked, dirt-smeared man stood in the doorway. His dirty blond hair was long and unkempt. A Larva perched on each of his shoulders, and he held another in each hand.

"Simon," Jake said.

The man's only response was a sick, gurgling moan. Faster than Sophie would have thought possible, the man Jake had called Simon brought up his left hand and slammed the Larva into Jake's belly.

Jake grunted and fell backwards, clutching his stomach.

Simon pulled back his hand and the Larva came with it. Sophie fought the urge to gag as she realized how the creatures were attached to him. Its spikes went clean through each of his hands. They were similarly impaled on his shoulders, and a thin greenish-red liquid ran down his arms and sides. Sophie wasn't sure what the liquid was, but it sure didn't look like human blood.

Sophie shoved Jake aside and brought her knife around hard, stabbing Simon in the neck. He didn't seem to notice.

"Get out of the way!" Logan yelled.

Sophie staggered to her right, dragging Simon with her.

Logan fired. The room exploded with the noise of the gunshot and a bullet hole appeared above the man's right eye. His head snapped back.

Sophie staggered backward as the sticky, not-quite-blood substance from the man's head splattered onto her arms.

Simon paused for a moment, and then shook his head, as if to clear it. His eyes were now fixed on Logan. He began walking toward her.

Logan fired again, once again landing a clean head shot. This time the man paused only a moment before staggering forward.

She fired again. And again. It barely slowed Simon.

"Damn it!" Logan shouted. "Anybody want to give me a hand here?"

Jake lay on the ground, clutching his stomach. "Kill the

Larvae first. Then subdue him."

Logan paused for a moment, then gave a quick nod and pulled out her knife.

Sophie yanked her knife out of Simon's neck. She thrust the knife back at him, stabbing the Larva on his right shoulder. Logan took out the one in his right hand. Frasier came forward and took care of his left hand.

Sophie killed the final Larva and nodded at Frasier. "Nicely done, old man."

He smiled. "I learned from the best." Then, as if suddenly remembering her new traitor status, he quickly looked away.

Sophie turned to Jake. "You okay?"

He grunted and pushed himself to his feet. "Yeah. It's not deep." He held up a hand covered in the blood that had leaked from his wounds. "Just messy."

Simon threw a wild punch at Logan. She easily deflected it. "Not so tough now, are you?"

Sophie noticed Mason peeking around his mother, his face pale with fear.

Jake's eyes searched for a frantic moment before resting on Mason, who was huddled behind Logan. Relief washed over his face. "You two okay?"

"Yeah," Logan said. "But what do we do with Simon?"

Jake shook his head. "I don't know. He doesn't die easy, that's for sure. Maybe we lock him in my office for now? Then we can gather all the others, make sure everyone's safe and—"

A loud whining noise from Simon cut Jake off. The naked man's head was thrown back and his arms were stretched out at his sides.

The sound pulsed in Sophie's ears like a painful drum.

"What the hell are you doing?" Logan yelled at him.

Sophie heard a chirping noise behind her and glanced over her shoulder. Two Larvae were rolling as fast as bowling balls. Another two flew through the air.

"Look out!" she yelled. She rolled to her side as quickly as she was able, and she felt a breeze as the Larvae sped past her.

The two on the floor leapt suddenly, impaling themselves on Simon's palms. The two in the air collided with his shoulders, taking the place of the ones Sophie had killed.

This time, the group moved as one. Logan took the left hand, Frasier took the right, Sophie took the one on the left shoulder, and Leonard dispatched the Larva on the right shoulder.

Simon was now streaked with the sludge left behind by the creatures. He snarled and threw back his head again.

Logan leapt at him, tackling him to the floor. She held his inky-black-smeared shoulders to the ground. He snapped at her with his dirt stained teeth. Her hands were barely out of his mouth's reach.

"We can't let him make that noise again," Logan said. "Bullet to the head didn't work. How about we try taking the head off altogether?" She looked at Taylor. "You mind?"

Taylor raised the ax over his head. For a terrible moment, Sophie was sure he was going to bring the ax down on Logan. It took everything she had not to stab him.

He brought the ax down hard, burying it in Simon's neck. The man's head rolled onto its side as it separated from his body. It came off a bit too cleanly, more like splitting wood than hacking flesh.

"Nice shot," Logan said.

Taylor nodded.

They all waited in silence, watching the body for any signs

of life. After a full thirty seconds, Nate said, "Well, that seems to work."

"Yeah," Frasier said. "Now if we can get them to all lie down nicely, they shouldn't be much of a problem."

Sophie took a deep breath. Her heart was still racing. Just when she'd gotten used to taking on the Larvae, here came the zombie plant monsters.

"How many of those things are there?" she asked. "How many more people have you banished?"

Jake glanced out the door. "Eleven. Not counting Zed."

"Great," Sophie said. "As long as they keep coming one at a time, we can handle them."

"Don't forget lying down nicely," Frasier said.

"Actually, that does raise a question." Nate glared down at the body. "Did Simon wander in here? Or was he sent?"

The room considered that in silence for a few moments. Then Jake said, "Nate, you know Zed better than anyone. Is such a thing possible?"

Nate thought about that for a moment. "On normal people, probably not. He can dig around in their heads, and he can manipulate like crazy. But he can't actually control a person's mind. These guys seem to be damaged though. So it's certainly possible."

Logan shook her head. "I don't buy it. If he's controlling them, why not send them all at once? There's no way we could stand up to all eleven."

Sophie said, "Unless he's trying to distract us. Or keep us busy."

Jake struggled to his feet. "Either way, we need to stick to the original plan. Sophie and I will go take care of Zed. Nate and Leonard, you knock on doors and let people know what's going on. I don't want anyone killed in their sleep by one of those bastards. Logan—"

"Yeah, I know." She clutched her gun with one hand and ruffled her son's hair with the other. "Protect the home front."

Jake nodded. "Maybe you all should hole up in an interior room. There's the bathroom upstairs. No windows."

Logan grimaced. "That's a damn tight spot. If a couple of those things come calling at once, we could be cornered."

Jake put his hand on her shoulder. "Okay. It's your call. I trust you. I know you'll protect Mason no matter what."

She smiled. "You better believe it."

Jake scooped Mason up in a giant bear hug. The kid looked a little daze, but he hugged his father back and smiled. "I love you, kid. Listen to your mother."

"Okay daddy."

"See you soon." He set Mason down and then nudged Sophie. "Break out the compass."

Sophie fished the compass out of her pocket, pressed the broken clock symbol, and thought of Zed. The needle moved immediately. "Got him. Let's do it."

Nate and Leonard followed Jake and Sophie out of the house. The two groups split at the path.

Jake patted Nate's shoulder. "Stay safe."

Nate nodded. "I appreciate you not asking, boss."

"Not asking what?"

"Whether you can trust me now that Zed's free."

Jake said, "No need to ask."

The groups went their two separate ways, one toward the cabins of Sanctuary and one toward the man who called himself Zed. Five minutes after they had left Jake's house, the next wave of attacks began.

* * *

4. Sanctuary

Jake marched down the trail. He hadn't even glanced at Sophie in five minutes. All these years, all the sacrifices he'd made, first coming here, and then capturing Zed. Deciding to live here forever rather than risk letting that madman loose on the world. Then realizing there may be a way home. Building the Sanctuary. Constantly second guessing himself. The hours spent lying awake at night, wondering if he was becoming a new version of Zed himself, with his rules and his banishments. Finding comfort in Logan's arms. Then breaking up with her. Then going back to her, over and over again.

What was it all for?

All he'd spent years building, and this woman had torn it down in less than a month.

"Jake," she said. "I'm so sorry for taking your book. For all of this."

He didn't reply.

"You wouldn't listen to me about Taylor," she said.

"I told you the score right away. This is a place without shadows. Someone wants their past to be known, they have to be the one to share it."

"He killed my sister," she blurted out.

He flinched.

"He didn't even know her. He picked her out at random and bashed her head in. Do you know what that's like?"

Jake didn't answer. He kept his eyes fixed on the trail.

"And you wouldn't listen to me. You threatened me. And then there were these trees. Messages started appearing. Messages for me. They told me how to bring Taylor to justice. All I had to do was follow their plan."

"Let me guess. The plan didn't work out quite the way the

trees promised."

"I feel so stupid."

He sighed. "Look, you're not the first person Zed has fooled. He did it to my whole damn town. Got us to agree to everything he said."

"Yeah, but you stood up to him."

He shrugged. "Eventually. But that was my wife's doing as much as mine. If it hadn't been for her, I wouldn't have had the courage." His eyes scanned the trees, searching for more Larvae. Or more naked men wielding them. "I was there in the crowd on Regulation Day. I listened to Zed. I voted for his Regulations. So you could say I took the bait just like you."

"So...you're not mad?"

He glared at her. "Oh, I'm mad. I'm beyond mad. I'm furious. But I also need you. Zed took an interest in you, leaving you those messages. Say what you will about him, but he's got an eye for talent. Nate was a dumb stoner when Zed found him, but Zed saw his potential. So I think you might have something Zed's scared of. Or something he wants."

"I do," she said, and she held up the compass.

"That's not what I meant. But that doesn't hurt either."

Sophie looked at the compass and frowned.

"What is it?" Jake asked.

"He must be moving. The compass is pointing to the left now."

"There's a fork up ahead," Jake said. "That'll lead us in the right direction."

As they walked, Jake said, "Sophie, I have to tell you something." He paused, but she didn't respond. So he continued. "I don't think I can do it."

"Do what?"

245

"The thing we're on our way to do. Banishing Zed."

"What are you talking about? I saw you do it the other day."

His feet suddenly felt heavy. It was like he was moving through knee-deep mud rather than over a beaten dirt trail. "I did it, but I had time to prepare. And it hurt. I was coughing blood for two days after that."

Sophie's brow creased at that, whether in concern or worry for her own safety, he didn't know.

"The book wasn't meant to be used by someone like me. A normal man. Or maybe it wasn't meant to be used so often. Either way, it's taking its toll. The words are getting cloudy. Harder for me to read. I'll try my best. I'll keep going until it kills me. But I'm not confident. I don't know if I could banish a normal man in the state I'm in, and Zed, well, that nearly killed me the first time, when I was fresh and doing the things in the book came easy to me."

"Then what the hell are we doing here? If you can't do it, then let's not do it. Let's figure out something else."

"What else are we supposed to do?"

Sophie bit her lip. "Show me how to do it."

Jake shook his head.

"What? You don't trust me?"

"It's not that. It's not exactly something I can teach you in ten minutes."

"I did okay unbanishing everyone."

"Don't remind me. Besides, that's different. It's like...untying a knot versus tying one. You could probably figure out how to untie most knots. It takes practice to tie a perfect one, though."

Sophie sighed. "So you can't do it. And you won't teach me to do it. Where's that leave us?"

How could he explain to her everything he was feeling...the way he knew this would end? The inevitability of it all weighed on him. Maybe standing up to a force of nature like Zed had been a mistake all along. Who was he anyway to defy a being who could bend and twist the very laws of nature? Jake was just a man. And not a very good one at that. He'd lucked into some good things, sure, like his family back home and his family here, and he'd avoided prison unlike some Hinkles he could name, God bless them. But at the root of it all, he was an average man.

He flashed back to that riverbank in Rook Mountain where Zed had held the gun to his head that day so long ago, only hours before he'd crossed through the mirror and came here. Maybe he should have died on that bank. A part of him wished he had. This, having lived so many years and suffered so much, only to die at the hands of the same madman, seemed too cruel.

But then he thought of Mason. The accidental son he'd never meant to bring into the world. He thought of Logan, and the strange, passionate, and wonderful relationship they shared. He thought of his unlikely friendship with Nate. And all the other relationships he'd had here in the place he'd built.

"I didn't make up the name Sanctuary, you know," Jake said. "It was already in the book. It was the secret name for this place. It was the book's name for it. When I saw that, I knew what I needed to do. I needed to create a safe place. A place where everyone was welcome. What I said before about Zed? He looks for talent. He finds the best people and twists them until they're doing his work and loving it. He finds the diamonds in the rough. But I wanted to be different. I took anyone. The book alerted me when someone was going to call for Sanctuary. It even allowed me to look at the person, to learn about them before I let them in. But I never did. Who am I to make that kind of choice? So I left it up to chance. I pulled people in at random. I never knew anything about them until they appeared."

"And what about me?" Sophie asked. "You said you never pulled me in. How'd I get here? How'd it work for me?"

Jake shook his head. "I don't know. Maybe it had something to do with that compass."

"Maybe." She glanced down at it. "Turn right ahead. So what's the plan? We hope he just stands there while you do your thing with the book?"

Jake couldn't help but smile. "The man does love to talk, so we've probably got five minutes while he gets around to saying hello."

He saw Sophie look down at the compass, then give it a shake.

"The needle," she said. "It's spinning like crazy."

A cold sweat broke out on Jake's skin. "We're too late. He's gone. He's back in Rook Mountain."

"You don't know that. Let me try again."

But Jake wasn't listening. Something had caught his eye. There was smoke in the sky. It was coming from the direction of the cabins. The blood drained from his face. Mason. Logan.

"We've gotta go back," he said. He pointed to the smoke rising from the forest.

Sophie gasped. "I'll lead the way. The compass will show us the fastest route."

They ran through the forest, sprinting down a winding trail until it spat them out of the woods in front of the Welcome Wagon.

Jake gasped when he saw the flames devouring the cabin.

And it wasn't just the Welcome Wagon. Judging by the pillars of smoke, at least ten other cabins were on fire.

"My God," he said. "We have to get back to my house. Now."

"Jake," Sophie said. "Look."

He turned back to the Welcome Wagon. There was a dark shape in the doorway. And it was moving.

A man stepped out of the house. He was covered in soot, but appeared to be unburned. Like the other banished people they had seen, he was naked, but there were no Larvae perched on his shoulders or hands. He had long dark hair and a massive bushy beard.

"Is that Zed?" Sophie asked. Her voice was a choked whisper.

"No," Jake said.

"Is it one of the people you banished?"

Jake shook his head. "I've never seen that man in my life."

The man walked toward them. "Where is Zed?"

5. Rook Mountain

Sean clutched the cut on his hand and watched the hypnotic swirl of the shadow creatures spinning overhead. They had done it. They had stopped time. Anger and panic bubbled up inside of him.

A few of the Unfeathered streaked across the sky, but they seemed to be keeping their distance. Perhaps they were afraid of the shadows creatures. If so, it would be the first time Sean and the Unfeathered had agreed on something.

He tried to clear his head. It wasn't the whole town. It couldn't be. The police cars less than a block away were paused. It was just them. Alone. Cut off from the world. Him, Wendy, and a dozen zealot teenagers.

He turned to the Zed Heads, and yelled, "Is this what you wanted? Congratulations. Things are back to the good old days!"

They looked at him, their eyes wide, a bunch of scared kids.

Wendy yelled, "Watch out!"

He looked down and saw another one of the round spiky creatures near his foot. He jumped back. "Damn it! These things just keep coming."

Wendy swung the hammer, cracking the creature in half. An image popped into Sean's head of going to Chuck E. Cheese as a kid and playing Whack-a-Mole.

The shadow creature wormed its way out of the broken shell.

"*The little one joins us! The little one!*" The sing-song collective voices sounded excited now. They spun faster and faster.

Sean put his hand on Wendy's shoulder. "They're waiting. Waiting for us to crack more of those things and hatch their babies or whatever."

"What do we do?" Wendy asked.

Sean shook his head. More of the round creatures were spilling through the doorway. If Wendy killed them, the population of shadow creatures would grow. They had already proven they could stop time. What would happen if they kept going faster?

Yet it wasn't safe to let the creatures live either. Colt's ruined face proved that. The boy lay on his side, curled in the fetal position and moaning.

"We need to run," Sean said. "Get the hell out of here. Maybe the creatures will clear out on their own."

He heard a crack as Wendy brought down the hammer, releasing another shadow. "You think time will start again?"

"I have no idea. But I think it's our only chance at this point."

Sean started to say something else, but then stopped. Something was approaching the doorway in the tree from the other side. Something much larger than the round creatures.

A dark figure filled the doorway and began to step through. The Zed Heads murmured with excitement.

A girl Sean didn't know knelt down and put her hand on Colt's shoulder. "It's happening. Just like he said."

"I can't see," Colt said. "Tell me when he gets here."

Sean drew a sharp breath as the figure stepped thorough the doorway. A familiar bald head emerged from the light, and then a long, well-muscled body. Zed.

He wore khakis that were a size too big and a worn tee-shirt, a strange ill-fitting version of his usual attire. His face, arms, and feet were smeared with dirt. Even the teeth revealed by his wide smile were speckled with mud.

The Zed Heads gasped when he stepped onto the pavement.

"My faithful children," he said. He looked at Sean and Wendy. "And you two. It's good to be home. You won't believe how I've spent the last few years."

"Zed!" a girl yelled. "Look out! By your feet!"

Sean squinted at the creatures surrounding Zed.

Zed chuckled. He crouched down and ran his hand along the spikes of the nearest round creature. "The Larvae? No need to worry about them."

Sean nodded toward Colt. "Tell that to your boy, here."

Zed clucked his tongue. "That's unfortunate. He probably spooked it." He reached out a hand, and the creature on the ground leapt onto it. Sean could have sworn he heard the creature purr as it rolled up Zed's arm and rested on his shoulder.

"They're so easy to control at this age," Zed said. "It's later you need to worry..." His voice trailed off, and the smile melted from his face. He looked upward.

It was then Sean noticed the silence. The shadow creatures were no longer singing. They weren't even spinning. They just hovered. It was as if they were surprised. Zed spoke again, quietly. "There's no need for trouble here. Let's all go our separate ways. You can return to your realm and leave this one to me."

Sean realized he was addressing the shadows.

"*It's him*," the shadow creatures sang. "*The one with the watch. He betrays. He hurts.*"

Zed said, "We've been over that. I've made amends. Haven't I helped? I provided a place for your young."

"*No amends*," the shadows said. "*No amends!*" Their voices were louder, so loud Sean wanted to put his hands over his ears. They started spinning now, and as they did they changed shape, forming into a funnel cloud.

"Go back to your own place," Zed said, more loudly now.

"*This is our place!*" they roared.

Zed looked at the Zed Heads, and Sean saw something like love in his eyes. "I appreciate your sacrifice. If I knew how to survive them, I'd tell you." He took another step backwards.

The girl who had warned Zed about the Larva spoke again. "What are you doing?"

Zed grimaced. "I'm going with Plan B." He glanced up at the shadow creatures one more time. "I'll send your young through the door. As many as I can. Think of it as a peace offering."

"*No peace!*" the shadows wailed.

But Zed was already stepping backward through the

doorway and into the tree.

"What's happening?" Colt asked.

"He's gone," one of the boys whimpered. "He left us."

Sean turned toward the Zed Heads and saw their faces fall as, one by one, they realized their savior had abandoned them.

"No!" Colt screamed. "That's not possible. This is a test. He's coming back for us."

Sean couldn't help it; he felt sorry for the kid. He'd been duped by Zed and his lies just like the adults had back in the Regulation days. Worse, really, considering he'd been brought up with Zed's laws. He'd been faithful to what his parents, his teachers, and his town had taught him.

Another one of the creature Zed called the Larvae passed through the tree's doorway. Then another two, side by side. True to his word, Zed seemed to be sending them.

"Wendy, give me the hammer." Sean said.

She put it in his hand.

He took a deep breath, pressed the broken clock symbol, and swung the hammer. It hit the doorway, and the hammer stopped like the door was made of rock, sending a jolt of pain up Sean's arm. He swung again, harder this time, and he cried out in pain as the hammer hit the door. He could have sworn it felt a little different this time. Like there was a bit of give to it.

"*What is the one with the hammer doing?*" the shadows sang.

"Wendy, listen. Those things aren't going away on their own. Not as long as their...Larvae keep coming through. I want you to take the kids and get the hell out of here."

Wendy shook her head. "I'm not leaving. I'll stay with you while you take down the doorway."

He grabbed her around the waist with his free arm, pulled

her close, and kissed her quickly but deeply. As they broke, he said, "Wendy, I love you, but that's the dumbest thing I've ever heard. Save these kids. Get out of here."

She gritted her teeth and nodded. She gave him another quick kiss and turned to the kids. She pointed at the two largest boys. "You two, come help Colt. We're getting out of here."

The kids didn't argue. The two boys hustled over and helped Colt to his feet, one supporting him under each arm.

Sean swung the hammer at the nearest Larva. He didn't want to take another swing at the door until Wendy and the kids were clear. He had a feeling the shadows weren't going to be pleased.

Wendy called back to him one last time. "Sean, do it quick and then run."

He nodded. "I will. I promise." Anything to get her moving. He wanted her safe. Her and those kids. That's what he had to think about now.

There were six Larvae around his feet. He hit one of them with the hammer, but two more came through the doorway before the shadow even left the one he'd hit. He had to act now, or he might not be able to finish.

He swung again, putting everything he had behind the hammer. It hit the doorway, and a bolt of pain shot through his arm. Without giving himself time to think about it, he swung again.

"*Stop!*" the shadow creatures sang. "*Let the little ones free!*"

He tried to ignore their song, though it was so loud his ears rang and his head pounded. He swung the hammer again.

A sudden pain, like a dozen knives, shot through his right calf. He looked down and saw one of the Larvae buried in his leg.

There was no time to worry about that now. He swung the hammer again. This time, he swore he heard a crack as the Tool struck the doorway.

He cried out in pain and dropped the hammer as one of the Larvae crashed into his right arm. He wouldn't make it much longer, he knew. He'd have to do this southpaw. He picked up the hammer with his left hand and swung again. And again. And again.

He could see tiny cracks spidering across the doorway now.

A Larva hit him in the lower back. He braced, willing himself not to fall. He knew if he did, he'd never get up again.

He swung the hammer again and again, making a little more progress with each hit. All the while, the shadow creatures were spinning faster and faster, singing more and more loudly.

He tried not to look around, tried not to notice the dozen or so Larvae around his feet. He could barely stand, and only three of them had attacked so far. How many more would it take to bring him down for good? He was all too afraid he knew the answer to that question: one. Or, none and a bit of time.

The creature on his back shivered, and Sean yelled in agony as the spikes covering the thing wedged themselves deeper in his flesh.

He took a deep breath and swung again. The cracks were spreading. It wouldn't be long now, but how much longer did he have?

Another swing. Another bolt of pain running through him. Another encouraging spread of cracks in the door.

He pulled back the hammer. He'd give it everything he had this time, do everything in his power to make this swing be the last. But before he could bring the hammer forward, a Larva launched itself from the doorway. It came at him in an arch that seemed almost lazy, but that he was still unable to stop.

The creature hit him square in the throat.

He dropped the hammer and fell to his knees. He wanted to grab the creature and tear it off, but he remembered the way Colt's hands had been punctured in a dozen places, and he forced himself not to touch the thing.

He concentrated on breathing. He was relieved to find he could still do so.

It was over now. He had failed.

He stayed there on his knees, his eyes growing cloudy. Everything in him wanted to lie down on the ground, but he was terrified of getting closer to the rest of the Larvae.

He heard a cracking sound, and he strained to see past the Larvae.

Wendy was swinging the hammer at the doorway. She looked back at him over her shoulder. He saw the pain and terror in her eyes, but she tried to keep her voice light. "The kids are safe. Now stay quiet and let me work."

He watched, though it was getting more and more difficult to do so, as she smashed the hammer into the doorway three more times. On the fourth hit, it sounded like thunder and glass shattering. The tree split.

The doorway grew dark, now nothing more than a crack in a tree that looked charred, as if it had been struck by lightning.

But Wendy didn't stop there. She hit the Larvae, one after another, taking the closest ones to her first and working her way outward.

Soon they were all gone. No, Sean remembered. Not all of

them.

"This is probably gonna hurt," Wendy said.

She started with the one on his leg. As the hammer hit, a stab of pain shot through his body like a bolt of lightning. Before the initial wave of pain had passed, she brought the hammer down again, this time striking the Larvae on his arm. Then the one on his back. Each blow was agony. Through the pain, he saw the shadows leak out each time the shell fell away.

Only the one in his neck was left now. She raised the hammer and paused.

"You ready?" she asked.

He wanted to yell *hell no* he was *not* ready, but he couldn't speak. He could barely even move his head. Anyway, she wasn't waiting for a response. She swung the hammer.

It felt like his windpipe was being torn out. It was the worst pain of his life. But then the shell fell away, and it was a bit better. The torture of the dozens of stabbing spikes was gone, but in its place, a dizzying amount of blood leaking out of him. He put his hands to his throat to try to stop it even as it poured down his chest.

Wendy stared at the shadows in the sky. "It's over! That's all of them! Now leave us be!"

"The little ones are home. They have joined the song. We will put you back in the river now."

The shadows spun faster and higher, until they disappeared from sight.

The air filled with the sound of police sirens. Two cars skidded to a stop behind them, and four car doors were thrown open.

"Where are those kids?" one of the officers asked. "I just saw them, and then they disappeared."

Wendy ignored them. She bent down next to Sean. "Hey, you're gonna be okay. No way am I gonna let you leave me alone to explain all this."

He tried to speak, to tell her he wasn't sure she had a choice, but all that came out was a croak.

She put her hand on his cheek. "You did it, you know. You stopped Zed from coming back. You saved those kids." She glanced down at the hammer in her hand. "Okay, maybe I helped a little. But you loosened it for me."

His eyelids were getting heavy now. He smiled at her, trying to get his face to express what he couldn't put into words anymore.

"Is that Sean Lee?" one of the officers asked.

"Ma'am, get away from that man!"

"Dispatch! We've got an officer down!"

Sean knew he only had moments left. He'd lost far too much blood already.

The voices blurred together. His vision was narrowing now, but he focused on her face. He concentrated on her eyes. He looked into them for as long as he could, until his own eyes closed. The pain faded, until it was like a distant speck of light. Then the world went dark.

6. Sanctuary

"Where is Zed?" the man with the beard asked.

Sophie nudged Jake's arm. "You sure you don't know this guy?"

Jake's eyes didn't leave the man. "Pretty damn sure."

The man kept walking toward them.

"Sophie, give me the book," Jake whispered. "Now."

She fumbled with the zipper on the backpack. She got it open wide enough to shove her hand inside and grab the book, then yanked it out and tossed it to him.

The man looked at Sophie and tilted his head, as if seeing her for the first time. "You've done well."

"What does he mean?" Jake asked.

Sophie shook her head. "I have no idea."

Jake suddenly thought of Carver, poor one-armed Carver. He'd been staying in the Welcome Wagon. "What happened to the man who was in the house?"

"He's still in there," the man said. "I made sure he couldn't leave after I started the fire."

Sophie gasped.

"You started all these fires?" Jake asked, a quiver in his voice.

"Yes."

"Why?" Sophie asked. "Why would you do that?"

The man shrugged. He was looking past them into the trees. "People aren't needed here. I don't like needless things."

"Who are you?" Jake asked.

The man looked at him, and Jake could feel that stare, like a hot thing burning into him. "I'm your better. Where is Zed?"

Jake opened the book and flipped through the pages. This would hurt. Usually he spent a day or so preparing his mind for the task. He'd only done it once before without the preparation, the time he had banished Zed, and that had hurt him. But there wasn't time to think about that now.

The bearded man squinted at the book. "How did you get that? It doesn't belong to you."

Jake ignored him and concentrated on the page in front of him. Usually, he could see the shape he needed to trace on the page, but it was fuzzy now, like it was hiding from him. He concentrated harder, willing his mind to see what he knew was there.

259

"How many?" Sophie asked in a brash voice. She was trying to distract the man, Jake realized. Trying to buy him a little more time to do what needed to be done. "How many people did you kill?"

Jake thought he had the shape now. He was almost certain he could see it. He set his finger on the book and began to drag it across the page. He grunted in pain and surprise. It felt like a razor was cutting into his skull. It had never felt like this before. But he had to keep going.

The man's voice sounded bored when he answered Sophie's question. "All of them. I killed all the ones in the cabins. I will kill the people in the big house after I find Zed."

"No!" Sophie screamed, and Jake pulled his eyes away from the book and looked at her. She had her gun pointed at the man.

The bearded man moved toward her with freakish quickness, caught her by the throat, and held her at arm's length, staring at her like she was an unidentified substance on the bottom of his shoe.

Jake turned back to the book. It was Sophie's only hope now. He worked faster, dragging his finger across the page. It was more difficult than it had ever been. Every millimeter of progress sent waves of agony through his brain. He felt wetness on his neck and realized both his ears were bleeding.

The man with the beard held up his empty hand and stared at it. His fingers were growing longer. He bared his teeth at Jake. "Stop that!"

Jake kept working. He wanted to help Sophie, but the best way to do that was by finishing. He was almost there, but it hurt so badly. This man was strong—maybe stronger than Zed—and he was fighting hard against what Jake was doing.

Jake thought of his family, both the one back in Rook

Mountain and the one here in Sanctuary. For their sakes, he had to keep going.

"No!" the man yelled. "I command you to stop!"

But it was too late. Jake was almost done.

The hand holding Sophie grew, and she slipped from his grip and fell gasping to the ground.

Jake was almost there. All he had to do was connect his starting point to his ending point. But, no matter how hard he pushed, he couldn't do it. His finger wouldn't move any further. It was like trying to move through concrete. His mind felt like it would explode, but he kept pushing. He kept pushing until he felt a hand on his shoulder.

"Stop," Sophie said in a scratchy voice. "You got him. You have to stop."

"No," Jake said. "It's not finished."

"But it is. Just look."

He looked up and saw a short, broad tree where the man had been standing a few moments before. It wasn't right. He knew it wasn't. He could make out the man's nose and mouth in the pattern of the bark. It wasn't finished. It might not hold.

But Sophie was right. He had to stop. He couldn't push any harder. He dropped the book and fell to his knees.

Sophie put her hand on his shoulder. "Are you okay?"

He started to answer, but a coughing fit came over him. When it passed he saw the hand that had been covering his mouth was wet with blood.

Sophie said, "Jake—"

A loud cracking sound interrupted her. Jake struggled to his feet and turned toward the sound. White light was pouring from the tree behind him. And a silhouette stood in the middle of the light. It was someone was trying to come through.

"What now?" Sophie asked in a weary voice.

"No," Jake whispered. "I think it's okay." He staggered toward the tree. When he reached it, he squinted into the light.

"Who is that? What are you doing?"

A familiar voice came out of the tree. "Jake! It's Frank."

IN THE WOODS (PART SEVEN)

1. From the Book of the Broken World

I'm from Sugar Plains, but so is everyone else. I mean, technically that's not true. Some of the older folk are from elsewhere. Some of them moved here when they were kids or whatever. But, seeing as Sugar Plains is the last town in existence (as far as we know), it's a pretty safe bet you already knew where I was from.

They tell me Sugar Plains was part of a group of towns called Illinois. The last letter was silent. The old folks always make a big deal if someone says it wrong. There were fifty of these groups of towns, and together they made an even bigger group called a country. But that was a long time ago, back when people traveled from town to town and even to other parts of the world. I don't really know why they even make a point of teaching that history stuff to us. It's like algebra. I'll never use it. That was a different time and a different world. People went wherever they wanted, even at night. The Unfeathered didn't even exist. Or maybe they did, but people hadn't discovered them. (Or they hadn't discovered how tasty people are—ha ha).

Anyway, the whole point of this assignment is for me to pretend you aren't from Sugar Plains. Like, maybe you found this paper a thousand years in the future and wanted to know what life was like in Sugar Plains in 2019. Like you don't have better things to do than read some

263

essay by a kid who barely passed Sophomore English. But, I'm trying to get into the spirit of things. I really am. My mom always tells me I am too literal. So, deep breath, serious face, here we go.

In 1985 (eighteen years before I was born, if you care), the Unfeathered showed up in Sugar Plains in the middle of the night. They killed a bunch of people. Everyone freaked out and hid in their homes. You get the idea. Have you seen Night of the Living Dead? (Do they have VHS in whatever year you are from?) It was like that, except with Unfeathered instead of zombies.

So, that all went on for a few days. Then this drifter dude named Zed goes to the mayor and says he can stop the Unfeathered. The mayor thinks he's crazy. In the mayor's defense, Zed supposedly slept on park benches and no one would go near him. But, what's the mayor got to lose, right? So he goes with it. And here comes the twist. Zed actually does stop the Unfeathered. It's like they're locked out of Sugar Plains. So as long as no one leaves town, we're all cool.

It turns out Zed's some kind of genius, and he starts figuring out how Sugar Plains is going to survive long term. He comes up with the Regulations to keep the town safe. He sends a few specialists out to gather food and supplies from surrounding towns. He starts a special school to train all the brainiac kids in town. (Guess what? Yours truly wasn't invited. Guess what else? His idiot sister was.)

Things went on like that for fifteen or twenty years. Sure, it wasn't all as smooth as I'm making it sound. I'm sure there are tons of details my teacher, the beautiful and talented Ms. Jones who is sure to appreciate my efforts on this essay, would prefer I include. But, honestly, the only thing you really need to know about is the rebellion.

This one happened while I was alive. Granted, I was only two, but still. A bunch of people in town decided they didn't like the way Zed was running the show, and they tried to kill him. They didn't have the manpower to fight the town head-on, so they started engaging in guerrilla warfare. They captured one of the police officers, tossed him across the town line, and watched the Unfeathered tear him apart. Stuff like that. Real swell group of fellas. They started fires and killed people and raised general mayhem. It went on almost a month before the police were able to stop it. They say Zed himself got involved.

Now I know what you're probably thinking. If things in Sugar Plains are as good as I am saying, why would anyone want to revolt? I guess we'll never know the answer to that question. But it's happened before, right? People don't know how good they have it. They start imagining things could be better. Maybe after a while simply following the forty-three Regulations started to feel like a burden. Maybe having their food and clothes and everything else they might need provided to them by the RESPys each week started to feel too comfortable and they took it for granted.

There's this story my mom told me. She heard it from a friend who heard it from a friend, so who knows if it's true. But I'm gonna tell it anyway. Sometimes the story and what it means is more important than whether or not it's true, you know? Zed has this pocket watch he always carries (that part is true for sure, I've seen it). Apparently during the rebellion the traitors stole Zed's watch. They had it for a few days before the police got it back for him. And what did Zed do when he finally captured those rebels? He didn't hang them or torture them or any of that stuff. He just made them disappear. Apparently a couple cops saw it happen. One second they were there and the next they were gone forever.

I tell that story to illustrate why the outlaws were wrong. They called Zed evil. Some of them even said he'd brought the Unfeathered here himself. But he proved them wrong with the efficient and merciful way he dealt with them. If he were evil, he would have made them suffer.

So if you're wondering why I have hope for the future, that's the reason. Forget everything that's happened lately. Trust is a must. That's what Zed always says, and I agree. While the rest of the world was being destroyed by the Unfeathered, Zed saved us. And he can do it again.

If you want the first-hand account of what happened next, here goes. I was eleven when it started. Things changed. Or shifted. I'm not sure of the best way to say it. I would be walking home from school and suddenly I'd be standing in a park on the other side of town. It wasn't like I moved. It was more like the town did. It was sort of chaos there for a little while, but Zed stepped in again with a new set of regulations to make things right. And then it got better. I mean, Regulation 35, no more cars, trucks, or motorcycles, how many lives has that one alone saved?

Other things started to change. These little trees started popping up around town. Zed figured out they could help us. Just like normal trees remove carbon dioxide from the air, these trees would help stabilize the town. And he was right. The shifting thing started happening less often.

The trees aren't so little anymore, of course. They grow much faster than any normal tree. The one in my yard has got to be fifty feet tall now. But the good news is the town's getting bigger too. It's like the land itself is growing with the trees. My walk to school used to be half a mile. Now it's three quarters. And the landscape is changing. Hills are developing. I remember when I was a kid this place was flat as a pancake (it is called Sugar Plains, after all). Now, not so much.

Zed has changed a bit, too. He used to be around a lot more when I was a kid. He was always making speeches at different events. He even talked at my grade school a couple times. Now, we don't see him quite as much. And, when we do, he's got this book with him. He says the trees are more than trees. They are locks. And he says the book is a way to unlock them.

Here's where it gets exciting. Once the trees are fully grown, Zed says we'll be able to use them as doorways to other special places, places that are important like Sugar Plains. He says we might even be able to use them to travel into the future. Or the past.

He did this little demonstration in town square last Regulation Day.

One of the biggest trees is there. He did something with that book of his, and a tiny beam of light shot out of the tree. It was about the size of a pea, and it only lasted for a minute. But Zed says as the tree gets bigger, so will the hole. Eventually, it'll be a doorway and we'll be able to leave it open for days at a time.

I don't know exactly how long it'll take before that happens, and I'm not sure if Zed does either. All I know is I hope I live to see it. I would love to walk through a doorway and be on the other side of the world. Or maybe go back to before the Unfeathered came. I think I'd love to drive a car. Maybe a convertible, like in the movies. I'd speed down the street, wind in my hair, not a single Unfeathered in the sky. Or maybe travel into the future and see how society turns out. I could see all the statues of Zed and the leaders of Sugar Plains

So, hypothetical future man or lady, that's the way things are in Sugar Plains in 2019. We live in a transitional time. That's what Zed always says. I am proud to be alive in this strange time, and I am proud to be a citizen of Sugar Plains.

I don't know what will happen next, but I trust it'll be interesting. Trust is a must.

2.

The entry ended there. Frank flipped through the rest of the book, but all he saw were drawings of trees and words written in a strange language he couldn't read. He closed the book and a shiver went through him.

The story of Sugar Plains eerily mirrored one that was all too familiar to him. The realization that Zed had done this before, that Rook Mountain wasn't Zed's first attempt to take over a town, hit Frank like a bowling ball to the gut. Those trees in the story...were they the trees that surrounded him now? Was he *in* the former Sugar Plains, Illinois?

He ran his fingers through his hair as he thought. It didn't make sense. If Zed had taken another town outside of time in 1985, wouldn't somebody have noticed? What about all the missing people? This should have been a huge news story.

Another chilling thought: what if Sugar Plains wasn't Zed's first time either? How many times had he done this?

He stood up and looked at the compass in his hand. He'd asked the compass for information on how to get out of here, and it had shown him those pages. Did that mean the trees were his way out? And if that was true...if the trees really were gateways to other times and places...if time was no longer an uncrossable barrier...

He pressed the broken clock symbol and spoke his direction aloud. "Take me to the tree that gets me to Jake."

The needle on the compass spun clockwise a quarter turn and stuck there. Frank took a deep breath to quell the rising hope within him and stepped out of the cabin.

He followed the needle for nearly half an hour. It was a nerve-wracking journey, his eyes constantly flicking between the compass, the ground, and the trees, hoping he wouldn't see any of the Larvae and at the same time hoping he'd see one so that it couldn't catch him by surprise.

He spotted four Larvae on his walk, but he managed to skirt around them without incident.

Finally, he arrived at the tree. He walked around it once and watched the needle turn with his movements, making sure this was the tree the needle was locked onto.

The entry said Zed used the book to open the gateway. *Thank God for this stupid compass*, he thought. Once again, the compass guided him to the correct page.

The page was covered with a dozen drawings of trees of various sizes in various artistic styles. The compass pointed him to one particular drawing.

He paused for a moment. What did he do now?

"You have to trace the picture with your finger."

The deep, baritone voice startled him. His head snapped up and he saw the bearded man, the man he had seen standing behind Mason at the stream, standing ten feet in front of him. Frank could see more than just his face now.

The man was dressed in what Frank could only describe as a tunic. It was a loose fitting bluish item of clothing that covered him from shoulder to ankle. It was sleeveless, revealing the man's thick, well-muscled arms. His beard was a bushy, dirty thing with bits of twigs lodged in it. His face and arms were splattered with mud.

"Who the hell are you?" Frank asked. Zed had seemed afraid at the mention of this man. Anyone who didn't get along with Zed could be an ally.

The man scoffed. "Please. Explaining myself to you would be like a mountain explaining itself to an ant."

"Huh," Frank said. So maybe not the friendliest of allies, then.

"Trace the picture with your finger, my little ant. Go to your brother. Serve your purpose."

Then, as if he had never been standing there, the man was gone. Frank didn't know if the man had quickly ducked into the foliage or if he had disappeared through some other means. All that mattered now was getting to Jake.

He put his finger on the page, then hesitated. What if he wasn't doing the right thing? Or, what if he was doing exactly what Zed wanted? Hadn't the entry said Zed wanted to open the gates?

The thoughts gave him pause for only a moment. To hell with all that; he wanted to see his brother.

He traced the picture with his index finger.

As he dragged his finger across the page, it felt like someone was dragging a finger across his mind. It was like something was being pulled out of him. Something vital.

Then it was over.

The bark in front of Frank split and hot white light poured through. Frank squinted at the opening, watching as it widened. Soon it was the size of a door. He reached toward the gap, slowly piercing the light with his hand.

Suddenly the dark silhouette of a man appeared. The shape was moving forward, but unsteadily, stumbling as it came. It paused near the doorway and tilted its head, as if looking out at Frank.

"Who is that?" asked the silhouette. "What are you doing?"

Frank's heart leapt at the sound of the voice he knew so well. The voice of the man he'd spent so long trying to find. "Jake! It's Frank."

3.

Frank squinted into the light at his brother's silhouette.

"Frank?" Jake asked. His voice sounded weak. Strained somehow. "My God, is that really you? What are you doing here?"

Frank couldn't help but grin. "I got your message." He held up the Cassandra lock.

"How did you open this door?"

Frank shook his head. "I'm coming through. I'll explain everything in a moment."

He pushed himself into the light. And the light pushed back. It gave off a painful white heat and it seemed to solidify as he pressed against it. It was like wrestling against a wall of earth.

"Frank, stop. You can't get through like that. I have to pull you."

Frank fell backwards a step, recoiling from the force of the light. He looked down at his hands, expecting them to be burned, but they were unmarked. "Alright. Pull me through."

There was a long pause. "Not now. Listen, some bad stuff is going on here. Very bad. Like, Zed bad. You need to stay in Rook Mountain. It's not safe here."

"No, you don't understand. I already left Rook Mountain. I'm in...Sugar Plains. I just got here later than you did. Way later. I came through the mirror."

Another long pause. "I thought you said you got my message."

"I did. That's why I came."

"But I said to meet me at the quarry—" Jake's words were cut off as a fit of coughing overtook him. Even through the muffled haze of the doorway, that cough did not sound good to Frank. Not good at all.

After Jake's coughing subsided, Frank said, "Will and Christine told me *meet me at the quarry* was your signal the coin wasn't safe at Sean's house. Look, Jake, it's not safe where I am either. I've got Zed problems of my own."

"You...you don't remember do you?"

Frank glanced over his shoulder making sure none of the Larvae were nearby. He'd spent all this time searching for Jake, and thirty seconds into their grand reunion, his brother was annoyed with him. "Remember what?"

"The quarry! When we were kids. Don't you remember the quarry?"

Frank had no idea what his brother was talking about. He stared at the light in stunned silence.

"That's why I used quarry as a codeword with Sean and the others," Jake said. "Because of what happened to us when we were kids. Are you seriously telling me you don't remember the quarry?"

Frank racked his brain. What Jake was saying didn't sound the least bit familiar. And yet...there was something there. Like a blank spot. Like a hole where something should be. But he couldn't think about that now. There was too much happening, too many moving parts. And if he was honest, he didn't want to think about it. There was something scary about that hole in his memory.

"Jake, please pull me through."

There was a long pause. Jake's voice sounded weary when he spoke. "Yeah. Okay. And Frank?"

"Yeah?"

"Thanks for coming."

Frank nodded, afraid he wouldn't be able to get his words around the lump in his throat.

Frank heard another voice, a woman's voice. Jake said something back to her. He couldn't hear what they were saying—they must have been turned away from the gate—but it sounded like they were arguing.

After a moment, he heard Jake's voice more clearly, as if he'd turned back toward the door in the tree. "Frank, I'm gonna pull you through now. You ready?"

Frank said, "Let's do it."

Then he waited in silence. He remembered his own experience with the book, the way it had pulled on his mind and his every bit of attention while he was using it. Was it the same for Jake?

He kept quiet. He didn't want to distract his brother. At the same time, the adrenaline was pumping through his veins. He was about to see Jake at long last.

This wouldn't be the end. They still had so much work to

do. They needed to figure out what exactly it was Zed wanted, and they had to figure out how to stop him from getting it. They needed to deal with this woman, the one Mason said killed Jake. They needed to keep Jake from dying and keep Mason from growing up alone in the forest with only Zed to take care of him. And they needed to figure out how to get back to Rook Mountain for good.

But whatever they did, they would do it together. They hadn't always been the closest of friends, but there was no denying their bond of blood. There was no one Frank would rather have on his side in a fight. Not Ty Hansen or Christine or Will or anyone. And that was saying something.

He felt a twinge, a slight push. It was as if a stiff wind was moving him toward the tree. He took a step forward and leaned into the light. It was warm now rather than hot, like slipping into a warm bath.

The bright light was all around him now, too bright to see in either direction, back or forward.

He heard someone yell.

Frank stepped out of the light and into the forest and froze. His brother's body lay at his feet.

4.

Mason watched the light coming through the door in the tree, his jaw open in shock. Frank had done it again. How long had Mason and Zed worked to find a way out? How many avenues had they pursued? How many hours had they dedicated to considering the problem?

And here comes Frank Hinkle. Not only did he best Zed on the roof of City Hall in Rook Mountain that day so long ago. Not only did he find the book. Now he also found a way out, and he did it mere hours after arriving.

Mason had followed the voices and the light to this place, and now, crouching and hidden in the ferns, he couldn't believe what he was seeing.

He had almost no sense of entitlement. He spent no time wondering why he, out of all the children in the populated world, had been born in Sanctuary. Or why his parents had died. Or why he had to grow up alone in the woods but for Zed's occasional appearance. But this—Frank finding a way out of the woods so quickly—this didn't seem fair to Mason. It should have been him. He was the one who'd grown up there, the one who knew the woods, even in its ever-changing state, like the back of his own hand.

If Mason had found a way out, he'd have humbly presented it to Zed. It would have allowed him to express his gratitude in a way words never could.

But not Frank. Oh no, not Frank. Even after all his promises of taking Mason with him when he left, there he was stepping through all by his lonesome. The evidence of Frank's betrayal was right there before his eyes.

He shouldn't have been surprised or upset by any of this. It confirmed what Zed had always told him. People were scum.

He rose and moved closer, the gun raised. He crept carefully, staying behind cover, but he quickly realized Frank was so enthralled with whatever was on the other side of the light that Mason probably could have tapped his uncle on the shoulder without the man noticing. He got as close as he could and switched to a two-hand grip.

Mason knew this wasn't his fault. He'd warned Frank. Now Frank had to pay. And Mason would be the one to show the open gate to Zed. Exactly as it should be.

He lined up the sites on Frank's head.

Frank stepped forward into the light. He was gone. And so

was the light. The tree was just an ordinary tree again.

Mason sat crouched in the ferns for a long time, his own failure lingering like a bitter taste in his mouth. After a while —he wasn't sure how long—he felt a presence behind him.

"I was close," Mason said. "He opened a gate in the door. Light came out and he disappeared into it. I couldn't stop him."

"Yes," Zed said. "It seems you've failed."

Mason turned his head. The look on Zed's face wasn't anger; it was sadness. That was far worse. "I had him cornered. I had my gun on him and he was unarmed. I should have shot him."

"That would have been a very bad idea. We still need him. How'd he get away from you?"

"He did this....whistle. And then one of the Larvae attacked me."

Zed shook his head. "My friend, believe me when I say I have felt your pain. Almost exactly. I forgive you. We'll be seeing your uncle again. Very soon."

Mason felt a hand on his shoulder, and then Zed continued.

"Have you ever wondered why I helped you? Why I showed you how to take care of yourself and survive in the forest?"

Mason licked his lips. "I never had to wonder. It was because of your generosity. You're a good person."

Zed chuckled. "I may do good things at times, but whether I'm a good person is highly debatable." He patted Mason's shoulder. "No, I took care of you because I thought I might need you. In my experience, Hinkles are unique talents. Your dad proved that with the way he used the book in Sanctuary. And your uncle has his locks and his impenetrable mind. But you turned out to be one of the most ordinary and useless human beings I have yet to encounter. You're completely worthless to me."

Mason looked at Zed with wide eyes. The lump in his throat made it difficult to speak. "Zed...I tried...I tried to bring him to you."

Zed's signature smile was back now. "Ah, Mason, that's exactly the type of incompetence I am talking about. Thankfully, Frank is proving to be much less clever than I remembered. The book can't pass through the gate. He was carrying it when he went through. Which means it's lying right in front of that tree." He winked at Mason. "Let's go get it, shall we?"

Zed walked to the tree where Frank had disappeared.

There it was on the ground. The book.

Zed picked it up and carefully brushed a bit of dirt off the cover.

A look of peace washed over his face. For the first time in the many years Mason had known him, Zed wasn't smiling or frowning. His face was relaxed.

After a moment, Zed opened the book, and his wide smile returned.

CHAPTER EIGHT: A PLACE WITHOUT SHADOWS

1. Sanctuary

Sophie scanned the ground for Larvae as Jake staggered to the tree. He stood there for a long time, hunched over and bleeding, talking into the tree like some kind of idiot. She felt uneasy as she watched. A change came over him. He seemed different than she'd ever seen him. He was animated in his movements.

Then Jake opened the book and put his finger on the page.

"Jake! What are you doing, man?" She sprinted toward him.

He looked up at her. His eyes were so bloodshot, she could barely make out any white. The skin seemed to be hanging off his face. The man looked like he'd lost thirty pounds in the last ten minutes.

"Sophie, I'm not going to make it. The book has used me up. Banishing the guy with the beard broke me. You need help."

"What are you talking about? Put the book away."

He scrunched up his face in a pained smile. "Trust Frank. Protect Mason." He turned back to the tree. "Frank, I'm gonna pull you through now. You ready?"

A voice from within the light said, "Let's do it."

Before Sophie could stop him, Jake dragged his hand across the page. As he did it, he yelled in pain. The light from the tree brightened ten-fold, enveloping them both. Then the light was gone.

Jake lay at her feet, his eyes wide open. He wasn't moving. Wasn't breathing.

She dropped to her knees and touched his cheek. His face was cold and stiff. It was like he'd been dead for hours.

Through the tears, she looked up and saw a man standing in front of the tree.

Sophie lifted her gun with a shaky hand and pointed it at him.

The resemblance to Jake was uncanny. This man was a little thinner, and his hair was a striking combination of black and gray instead of the blondish gray mix of Jake's hair. He may have been a bit taller too. He was shirtless, and his arm was wrapped in a blood-soaked tee shirt. But around the eyes, this man looked like Jake.

The man stared down at Jake, his mouth agape.

"Don't move!" Sophie yelled. The man looked up at her, and she saw the tears in his eyes.

"Did you shoot him?" he asked, his voice choked with emotion.

"What? No. Why would you ask that?"

He shook his head. "Who are you? What's going on here? What happened to my brother?"

"Brother?"

He nodded. "My name's Frank Hinkle. Jake's my brother."

Sophie suddenly realized she hadn't even known Jake's last name.

"Damn it!" Frank said. The tears were coming now. "I

finally found him. I've been looking for so long. And now…"

Sophie wiped at the tears running down her face with an angry hand. Jake had told her to trust this man, but she couldn't help but be furious at him. "He died bringing you through."

Frank look stunned. "No. Why would he do that?"

"Because he needed your help. Bad things are happening here. So bad, I don't even know where to—"

Sophie stopped. Frank was reaching for the book lying next to Jake.

She brought her gun back up. "You stay away from that book."

Frank looked up at her. Tears streaked his face.

She said, "If you're his brother, you must be from Rook Mountain. I take it you know about this Zed guy."

Frank nodded. "I'm sorry to say I do."

"Well, he screwed me over."

"Join the club."

"He's loose. Jake was gonna try to use the book to banish Zed."

"Banish him?"

"Yeah, um, turn him into a tree. God, that sounds stupid when I say it out loud. Do you know how to use the book? Could you banish Zed?"

He shook his head. "You're from Sanctuary? And you say people are dying?"

She nodded.

"Well, Sophie, I'm not sure how to say this, but, you and I? We aren't gonna live through this thing. You know that kid, Mason? He's the only one who makes it."

She shook her head. "How could you know that?"

He smiled weakly. "I come from the future."

She started to say she didn't believe him, but then she remembered she'd just suggested they turn a man into a tree.

"Wait," Frank said. "There might be a way. Do you have the compass?"

"How do you know that?"

"Mason. He told me there was a woman who...who had the compass." Something about the way he said it made her think Mason had told him more than that. "I was wondering if it was you. Anyway that's how I got here."

"What do you mean?"

He held out a hand, indicating the forest around them. "These trees are doors. Well, I guess you saw that. But some of them take you to different times. I had the compass. All I did was hold it and ask it to take me to Jake."

She nodded slowly. What he was saying made sense. If the trees could really take you to different times...

She pulled out the compass, and thought Jake. Living Jake, not the dead one here in front of me.

"It's not working."

Frank frowned. "Did you press the broken clock symbol? You have to do that."

She glared at him. "Yeah, I've used this thing a time or two."

"I'll try too." He reached into his pocket and pulled out an identical compass.

"There's more than one of them?" she asked, her eyes wide with surprise.

"No. This is the same one as yours. It's the future version." He tapped the side of it. "It's not working for me either. We need to hide the book. That's what Zed wants. And if he gets it..."

"What? What will happen if he gets it?"

"Well, honestly, I have no idea. But prior experience leads me to believe it won't be good."

"And you know where you can hide it?"

Frank nodded. "Yeah."

He bent down and kissed Jake's forehead. He said it quietly, but Sophie still heard. "I'm sorry I didn't get here sooner." He paused for a moment, his mouth a thin line, his face streaked with tears. Then he took a deep breath and said, "Here's the thing. I have reason to believe I shouldn't trust you. Granted, it came from a very unreliable source. But still, I can't take the chance. So, apologies in advance."

He stuck his hand into his pocket and disappeared.

Sophie gasped. She brought the gun up and held it in front of her.

The book, which had been lying near her feet, disappeared too.

"Hey man, show yourself."

Frank said, "I've got to fly solo on this one."

She couldn't even tell which direction his voice was coming from. She waited to see if he'd speak again, but he didn't. She was alone.

2. Sanctuary

For the past few years, Nate had often wondered what would have happened if he'd never gone to see Zed speak in the park that day so long ago. He'd been drawn in from the moment Zed opened his mouth. What other people in town had seen as weirdness, Nate had recognized as genius. And the best part was Zed had seen something in Nate as well.

A fairly large group had been coming by then. Not huge, but probably two dozen. Zed had taken one look at Nate and invited him to talk one-on-one. And that had been that. Zed was the first person in Nate's life that had seen him as special. Oh sure, a few others had said it. His parents. The occasional teacher. Mr. Rogers on TV. But there had been something different about the way Zed had said it. It wasn't like he was saying it to make Nate feel good. He was simply stating a fact.

It had taken a long time, but, after watching Jake's leadership style and thinking back on what had gone down in Rook Mountain, Nate had finally realized something: Zed was an asshole.

Now that theory was confirmed.

He was still reeling from the death and destruction he and Leonard had seen. They'd gone to warn the others, to make sure they weren't caught unaware by the unbanished people and their Larvae. But they had been too late. The first cabin they came to was Yang's. He laid dead the middle of his living room. Pieces of him were gone, presumably carved away by the Larvae. Or maybe their naked friends. Or both.

When they left Yang's cabin, they saw the fires. Someone was burning the cabins. They saw shapes through the smoke, shapes with round things on the tops of their shoulders and the ends of their hands. At that point, Nate decided it was time to start thinking about survival, and he and Leonard retreated to Jake's house.

"So what's the plan?" Nate asked after they were inside. Three of the formerly banished residents of Sanctuary were slogging toward the house, each wielding four Larvae. Nate and Logan watched the approach through the window.

Logan nodded toward the two on the right. "The woman's Rosenberg and the guy's Harris. Old pals of mine."

Nate recognized the other one. His name was Gilbert. Logan said, "Let's see if they get through the door. If they do, Nate, Leonard, you take down Rosenberg. Kill the Larvae

first. Then hold her down and Taylor will chop the head off.
Evan and Gail, you do the same for Harris. Frasier and I'll
take Gilbert." She turned to Mason who was still standing
behind her. "Honey, I need you to go in the bathroom
upstairs. Lock the door and don't come out until I tell you.
No matter what you hear. Try to be as quiet as you can.
Understand?"

The boy nodded.

"Good," Logan said. "Go. Now."

He hurried off down the hall.

The three unbanished reached the house, and there was a
banging, grinding sound. Larvae spikes broke through the
door, splitting the wood, and then disappeared again, leaving
long thin gashes.

"That door's coming down in a minute," Logan said.
"Everybody ready?"

No one replied. Their eyes were glued to the door.

Fear hung thick in the air. Nate felt it penetrating his every
pore. These weren't soldiers. They were just people. And now
they were being asked to fight monsters. It wasn't fair, and it
was a wonder they were holding up as well as they were.

The wood buckled inward, and Gilbert was the first
through the gap. Logan and Frasier rushed toward him.

Nate looked at Leonard. "Ready?"

He had his knife gripped tightly in his hand. He nodded.

"I'll take the right side, you take the left." Nate didn't wait
for an acknowledgment. Rosenberg was through the door
now. He rushed at her.

He saw the soft spot, the spot Sophie had shown them, on
the Larva on Rosenberg's right shoulder, and he stabbed at it.
His knife sunk into the creature with a satisfying crunch. He
felt spikes brush past his cheek as Rosenberg tried to grab

him.

He grabbed the wrist as her right hand flew past him, and dispatched that Larva too. The smell of the dissolving Larvae hit his nose, an intensely sweet stench like rotting fruit.

Leonard moved in, taking out the one on Rosenberg's left shoulder.

Nate felt his arm go numb as Rosenberg slapped him in the shoulder with the creature in her left hand. His first thought was of Carver and how he'd lost his arm after a similar injury. He pushed the thought away. He needed to concentrate, and thoughts of amputation, let alone thoughts of how Carver was likely burning in the Welcome Wagon right now, weren't helping.

Leonard stabbed the Larva.

"Thanks," Nate said. He tried to block out the pain in his arm. He knew they had to take Rosenberg down quick before she could call for backup. He wrapped his arms around her, fighting the urge to recoil at the texture of her cold waxy skin, and threw her to the ground. "Grab the legs!" he shouted to Leonard.

Nate pinned her arms to the ground. "Taylor! We've got her."

Taylor sprinted toward them, and Nate barely had time to lean back as the ax whizzed past his face and separated Rosenberg's head from her body. A spray of greenish-red liquid caught Nate in the face, and with it a rotten smell like decomposing vegetables.

Nate looked at Leonard. "You all okay?"

The man nodded, but he was deathly pale.

Leonard pointed. "Looks like Evan could use a hand."

Nate spun his head around. Evan held Harris by the wrists, and he was backpedaling while desperately tried to keep out of the reach of the Larvae on the man's hands and shoulders. Gail was on the ground next to him, struggling to find her feet. Blood oozed out of a nasty gash in her left cheek.

Nate and Leonard ran to their aid. With Evan holding Harris's wrists, they made short work of the Larvae.

Nate tackled Harris and the group held him down. "Taylor, we've got him ready!"

Taylor stood over Rosenberg, looking down at her. He slowly wiped the blade of his ax on his shirt, his eyes distant.

"Taylor, wake up!" Nate screamed. "We need you here!"

But it was too late. Harris threw back his head and let out the piercing whine Nate had heard earlier.

"Taylor, now!"

Taylor finally looked up. His eyes were alive, and Nate didn't like what he saw there. It looked like a strangled mix of anger and pure joy. He galloped to them and swung the ax, removing Harris's head in one stroke.

Four Larvae had answered Harris's call and were speeding through the door of the building. Frasier was on the ground, still on top of the now headless Gilbert. He didn't see the Larva rushing toward him. It slammed into the back of his skull, and he fell to the ground.

Logan quickly stabbed the Larva and it fell away. Nate, Gail, and Leonard dispatched the other three creatures.

Logan rolled Frasier over. "Frasier! You still with us."

Frasier groaned weakly. His eyes were cloudy and unfocused.

Nate leapt to his feet. "Damn it, Taylor! What the hell's wrong with you?"

He was once again wiping his ax on his tee shirt. "What's the problem?"

Nate rushed toward him, getting up in his face. "The

problem? I was calling you and you didn't come! You just stood there!"

Taylor didn't flinch. "Yeah, sorry about that," he said, looking anything but. "I guess I spaced out for a second."

Nate wanted to punch the guy, but he knew he needed to save his strength. "You spaced out? Really? In the middle of a fight for our lives?"

Suddenly, Nate felt something. Something he hadn't felt in a long time. Back in Rook Mountain, Zed had given Nate and the other selectmen a bit of telepathy. The power had vanished when Zed disappeared on the roof of city hall, but Nate felt a tiny twinge of that old telepathy now. He saw a flash of something in Taylor's mind. Something dark.

Then it was gone.

"Okay, enough," Logan said. "Look."

Darcy, a woman of fifty, came running into the room. Her clothes were torn in a dozen places, and her face was bloody. "They're coming! They're on their way!"

Logan grabbed her shoulders. "Whoa. Calm down. Explain."

Darcy took a deep breath. "They went cabin to cabin killing everyone inside. They're burning the cabins. There's blood everywhere. Must have been seven or eight of them. And there was a man with a beard. He seemed to be leading them."

Nate felt his heart sink. How many were dead? How many of his friends? Hell, he might as well say it: these people were his family.

"I went out the window," Darcy said. "I thought I was dead, but I killed the Larva on its hand like Sophie showed us. Then I slipped away. They're on their way here right now. They're traveling like a pack."

"What do we do?" Nate asked. "Run? Scatter into the woods?"

Logan shook her head. "It takes at least two of us to take down one of them. If we scatter they'll pick us off one by one."

"Alright," Nate said. "Maybe I can talk to Zed. He and I were close once. Maybe I can bargain for our lives."

"Don't be an idiot," Logan spat.

"Why is diplomacy idiotic?"

"You really need me to list the reasons? First, you don't know where he is. Second, Jake and Sophie are already out there trying to find him. Third, he probably sent a hoard of zombie plant monsters to kill us, so he doesn't seem reasonable. Fourth, we don't even know he's the one controlling them. Maybe this is what people are like when they come back from banishment."

Nate opened his mouth to respond but then paused. He couldn't refute any of her points. "Okay. I give. What do we do?"

Logan looked out the window down the trail and Nate followed her gaze. There they were. A hoard of eight people wielding thirty-two Larvae.

She sighed. "Maybe we can do this different than last time. Their heads seem to come off pretty easy. Let's gather near the door. They can only come through one, maybe two at a time tops. Taylor, give me your ax. I'll take off their heads as quickly as I can. Then the rest of you'll deal with the Larvae. Deal?"

She held out her hand. Taylor frowned at the ax for a long moment, his brow furrowed.

"Come on, man," Logan said.

He handed over the ax, then pulled a knife out of his belt

with what looked to Nate like melancholy.

"Logan," Nate said, "you sure you don't want me to take ax duty?"

"You don't think I can handle it?"

"That's not what I'm saying. At all. But that kid needs you."

Logan smiled. "That's exactly why I can't trust one of you nerds with the ax. Or Captain Space-Out there. I want us to survive this."

Nate held up his hands in mock surrender. "Okay, okay. Just thought I'd offer."

The unbanished were almost at the door.

Nate gripped his knife. "Everybody ready?"

A chorus of tentative, vaguely affirmative noises came back to him.

Logan raised her ax. "If we make it through this, we really need to start having cadence drills or something. That was weak."

The first naked man stepped across the threshold, and Logan swung her ax.

What happened next was a blur to Nate. The battle may have lasted three minutes and it may have lasted thirty. All sense of time and reality was lost for him. All he knew was the glint of his knife blade, the sharp cries of the injured, and the terrible sights and smells of wounds and death.

Logan neatly knocked off the heads of the first four banished. Leonard took a bad wound to the side, but, other than that, they killed the first twenty Larvae without trouble.

Logan moved like an unholy force of nature. There was no hesitation, no sign of concern for her own safety. It was as if she had been born for this moment.

The fifth man through the door was smarter or luckier than the rest. He lunged a step to the left as Logan swung at him, causing her ax to ricochet off the Larva on his shoulder.

"Logan!" Nate yelled, but it was too late. The man in the doorway grabbed the Logan's ax and pulled, dragging her outside. There was flurry of movement, and Logan went down. He never even heard her cry out.

He choked back his emotion. He couldn't lose it. Not now. Not with the rest of them trying to survive. He saw the handle of the ax sticking inside the doorway. He reached out, intending take over for the fallen Logan, but another arm snaked past him and grabbed the ax.

"I got this," Taylor said, lifting the ax.

Nate paused, then nodded.

True to his word, Taylor quickly decapitated the next two who tried to pass through. The third one got by him as he was trying to pull his ax from the stubborn neck of the last man he'd taken down.

The man sprinted forward and drove a Larva-baring fist into Leonard's face. He spun and shoved the other fist into the side of Darcy's head.

Nate screamed in rage, and dropped the two Larvae who were hurting his friends. Gail felled the two on the man's shoulders, and Taylor quickly followed up with an ax to the neck.

It was too late for Leonard and Darcy, though.

Nate looked around. It was only him, Taylor, and Gail left. And Mason, of course, who was still locked in the bathroom.

They all turned toward the door. Only one of the unbanished left. He moved toward the doorway, seeming to walk slower than the rest of them had. Nate recognized this one. Dale. He'd been banished for attacking a woman a few years ago.

Taylor moved back to the door. As Dale approached,

Taylor swung his ax hard, taking off the man's head in a single blow. Nate and Gail dove forward, killing the Larvae.

Nate was almost sad as he stabbed the last of the creatures. He wished he could kill it again. Kill it a hundred times for the damage its brothers and sisters had done to the people of Sanctuary. Instead, he sat there, dazed, watching the black sludge run off his knife blade.

There was a flash in his head, another tiny bit of his old telepathy. Something powerful was happening in Taylor's mind. Something primal.

Suddenly, Gail cried out in pain and surprise. Nate spun around. Had they missed one of the Larvae?

What he saw stopped him cold. Even now, even after all this, he wasn't prepared for what he saw. Then there was a blur of movement, and it was his turn to cry out.

3. Sanctuary

Sophie made her way up the path toward the house, silently cursing Jake's annoying, untrustworthy, and apparently magical brother. It hardly seemed fair; invisibility was cheating.

He had the book. He had a compass. He claimed he wanted to hide the book from Zed, but who knew for certain?

Worst of all, her own compass couldn't seem to locate him. He'd somehow made himself invisible even to the Tool.

Jake was dead. The book was gone. She had no way to find Frank. All she could think to do was head back to Jake's house. The men and women there could be fighting the unbanished people right now. She had to try to help them.

Thankfully, today the trail back to the house wasn't long. It took her less than fifteen minutes.

When she was almost there, she stopped and gasped. She surveyed the carnage on the porch. Bodies. Heads. So many of the unbanished. Then she saw something else out of the corner of her eye, a swatch of clothing. She put a hand over her mouth.

It was Logan, dead on the ground. Tears sprang to her eyes.

There was Darcy. And Evan. And Leonard, sweet Leonard, who'd had such a crush on her. And, oh God, there was Frasier.

All dead. Them and more.

She had done this. It was her fault. It was all on her.

A sudden noise made her look up.

Taylor sat on the floor near the open doorway, a bloody ax lying across his outstretched legs.

"Hello, Sophie Porter."

Sophie stepped back. "What happened here?"

Taylor smiled. "I think you know. You set them free, and they came here to kill us." He picked up the ax and twirled it in his hands. "Hell of a thing, isn't it? I'm the one person you wanted dead, and here I am the only one to survive the attack you started."

Tears were running down Sophie's face now.

Taylor pushed himself up and struggled to his feet.

Sophie saw Nate on the ground inside the door and let out another cry of sorrow. He lay on his stomach, his left cheek against the floor. The back of his head was split open. That was no Larva wound.

"Taylor, what did you do?"

He was walking toward her, sauntering forward, using the ax like a cane. She cursed herself for not running the moment she saw him.

"Come on," he said. "It's not like any of us were gonna survive anyway. I'm done playing house."

She swung her backpack off her back and quickly unzipped it. She reached inside, searching for the gun. Her hand closed around something else instead, something metal. The compass.

Taylor was moving toward her now, much faster than she would have thought possible for such a big man. And he was swinging the ax. She tried to backpedal, but he was coming too fast.

He was holding the head of the ax and swinging the handle at her, she realized. He wanted to bludgeon her. Just like Heather.

The ax handle collided with her head, and she collapsed. Everything went dark.

She opened her eyes and saw two small legs in front of her. The boy bent down and took the compass out of her hand. She tried to speak, but everything went dark before she could.

The next time she opened her eyes, she heard Taylor whistling.

Her first thought was relief. She was alive. She reached up and felt her head. God, it hurt. But it wasn't split open. There was no blood on her hand when she pulled it away from her head.

Taylor was crouched on the ground across the room, watching her. Had he been watching the whole time she was passed out? "Glad you're awake. I was afraid I might have swung too hard. I get carried away sometimes. Like with your sister."

She groggily raised herself to a sitting position. The world was swimming before her eyes. She blinked hard three times and things cleared up a little.

"You know, I actually like you. You've got a lot of fight. This is gonna be fun." He smiled a toothy grin, his misshapen face wrinkling like a rotten apple.

Sophie looked around, searching desperately for her backpack, but it was gone. Her gun had been in there. She felt her belt. The knife was gone too.

Taylor got to his feet. "The challenge is to see how many times I can hit you in the head and keep you alive. Sort of an exercise in self-restraint. I gotta hit you hard enough that it'll be satisfying, but not so hard that you die. Understand?"

"Go to hell!" Sophie yelled. She crab-walked backwards away from him. He followed, the ax over his shoulder, taking one long slow step at a time.

"I'm betting I can do four. Maybe five. But, like I said, I do get carried away sometimes."

Behind Taylor, Sophie saw Nate's body roll over. That was impossible. She'd seen the way his head was split open. There was no way he could be alive. It was almost as if someone were moving him.

Taylor shifted the ax to a two hand grip. "Okay, ready to get started?"

Something flew through the air and landed on the ground next to Sophie. A knife.

Taylor squinted at it. "What the hell?" He spun around to see who had tossed it. That was all the time Sophie needed.

She grabbed the knife, tucked her feet under her, and sprang up. Taylor turned back, a confused look on his face. The confusion quickly melted into shock as Sophie brought the knife around and stuck it in his neck.

He staggered backwards three steps and collapsed. Sophie picked up the ax off the ground. She paused wondering if she should say something. Something like, *This is for Heather.*

293

But no, there was no joy in this. It was just something that had to be done. She wouldn't gloat.

She lifted the ax and finished the job.

Looking toward the doorway, she said, "Thanks."

Suddenly Frank was standing there next to Nate's now face-up body. "You're welcome." He stepped forward. "I, uh, thought about taking him out. Seemed like maybe it was something you needed to do yourself. From what he said about your sister and all."

Sophie shuddered. She suddenly wanted nothing more than to leave, to be away from all this death and destruction. "So, you got a Bilbo Baggins ring or what?"

"Huh?"

"The invisibility thing."

"Oh. Come on, I'll show you." He ducked into Jake's office. Sophie followed him, carefully sidestepping the bodies in her path. The old lockbox was sitting on the desk.

"I found this under the desk. I put the book inside," Frank said. "Now watch this."

He pulled a strange metal object out of his pocket. It was a silver hoop hooked into a metal square.

"What is that thing?" she asked.

"It's a lock. To open it, you twist, squeeze, and then pull. Watch." He demonstrated, and the lock popped open. "Now, here's the cool part." He put the lock on the box. When he snapped the lock shut, the box disappeared.

"No way." Sophie reached out and touched where the box had been. Her fingers passed through the air as though nothing was there.

He looked at her. "It'll be safe from Zed."

"You sure?"

He smiled weakly. "I'm from the future, remember?"

She grunted in reply. "So you trust me now?"

Frank ran a hand through his hair. "I don't know. Turns out the info I had on you was a little off. I trust you more than Zed. I know that much."

"What do we do now?"

Frank shook his head. "Mason told me you were dead by the time he took the compass from you. And he didn't mention me being here. I don't know how this ends."

"Mason," Sophie said. "We need to find him. Before Zed does. Then we need to search for survivors. Maybe try to put out the fires. I don't know. I wish I still had the compass."

"I've got mine."

"What do we do if we run into Zed?" she asked.

"I don't know. I've got another lock. We can hide if we need to." He pressed the broken clock symbol and closed his eyes for a moment. "Okay. Let's go."

They made their way out of the house, past the bodies of the people Sophie had known and the unbanished that she hadn't. Past the bodies of strangers and friends.

"What are we gonna do when we find Mason?" Frank asked.

"I don't know. But we can't leave him alone out there."

They didn't have to walk far before they saw a figure standing in the middle of the trail. Zed.

"Well, this ain't good," Frank muttered.

Zed wore a set of loose, ill-fitting khakis and a tee-shirt.

"Good Lord," Zed said, a quizzical smile on his face. "Is that Frank Hinkle?"

"Nice outfit," Frank said.

"Thank you. I got it out of one of the cabins before that idiot burned it." Zed said. "Where in the world did you come from? I take it you came through the mirror?"

"Where's Mason?" Sophie said.

"The kid?" Zed asked. "He's hiding in the woods a little way from here. I'll deal with him next."

Sophie pulled out her knife. "Leave him alone."

Zed waved a dismissive hand toward her. "It's beautiful, isn't it, Frank? You see now what I had planned for Rook Mountain. After the people are gone and the town is disconnected from reality, there are so many wonderful things you can do."

Frank spoke through gritted teeth. "This is your master plan? To turn towns into weird little forests?"

Zed chuckled. "They're so much more than that. These weird little forests are the only places I'm safe. Think of it as building a castle with a moat around it. And, the forests provide me what I need to do my real work."

"What's that?" Frank asked. "Babysitting Larvae?"

Zed's smile wavered for just a moment. "The Larvae are an unfortunate side effect. They grow up to be the Ones Who Sing, after all. And trust me when I say I don't want that."

Sophie glanced at Frank. "What do we do?"

"I am still getting re-acclimated to my body," Zed said. "My original plan for getting back to Rook Mountain today failed. I'm the weakest I've been in a long, long time. You might even be able to kill me right now. That's why I've decided to deal with you later."

Sophie felt something like a meat hook tear into her back. The air rushed out of her lungs. She felt herself flying through the air, and then the world changed.

IN THE WOODS (PART EIGHT)

"Glad to see you both," Zed said.

Frank doubled over, gasping for breath. He saw Sophie next to him, doing the same. After a moment, he looked up and blinked hard. It was like decades had passed in a moment. Zed stood in the middle of the path, exactly where he'd been a moment ago. Now Mason—sixty-year-old Mason—stood next to him.

The path had changed. It was thinner now, and partially grown over.

The only thing unchanged was Zed. He was wearing different clothes, but, other than that, he looked exactly the same. No, that wasn't quite right. He hadn't been holding an open book in his hands.

Zed had the book. Jake had died bringing Frank to the past. And for what? The people of Sanctuary were still dead and now Zed had the book. Zed had won.

White light poured out of a door in the tree next to Frank. "You pulled us through the tree?" he asked.

Sophie shook her head. "Jake said that couldn't be done."

"It can if you know what you're doing," Zed said. "And if you don't mind hurting people a little."

297

Frank's back felt like it was on fire from whatever mystical force had grabbed him and pulled him through. It seemed to be intact though.

"I'm in a better position to deal with you now," Zed said. "A much better position. I've been waiting more than fifty years to be strong enough to pull you through and save my younger self." He pointed toward Frank's hand. "Is that the compass? If you don't mind..." He slid a finger across a page of the book, and the ground under Frank shifted. It was like being on a moving sidewalk at an airport. The ground carried him twenty feet down the path, and in a moment he was standing in front of Zed.

He grabbed Frank's wrist and squeezed with hellish strength. Frank cried out and dropped the compass into Zed's outstretched hand. "Glad to have this one back. You know, if I'd had this in Rook Mountain, things would have gone very differently." He glanced down at the compass. "Well, now, isn't this interesting? The compass is pointing at Ms. Porter."

"What does that mean?" Sophie asked. "Why does it do that?"

Zed's smile widened. "It only points to the worst of the worst. If you press the broken clock symbol and concentrate, you can move the needle in another direction for a while, but evil is this compass's true north. It would seem you have the potential for great evil, my dear. Maybe we should keep you around for a while."

Mason raised a pistol and pointed it at Sophie. "You killed my mother."

"What?" Sophie asked. "I've never even seen you before."

Zed sighed. "Catch up, Ms. Porter. This is little Mason Hinkle, all grown up."

"Mason, I was there," Frank said. "I saw it. She didn't kill your mother. Zed's been lying to you."

Mason's eyes narrowed. "Like I'd believe you."

Zed pushed the pistol down. "Mason, please. Not now. There'll be plenty of time for killing her once I leave."

Mason's eyes widened. "You're leaving?"

He nodded. "I have to finish the work I started before your uncle and his friends stopped me."

Zed's hands flew over the pages of the book. With each stroke of his finger, the forest changed. Trees zoomed around, reorienting themselves. Hills flattened. Paths grew and twisted and disappeared.

Frank wanted to throw up. It was like the world was spinning around him. It hurt his eyes, his brain more so. Even after everything he had seen, this was too much for him.

"What Jake didn't realize when he…banished me," Zed said, working the book as he talked, "was that he was connecting me to all sorts of other places and times. The roots of the trees here reach far beyond this soil. I found I could influence things very far from here. I could even appear briefly in an almost physical form with a little help. I did that a few times in Rook Mountain. So, I created the legend of Sanctuary and put it into as many times and places as I could. Sanctuary is the book's secret name for this place. I knew the book would make sure Jake heard the people when they called for his help. And, kind-hearted fool that he was, I knew he'd help them. The more people he brought here, the better the chance someone would screw up and I'd be able to make my escape." He smiled at Sophie.

Sophie glared at him. "Is that why you brought me here? Is that why you left me messages? So I could help you escape?"

A dark cloud passed over Zed's face. "My powers were limited when I was banished. I could influence things in small

299

ways. I left a few messages for my friends in Rook Mountain, but it hurt every time. Someone else brought you here and left you those messages."

Sophie laughed. "Right. Who was it then?"

Zed grimaced. "The same man who killed your friends. The man who drove the banished people to attack. The man who started the fires." He glanced at Frank and saw the skeptical look on his face. "Come on. Why would I kill all those people? You know I love working a crowd. I'm an idealist at heart. I believe in people."

Zed tapped his fingers on the page like a pianist coaxing out a complicated concerto. Suddenly a man stood next to Frank.

It was the bearded man. The man Frank had seen over Mason's shoulder when he first arrived here.

The man looked around, confused.

"I don't understand," Sophie said. "Jake banished him. Did you change him back?"

"Noooo," Zed said. "I was the one who transformed him into a tree originally many years ago when this place was still called Sugar Plains. And then you released him. And Jake did his half-assed job of changing him back into a tree. It took a while, but our friend Vee here broke free. He did that...what was it, Vee...two years ago? That was impressive. He's been sulking around the woods since then. Thinking he was hiding from me. Waiting for his chance to take me out. Well, here I am, Vee."

The bearded man smiled, revealing dirty teeth. "Zed. I have a message for you."

Zed waved his hand at the man. "I don't want your message."

"You need to hear it, nonetheless," Vee said. "Come

home."

Zed scowled at the bearded man. "I am home. You tell them that. I am home."

Vee said, "That message will not be well received."

Zed shook his head as if dismissing the idea. "You gonna tell Frank and Sophie how you killed their friends? How you brought poor little Sophie to Sanctuary? Tricked her with your messages?"

"Why should I tell them anything? You've been living among them far too long if you think they matter."

"That's where you're wrong," Zed said. "They are wonderful tools. You just don't know how to use them properly."

Vee let out a bark that might have been a laugh. "You were always the smart one."

Zed's smile widened. "And you were always the strong one. The way you did all those things while you were in tree form, it was mighty impressive. I watched in awe as you made things happen here and in Rook Mountain. Your message even helped my friends locate the hammer."

"I wanted them to open the door, same as you. I want out of this place as badly as you do."

"I couldn't have done all that," Zed said. "Like I said, you're the strong one. We both know I'm no match for you in a straight up fight."

"Then why are you smiling?" Vee asked.

"Because I'm the smart one."

Zed slid his fingers across the page in front of him, and light burst out of the two trees nearest to Vee. He flipped onto his back as if his legs were being pulled in one direction and his arms in the other. He hovered three feet off the ground, a pained looked on his face, his arms and legs stretched in opposite directions.

Frank remembered the irresistible force that had pulled him through the tree moments ago. It appeared a similar force was pulling Vee. Toward two separate trees at once.

Vee groaned, his eyes wide.

"You had to come after me," Zed said. "You couldn't leave well enough alone. They need *me* even if they don't know it. Screw the Ones Who Sing. And screw you. They need *me*. You tell them that."

Vee grunted, as if he were trying to speak but was stretched too far to let any words out.

Zed flicked the page, and Vee cried out, releasing a guttural shriek of pain. His body quivered, and then his arms were ripped from his body and flew through the door behind him even as the rest of his body flew through the door in front of him.

Vee was gone. Only a splatter of blood on the ground remained.

"There," Zed said. "That's taken care of."

"Jesus!" Sophie yelled. "You tore him in half."

"Hush now," Zed said. He put his hand back on the book and his fingers started dancing.

Frank looked around and let out an involuntary gasp. The trees were lined up in orderly rows as far as the eye could see. White light poured from each of them.

Frank stumbled backwards toward Sophie and put his arm around her. As they clung to each other, he realized they were both shaking.

"I'm pretty good with this thing, right?" Zed asked.

"Who was that man?" Frank asked.

Zed grunted. "He was no one. Someone who thought he was entitled to power."

"What is that book?" Frank asked. "Where did it come from? Did you make it?"

Zed paged through the book as if trying to find a particularly interesting passage. "No. Every special place has a book. I'm just skilled at finding the important ones."

Frank asked, "Even Rook Mountain has one of these books?"

Zed looked up, his eyes wide with surprise. "Frank, your mind is a strange and beautiful thing. You really don't remember?"

"Remember what?"

Zed tilted his head and squinted at Frank, as if trying to figure out if the man was kidding. "Rook Mountain did have a book. You burned it."

Frank shook his head. "I don't know what you're talking about." He suddenly felt like the world was twisting again. Something strange was happening in the back of his mind, but he didn't know what it was.

Zed chuckled and shook his head. "And that's exactly why I'm not going to kill you. I might need some of what you have locked away in your head. If either one of us can ever figure out how to access it."

Sophie nodded her head toward the tree next to her. It was an especially tall tree with a complex and twisted root structure. Frank didn't know what she was trying to tell him.

Zed flicked the page with his finger, and the white light coming out of one of the trees disappeared. He flicked again, and another light went out. He did it again and again, faster and faster.

"Frank, give me your lock," Sophie whispered.

Frank squinted at her, wondering what she was talking about. Then he remembered there were two lock. The one he'd brought with him from Rook Mountain and the one he'd taken off the lockbox. He still had one in his pocket. He passed it to her.

"Zed, what are you doing?" Mason asked.

Zed kept moving, putting out lights as he answered. "I only need one of these doors. And I might not be the only person trying to use them. Better to destroy them. Besides, there's only one place left I need to go."

Frank noticed Sophie was crouched near the ground, but he couldn't tell what she was doing.

Finally, when all the lights were out but the one on the tree directly in front of Zed, he closed the book and looked at Frank. "I'll come back for you," he said. "I may have work for us to do together." He stepped toward the doorway, and then paused. "I've set this door to burn out after I step through. But you have food and supplies. Try to stay alive until I get back."

He gently set the book down in the dirt.

"Wait," Mason said. "You're taking me with you, right? Like we talked about?"

Zed smiled at him. "As much as I appreciate your loyalty, the answer to that question is a resounding no."

Mason bit his lip. "Can I have my compass?" His voice was shaking.

"Son, it was always my compass. You were just holding it for me."

Zed winked at Frank, then stepped through the door in the tree.

As soon as he'd passed through the tree, the light blinked out.

"No," Frank whispered.

"What's happening?" Sophie asked. "What does this

mean?"

"He's gone," Frank said, struggling to keep his voice steady. "He's probably going after my family. My friends. He'll kill them all."

"Well then we find him. We use the book. Like you did before when you found Jake."

"No. I had the compass. And even then Jake had to pull me through. He said he destroyed the doors."

Mason picked up the book and flipped it open.

"There has to be a way!" Frank said. "Maybe we can learn to use the book. Study it."

Sophie said, "I don't know. Jake studied it for years. Like, a decade. But if we can figure out the book, there might be a way."

The tree in front of them suddenly moved. It shifted horizontally to the other side of the trail. Then it moved back again.

"Not bad!" Mason said. He dragged his finger across the page and the tree shot fifty yards away. He ran his finger the other way, and the tree raced back, stopping inches away from Frank's nose.

"Why didn't you tell us you knew how to use the book?" Frank asked.

"I didn't know I did," Mason said. "I haven't seen it since I was a kid. It was locked in that box, remember? But it all looks pretty straight forward. The instructions are written right here."

"You can read it?" Frank asked.

"Yeah." He chuckled wearily. "Funny. I haven't read a lick in more than fifty years. I wasn't much good at it then, either. But this is all crystal clear." He shrugged. "It just seems to make sense. This book is of this place, like me. And Zed thought I was useless."

Frank put his hand on his nephew's shoulder. "Mason, you have to take us through the doorway. We have to follow him to Rook Mountain."

Mason frowned, flipping through the pages. "The tree he went through doesn't go to Rook Mountain."

"Where's it go?" Frank asked.

Mason scanned the page. "King's Crossing, Wisconsin. He did something to all these trees, though. The doorways don't open like the book says they should."

"Maybe you're not using it right," Frank said. "It might take some time to figure it out."

Sophie crouched down and fiddled with something on the ground. Suddenly a tree appeared next to her. And the white light was still pouring out of it.

She held up the Cassandra lock and smiled. "I figured we should hide one of the trees from Zed."

Now Frank was smiling. It was the tree he had seen next to her before. The one with the twisted root structure. "You used the lock."

Sophie nodded. "I put the lock on one of its roots. This is the Rook Mountain tree."

Frank glanced at Mason. Mason flipped a page of the book and nodded. "She's right." A smile crept onto his face. "And the door seems to be working. I've never done this before. Give me a second."

His finger twisted on the page. Sweat beaded his weathered brow. After a few moments, he looked up at them and said, "It's ready for us."

Frank grinned at Sophie and Mason. "Ready to go home?"

Sophie smiled back at him. "Hell yes."

Mason frowned. "I was born here. I've never been

anywhere else. I'm—"

Frank cut him off with a hand on his shoulder. "Come home."

Mason nodded.

Frank, Sophie, and Mason stepped into the light and went home to Rook Mountain.

EPILOGUE

Rook Mountain—May 29, 2015

Mason stood at the window, peeking through the curtain.

"Geez, man, she'll get here when she gets here," Frank said.

Mason nodded. "I know. I'm just checking."

Frank couldn't blame Mason for his anxiousness. He'd had to adjust a lot of new things over the month since they'd returned to Rook Mountain. Running water. Cars. Toothbrushes. And people. Mason got pretty jumpy around them, and in the non-Sanctuary world, they were just about everywhere. Frank couldn't blame Mason for being excited about seeing someone slightly more familiar.

But at least he got to go out and experience things, unlike Frank who'd been stuck in Sean's house for the last month, afraid he'd bump into Christine, Trevor, or Will. It wasn't that he didn't want to see them. He did. Badly. But there was no way he was bringing them back into this. And if they knew he was back, they would insist on trying to help. Frank couldn't allow that.

Frank had wandered out into town a few times, using the Cassandra lock to render himself invisible, but that had only made him feel more alone. The streets of Rook Mountain felt haunted; he saw reminders of Zed and the Regulations everywhere he went.

He felt a hand on his shoulder and he turned. Sean stood behind him.

"You sure you won't reconsider my offer?" Sean asked. "I do come in handy every once in a while."

"That's what I hear," Frank said with a smile. "Still waiting to see proof of that myself."

Sean pointed at the scars crisscrossing his neck. "There's your proof. For real, though. It's not too late. I can have a bag packed and be ready in ten minutes."

Frank shook his head. "I need you here. This place is important to Zed. I know it. He'll come back here, and I want you to be ready when that happens. Besides, you've got Wendy to think about."

"True. No way would she stay behind."

"You see? We just don't have room in the car for all of you."

The smile drifted away from Sean's face. "Are you sure you want to do this? You've put in your time. Maybe it's someone else's turn to take a crack at Zed."

Frank turned away. "No one else understands him like we do. And then there are the locks."

Sean frowned. "You sound like Jake. He insisted we stand up to Zed."

Mason turned away from the window. "And look how far that got him. He wanted to save people by bringing them to Sanctuary, and they all ended up dead."

"Is that what you think?" Frank asked. He searched Mason's face. The older man wasn't speaking emotionally. He was just stating a fact he had learned long ago.

Mason turned back to the window. "Of course. Dad tried hard. And he had good intentions. It's wasn't his fault he failed."

"I don't know about all that," Sean said. "If it wasn't for your dad and his message, Frank wouldn't have been let out of jail. Zed might still be ruling over Rook Mountain."

"Exactly," Frank said. "Look, he originally went through that mirror to find help for his family. Because of that, I got out of prison and was able to do my part. And when we sent Zed through the mirror, your dad was waiting there and he banished him."

"Sure, for a little while," Mason said.

"Long enough for his family here to be safe. And long enough to create a new family. Mason, your dad was all about keeping people he loved safe. He died doing that. So don't think for a minute that he was a failure. He gave every person in Sanctuary a new life, even if it didn't last forever. He gave me one too."

Mason turned just enough for Frank to be able to see the hint of a smile on his face. "Yeah, I guess he did."

Sean cocked his thumb toward the window. "Looks like your ride's here."

Sure enough, Frank saw a tan Honda Civic roll to a stop in front of the house.

Sean pulled a surprised Mason into a bear hug. "My friend, it was super weird teaching you how to operate a faucet. I wouldn't have traded it for anything."

Mason just grunted, clearly desperate to have the hug end as quickly as possible.

Sean hugged Frank. Then he handed Frank something.

"What's this?" Frank asked.

"Pre-paid cell phone," Sean said. "My number's

programmed in there. If you need help, I'm the first call you make. Deal?"

Frank smiled. "Deal. Thanks, man. For everything." He slipped the phone into his pocket. "Same goes for you. Watch out for them. Christine and Trevor, I mean. If you need anything, or if they do, don't hesitate. I'll come back here on the run the minute you call."

"Of course," Sean said. "It seems like you are always leaving. Going off somewhere new and exciting."

"Not forever," Frank said. "I'm coming back here soon. For good. Just got to take care of this little Zed problem first."

Sean smiled. "Oh, is that all?"

A few moments later, Frank and Mason threw their bags into the trunk of the Civic and climbed into the car. Mason got in the back seat slowly and carefully. He was still getting used to the idea of vehicular travel.

Sophie smiled at them. "Hello, my fellow idiots."

"Right back attcha," Frank said. "You get everything straightened out with your parents?"

Frank knew what she had told them about the time she was missing. She said she remembered being held at gunpoint by Rodgers and then she didn't remember anything else until she reappeared in Rook Mountain. The story might have been easier to believe if the Rook Mountain tree hadn't spit them out in April, 2015, a full six months after Sophie had disappeared. Still, she'd stuck to her story through all their confusion and questions, and she hoped they at least half-believed it. It was Rook Mountain after all. Weird was what this town did.

Sophie shrugged. "Near enough. I told them I got a job interview up north. They are all about job interviews so they liked that."

"Let's talk while we drive," Mason said. "I want to get to the part where we kill Zed."

Frank chuckled. True enough, he too wanted to kill Zed. He did feel it was his responsibility. He hadn't lied to Sean about that. But there was another more selfish reason for going. Zed had gone to another one of the special towns. A place that was special, Frank had to assume, like Rook Mountain and Sugar Plains were special. And Zed had told him all special places had a book.

So maybe King's Crossing, Wisconsin had a book. Maybe it was a book that would allow Frank to reach through time.

Maybe Jake didn't have to end up dead on the forest floor.

Frank hadn't spoken those words aloud to anyone; he kept that secret hope locked away in a special place in his mind.

He reached into his pocket and pulled out a small box. He tossed it to Sophie. "Made you something."

She scrunched up her face. "Seriously?"

"Just open it."

She lifted the lid on the box and pulled out a silver necklace with a tiny lock hanging from the end of it.

"It's a new design," Frank said. "Put it on. It'll hide you from the compass. So Zed won't see us coming."

Sophie put the chain around her neck. "I don't know what to say."

"You don't have to say anything," Frank said. "I made one for Mason and one for me, too. More manly versions, of course."

"Of course."

"Sophie," Frank said, looking into her eyes. "I really appreciate you volunteering to do this with us."

"I'm young and single. The ideal time in life to fight bad

guys." Sophie shifted the car into drive and pulled away from the curb. "So…King's Crossing, Wisconsin. How do we know Zed didn't already take it out of time?"

"For one thing, it's still on the map," Frank said. "Besides, Zed doesn't have the pocket watch anymore. He has the compass. Whatever he does next, it's gonna be something different."

She fingered the lock dangling from her neck. "At least he won't see us coming."

Frank smiled. "No he won't."

Sophie, Frank, and Mason left Rook Mountain and headed north.

TO BE CONCLUDED...

The third and final book in the Deadlock Trilogy, The Broken Clock, is available now. Visit pthylton.com/book/broken-clock for more details.

As a way of saying thanks for reading, I've also included some bonus features.

- A deleted scene showing how Nate came to be in Sanctuary (featuring a few familiar faces from Regulation 19)
- The writing tips video series 'Writing the Lights Out'
- 'A Place Without Shadows' music playlist
- And more!

Visit *pthylton.com/place-shadows-bonus-features* to view the bonus features.

If you enjoyed **A Place Without Shadows**, please consider leaving a review wherever you bought this book. As an indie author, I count on reader reviews to help my books reach a wider audience.

If you just want to say hello, email me at pt@pthylton.com

Thanks for your support!

ACKNOWLEDGEMENTS

This book would not have been possible without support from the following people:

My wife, who was once again my rock and my source of inspiration.

My daughter, who asked me, "Are you still working on that book where people turn into trees?"

My editor, Kirsten D, for her wonderful suggestions, her level-headedness, and the way she kept me honest about my rules for time travel.

My beta readers, who I will not call out by name here. This book is *very* different—and I think much better—than the one they first read, and it's all thanks to their wonderful comments.

My fellow indie authors, who supported me and advised me via dozens and dozens of email conversations.

And thanks to you, dear reader, for your continued support.

ABOUT THE AUTHOR

P.T. Hylton is a writer, podcaster, and instructional designer. He lives in beautiful Eastern Tennessee with his wife and daughter. Check out his blog at *pthylton.com*.